The Minister's Daughter

The Minister's Daughter

JULIE HEARN

Simon Pulse
NEW YORK LONDON TORONTO SYDNEY

SIMON PULSE
An imprint of Simon & Schuster Children's Publishing Division
1230 Avenue of the Americas, New York, NY 10020
Copyright © 2005 by Julie Hearn
Originally published in Great Britain in 2005 by Oxford University Press
All rights reserved, including the right of reproduction in whole or in part in any form.
SIMON PULSE and colophon are registered trademarks of Simon & Schuster, Inc.
Also available in an Atheneum Books for Young Readers hardcover edition.
Designed by Kristin Smith
The text of this book was set in Adobe Garamond.
Manufactured in the United States of America
First Simon Pulse edition December 2006
2 4 6 8 10 9 7 5 3 1
The Library of Congress has cataloged the hardcover edition as follows:
Hearn, Julie, 1958–
The minister's daughter / by Julie Hearn.—1st American ed.
p. cm.
Published in Great Britain under the title "The Merrybegot."
Summary: In 1645 in England, the daughters of the town minister successfully accuse a local healer and her granddaughter of witchcraft to conceal an out-of-wedlock pregnancy, but years later during the 1692 Salem trials their lie has unexpected repercussions.
ISBN-13: 978-0-689-87690-5 (hc.)
ISBN-10: 0-689-87690-4 (hc.)
[1. Witchcraft—Fiction. 2. Trials (Witchcraft)—Fiction. 3. Fairies—Fiction.
4. Supernatural—Fiction. 5. Pregnancy—Fiction. 6. Sisters—Fiction. 7. Hopkins, Matthew,
d. 1647—Fiction. 8. Great Britain—History—Civil War, 1642–1649—Fiction. 9. Somerset
(England)—History—Civil War, 1642–1649—Fiction. 10. Salem (Mass.)—History—
Colonial period, ca. 1600–1775—Fiction.] I. Title.
PZ7.H34625Mi 2005
[Fic]—dc22
2004018324
ISBN-13: 978-0-689-87691-2 (pbk.)
ISBN-10: 0-689-87691-2 (pbk.)

In memory of Shoe Taylor

Something still dances
Just out of your sight
It's the voice from the well
The trick of the light
It's something like water
you hold in your hand
While it's business as usual
In Merrie Olde Englande.
—*Robb Johnson*

"That as there have been, so ther are & wil be,
witches unto the world's end."
—*John Gaule, preacher, 1646*

The Confession of Patience Madden

THE YEAR OF OUR LORD 1692

Good day, brothers. I am ready to talk to you now. Ready to tell you the truth. Pray forgive the croak in my voice. It has been . . . it has been . . .

    Water? Yes. Thank you.

    Are you listening? I can barely see you. It is so dark in here. . . .

    Are you ready?

    Then I will begin.

I never meant it to end the way it did. Grace might have done, but not me. Grace was fifteen, as artful as a snake, and already on the slippery slope to Hell. But I, Patience Madden, could have stopped at any time—uncrossed my eyes, made my arms and legs be still, and called a halt to the filthy words jumping out of my mouth like toads. I could have spat the pins from under my tongue and admitted they came not from the

1

Devil, but from the cherrywood box our mother kept tiny things in.

I could have sat up in bed, looked around at the villagers come to whisper and gawp, and said, No. Stop praying for me. Stop bringing me bay leaves and splashes of holy water. For I don't deserve your lucky charms, nor any help from the Lord. Neither does my sister. She deserves them even less. It was her fault. She started it. And now she's hurting me. Yes, she is. Pinching me black and blue, beneath the coverlet, lest I weaken and tell you the truth.

"Grace," I whispered on the third evening, after our neighbors had drifted away, to feed their hogs, their children, or their own nosy faces. "Grace, I'm scared. I want to get up. Grace, I'm hungry."

"Be silent," she hissed. "Or, if you can't be silent, call out some more about imps at the window and a crow in the corner. That was good. They liked that. We'll do more with the imps and the crow."

She promised me I would not have to behave like this for much longer. In a day or so, she said, we would stage our recovery. Wake up all smiles, ready to put on our itchy bonnets and do our tiresome chores, like good, obedient girls.

A few days more, she said, and our lives would go back to normal. As dull as scum, but blameless.

It did not happen like that. It went too far.

We went too far.

APRIL
1645

The cunning woman's granddaughter is chasing a pig when she learns there is to be no frolicking in the village on May Morning. Minister's orders.

"Bogger . . . that," she pants. "And bogger . . . this . . . pig. There's no . . . catching . . . him. . . ."

Clutching her sides, she gives up the chase and collapses, laughing, against the gnarled trunk of a tree. Above her head pink blossoms shake like fairy fists. Spring has arrived. A beautiful time. A time when it feels absolutely right to think of dancing barefoot in the dew, and absolutely wrong to dwell on the new minister, with his miserable ways and face like a trodden parsnip.

"That's what they be saying," the blacksmith's son tells her. "No pole. No goin' off into the woods. No nothing. It ain't godly, Nell, to frolic so. That's what the minister reckons."

Nell picks a blade of new grass and begins to chew it. Her stomach rumbles beneath her apron, but she is used to that.

Out of the corner of her eye she can see the pig rooting around. It is a bad pig. A bothersome pig. Her granny will sort it out. This is how:

A SPELL TO SOOTHE A TRUCULENT PIG
**First, catch your pig. Do it on a Monday,
on a waning moon, when the time be right for healing.
Point him to the north, and hang on tight.
Rap his snout three times with a wand of oak, and call:
"Powers of earth, tame and soothe this creature that he
may become docile and no longer a bogging nuisance."
Wait seven beats of the heart, then let him go.
So mote it be.**

A light breeze frisks the orchard. There are things Nell ought to be doing, but she stays where she is, squinting up at the blacksmith's son and thinking about May Morning.

"And who be you wishing to frolic with, anyway, Sam Towser?" She chuckles. "As if I couldn't guess . . ."

The lad reddens. He is a month short of sixteen and all swept through with the kind of longings that can tie up a boy's tongue and have him tripping over everything, from clods of earth to his own great feet, twenty times a day. He has a mop of corn-colored hair and a cleft in his chin so deep, it might have been pressed there by his guardian angel. He is too ungainly; too unfledged, as yet, to be truly handsome. But he will be. The promise of it is all about him, like the guarantee of a glorious day once some mist has cleared.

"No one," he mumbles. "I got horses to see to. No time for

fumblin' around with some daft maid on May Mornin', nor any other time."

"Pah! That's a fib!" Nell flings both arms wide and twists her face to look like a parsnip. "Beware, sinner! Beware what you say! Repent! Repent! For Satan loves a fibber and will carry you off to burn in Hell. In Hell, I tell you, where fibbers go. And frolickers. And women who wear scarlet ribbons or sweep their hearths on Sundays—"

"Hush . . . Hush up, you daft wench."

"Repent! Repent! For I am your minister. God's representative in this heathen place. Repent! For though my nose drips, and I do not know a hoe from my—"

"*Nell,* hush!"

"—elbow, I know a sinner when I see one. And a fibber. And a frolicker. All rolled into one vile, wretched—"

"Right!"

"—body and a . . . *yieeek!*"

He has pounced and is tickling her—tickling her to what feels like a giggly death—while the sun pours down like honey and the truculent pig looks on in mild surprise.

"You two! Have a care! Mind that tree, and stop your messing."

A woman has entered the orchard. She stands some distance away, almost in the nettles. Her face, beneath a bonnet the color of porridge, is grave.

"What?" Nell scrambles to her feet. "What is it, Mistress Denby? What's happened?"

The blacksmith's son gets up. There are twigs and fallen petals in his hair. He looks like Puck. He looks drop-dead frolicsome.

5

"Gotter go," he mutters. "I got horses to see to."

The woman and the girl pay him no mind. They have already jumped the stile and are hurrying away, along the crooked path leading down to the village. Women's stuff, he supposes. Someone getting born. Or dying. Or doing both in the space of a few breaths.

He doesn't want to be seen trotting at the heels of womenfolk, toward whatever, or whoever, needs their attention in some fusty room. The sun is high now, and he has his own ritual to perform.

The apple tree he chooses is truly ancient; its timber as knotted as a crone's shins, its blossom strangely pale. No one knows how long it has stood here or why it was planted alone. Much older than the rest, it continues to bear fruit so sweet that to press cider from it, and drink the stuff, is said to send the mind dribbling out of the nostrils and the legs in several directions at once.

It is to this tree the Apple Howlers come, on Twelfth Night, to scare away evil spirits. It is here that they form their circle— raggle-taggle villagers, young and old, banging pails and pots and howling "Hats full! Caps full! Bushels, bushels, sacks full!" loud enough to wake the dead.

It is on these branches, and around this trunk, that the Howlers hang their amulets and leave cider-soaked toast for the piskies. The orchard swarms with piskies. Everyone knows that. Little folk in rags, their skin as rough as bark, their heads sprouting lichen and moss. A few are downright malicious; the rest, merely troublesome and high-spirited. All are uglier than dead hedgehogs and as greedy as swine.

Over the hills, in a neighboring county, lies fairy territory—a prettier species, by far, the fairies, but just as pesky, so rumor has it . . . just as demanding of treats, and remembrance.

Be good to the piskies, the old folk say hereabouts, and they will be good to you. Treat them with respect, on Twelfth Night, and they will stay by the trees, watching over the fruit until picking time comes.

The cider-soaked toast has been eaten long ago by robins and other things. But the amulets are still here, swaying gently at the end of their strings, like small, hanged felons.

"May I?" says the blacksmith's son before pressing the point of a horseshoe nail into the old tree's trunk.

Yep, something replies, the sound of it such a faint rasp that the blacksmith's son assumes the pig has farted.

Slowly, carefully, he begins to cut. Not his full name—Samuel—for he isn't sure of all the letters. A single "S" is the mark he makes, the downstroke wobbly as a caterpillar against the wood. He can't spell the other name, either. The one that is on his mind day and night. The one he only has to hear, in passing, for a fluttering to start in his belly, as if larks are nesting there.

He knows his alphabet, though. Just. And he knows, from the way the girl's name is said, which letter he needs to entwine with his own. It is one of the tricky ones that sound different, depending on the word. As the metal point of the nail forms the letter's curve, he finds himself wishing it made a soft sound like the beginning of "gentle." He would have liked that. It would have seemed significant.

The girl's name, though, begins with a hard "G," like "gallows" or "god."

When he has finished, he steps back to inspect what he has done. And then he sees one. At least, he thinks he does. There and gone it is, between knots of blossom, its face as coarse and gray as the tree, its small, bright eyes fixed intently on the "S" and the "G."

Oh . . .

He looks quickly, all around, and then back again. Nothing. There is nothing there. A trick of the light, perhaps? But, no . . . His sight is good, and he isn't given to fancies.

He stays a minute more, half dreading, half hoping to see the thing again. What did it mean? Was it lucky, to see a piskie when you were a month short of sixteen and so desperate to get your hands on a certain someone that you would probably die of frustration if it didn't happen soon?

Did it mean that he would?

Did it?

It takes just seconds for the blacksmith's son to convince himself that he has been sent an auspicious sign. That, come May Morning, he will be frolicking away to his heart's content with the girl whose name begins with a hard-sounding "G."

She will be all over him like a vine—yes, she will—for all she is the minister's daughter and seems as distant, and cool, as a star. He will have her. No doubt about it. For they are joined, already, in his mind, and on the tree. And their union has been blessed. He has the piskie's promise.

The blacksmith's son feels light on his feet as he swings himself over the stile, and he is whistling as he strides away.

Silly young bogger . . . goes the sighing and the rasping among the topmost branches of the trees. *Silly little whelp.* And the letters "S" and "G" begin slowly turning brown, the way a cut apple will do or naked flesh beneath hot sun.

All the way down the path, Mistress Denby had gone rambling on about a pot lid: "That pot lid's about to fall. Things be boiling up quick—a bit too quick, if you asks me. There'll be trouble with this one, you mark my words."

Nell had simply nodded and hurried on. She understood. The Bramlow baby is coming, and coming faster than a snowball down a hill. But you never, ever, spoke of these matters outdoors, lest piskies should overhear and come to steal the newborn away. No piskie would be interested in something as boring as a pot lid—although Nell often wonders what they make of a village in which pots boil over with alarming frequency, and their lids, when that happens, seem so fragile and important.

Now, beneath the eaves of a squat little cottage, the Bramlows' pot lid is giving everyone the worries. The Watchers—all mothers themselves—shake their heads and grunt, sympathetically, as the person lying prone on a straw pallet arches her spine and hollers. Her belly, rippled across by contractions, is so huge that she can barely lift herself.

Somewhere in the room a fly buzzes. It has been trying to escape, but the bedroom door is closed tight, and a rough piece of wood, wedged into the window space, is keeping light, air, and piskies out and heat, flies, and anxiety in.

Nell takes a damp rag from her grandmother and begins to wipe Mistress Bramlow's face. She does it reluctantly but with care, as if the sweaty forehead and cheeks were made of red glass.

This is her first time in a birthing room, and she has to get everything right. It is important.

The Watchers' eyes, flint-sharp above the glow of their candles, follow every dab and stroke of that rag. Nell takes a deep breath, dips the wad of material three times in a bowl of water, whispers five words, then wrings it out.

"Good girl. That's the way," murmurs the cunning woman. But whether she means her granddaughter or the heaving, panting soul beneath her hands, Nell cannot tell.

The Watchers shift. It isn't regular to have an unwed maid in on a birth. It goes against the grain, and who knows what trouble that might lead to? The Watchers know best—or, at least, they think they do. There are gaggles of women like these in villages all over England. Women who gather, as a matter of course, at every birth and death within walking distance. Women who are always first to throw something pulpy and rotten at whoever is slumped in the stocks. Women who like nothing better than a good hanging.

Elsewhere, they are known by other names. Here, though, everyone calls them the Watchers. No one can remember why, but it is probably because whole generations of them have been particularly dour and scarily attentive.

Right now they are directing black looks at Nell, as if they don't even trust her to wipe a birthing woman's chin without mishap.

The cunning woman, sensing an ill mood, looks up, frowning.

"My granddaughter is here to learn," she says. "Or would you rather those yet to be born were left to the mercy of nature and your own cack-handed tuggings once I am dead and in my grave?"

The Watchers lower their eyes. They will keep their own counsel—for now.

"Right." The cunning woman bends back to her task. "Good girls."

The trapped fly is crawling up the pallet. It can smell birth fluid and will soon be landing where it shouldn't. Once, the cunning woman would have known it was there and willed it away. Not anymore. She has aged much over the last few moons. Her touch has a tremble to it, and she has difficulty, sometimes, recalling a surefire cure for warts or the correct spell to mend a broken heart. This vagueness has come upon her suddenly, and no one—not even the Watchers, who don't usually miss a thing—knows quite how splutter-minded she has become.

Time is running out for the cunning woman, and there are certain skills she needs to pass on. Nell is young and wild, but the gift of healing is in her. She will learn fast and make a fine midwife.

The laboring woman howls like a thing in a trap as a fresh wave of pain grips her innards. "Get away from me!" she yells, hitting out at Nell's hands. "Go play hide-and-peep out-o'-doors with all the other brats. Go on, you little streak of cat's piss. I want no unweds here."

Knowing looks pass among the Watchers.

Nell flushes to the roots of her raggedy hair. "Bogger it," she says, setting aside the sweaty rag. "I'm off."

She stamps her feet, deliberately, as she heads for the door. The Watchers tut as she passes, cupping work-swollen fingers around their candle flames so they won't blow out in the draught of her leaving.

"You'll stay," snaps the cunning woman. "And you'll learn.

11

And the first thing you'll learn is that when a birthing woman gets nasty, 'tis time for her to push."

"Oh," says Nell. She is at the door now and can see most of what is happening to the parts of Mistress Bramlow where pot lids come out. "Oh," she says again.

It's not that she is squeamish. No country girl, used to the birthings of piglets and calves, kittens and lambs, would find any of this repulsive. It is just . . . it is just . . .

"Think I'll go anyways," she murmurs. "Afore I does something wrong."

"You'll stay," the cunning woman repeats. "And the second thing you'll learn is whether an unborn be ripe enough to drop. Get here. Aside of me. Now."

Slowly, dragging her dirty heels, Nell does as she is told.

Mistress Bramlow has heaved herself up onto her elbows and is glaring over the mountain of her belly. "'Tis coming too fast," she pants. "Too fast. . . . I ain't had the pains more than two blessed hours."

The Watchers' heads nod. *Too fast . . . Not good . . .*

"Hush now." The cunning woman is greasing her granddaughter's right arm with goose fat. Up and around each finger she goes, then over the wrist and down to the elbow, with swift, slick strokes.

Nell blinks. "That pig be on the loose still, up in the orchard," she says. "'Tis him I oughter be gettin' to grips with this day, not no unborn. Don't you think so?"

The Watchers clearly think so. The Watchers think Nell should be just about anywhere except at the foot of this pallet, preparing to stick her fist into a birthing woman.

"Now," says the cunning woman. "Between pains. I'll guide you."

And Nell scrunches her eyes shut tight as her grandmother forces her slippery fingers into slippery flesh and then presses her arm to follow. *This can't be right,* she thinks, the sweat gathering on her. *You could kill a person doing this, surely?* Mistress Bramlow is certainly yelling fit to bust. But: "When you reach the top, feel what's there," says the cunning woman. "Go on, girl. Feel what's there and tell me."

Cautiously, carefully, Nell moves what she can of her fingers. It is like groping along a stovepipe, full of hot sludge. Any second now Mistress Bramlow is going to kick her in the teeth, and who would blame her?

"Gently," urges the cunning woman. "But quickly. As quick as you can, or a pain will be on her, and you'll lose the chance."

Even with her own eyes closed, Nell can sense each Watcher willing her to fail . . . to cry, perhaps . . . to admit defeat, anyway, and leave the whole messy business to her grandmother.

I'll show them, she tells herself. *I'll show those old sows . . .*

"Well?" says the cunning woman. "Well, girl? What is it you feel?"

Cautiously, carefully, Nell waggles the tips of her fingers. "I feel . . . ," she murmurs. "I feel . . ." Drops of sweat trickle from her hairline as she probes. The straw of the pallet is too damp and hot to crackle, but it makes a slipping sound as Mistress Bramlow braces herself for another contraction.

Too late . . . Too late, girl.

Then something pulses. Just once. Out, then in. And something wet . . . something matted and warm, soft yet solid, meets the cramped spread of Nell's fingers. Amazed, Nell wills those fingers to be welcoming, and still.

"A head," she breathes. "I can feel its head."

She moves her hand, just a little.

A person, she thinks. *A new person. And I be the first to touch it. The first thing it knows.*

"Be sure," says the cunning woman. "Be very sure. For the top of an unborn's head can feel much like anywhere else, to a learner."

"I'm sure," whispers Nell.

"Good," says the cunning woman. "Now get out of there, and let this woman push."

Mistress Bramlow curses and thrashes as Nell pulls her arm out. Then she sets about pushing as if her life depends on it. Which it does. The Watchers shuffle closer, and Nell backs away.

Be alive, she wills the unborn. *Just be alive, will you?*

From her place beside the door, she can see her grandmother's hands at work. Probing and twisting. Probing and twisting. The old woman's face is in shadow, but Nell knows that her lips will be moving as she mouths a silent spell. There are swaddling clothes beside the pallet and a pail of water, its surface dappled with herbs. There is a name waiting for this unborn, along with five sisters, a cradle, and a beautiful spring day.

Then: "'Tis done," announces the cunning woman. And something slithers out of Mistress Bramlow in a sudden, watery rush.

Nell takes a step forward, but the Watchers have closed ranks, their shoulders and rumps as solid as a wall.

"Let me see!" Nell takes another step, but no one else budges.

Your fault, implies the silence. *Wretched little unwed. This is all your fault.*

Shut out, behind a blockade of fat bottoms, Nell can feel her fingers tingling where she touched the unborn's head. It was living then, she knows it was. Living, and sensing, and pulsing with the will to arrive. To begin.

If it dies now, will it really be her fault? Just because she is an unwed and has touched it? She can't bear to think this might be true. It seems so unfair—to both of them.

Although prevented from seeing, she can hear: the mutterings of the cunning woman; the keening sound of Mistress Bramlow's weeping; then a light splash as if something small has been dropped into the pail.

"Granny!" she cries. "What's wrong with it? What have I done?" And she butted the nearest bottom, so hard that the Watcher attached to it swivels in astonishment, creating a space.

"Does it live?" Nell careens through that space so fast, she almost topples over the pallet.

The cunning woman is holding the unborn—the newborn now—up toward the roof space. It lolls from her hands, like something made of dough. It is blue, and it is slimy, and it makes no sound at all.

Down into the pail of water it goes again, and then again, and then onto the straw, where the cunning woman sets about kneading its flesh, pummeling and pressing and murmuring all the while.

"Powers of the air . . . of the wind that howls and the breeze that blows . . . Powers of the air, I summon you . . . I summon you . . . Come unto this newborn that it may breathe and know its life . . . Powers of the air, be here now. So mote it be."

And as Nell watches, and the Watchers lick their lips, and Mistress Bramlow continues to moan, the scrap of skin and bone beneath the cunning woman's palms begins to twitch, and then to wriggle, and then to cry.

"It lives," announces the cunning woman, grabbing it under the armpits and holding it aloft, in the general direction of the sky. "It lives. And it's a boy."

A boy . . .

Mistress Bramlow carries on crying, but softly, out of relief. Nell senses the Watchers pressing in. She feels like spinning round, to give them a mouthful, but her fingers are tingling still, and she wants, more than anything, to touch the newborn's head again.

"But he be feeble," the cunning woman adds. "So if it's baptism you're wanting, Mistress, best do it without delay." She looks up, straight at her granddaughter.

"Go fetch the minister," she says.

Nell scowls. "But—"

"Now! Go now. Straightaway."

She has swaddled the baby boy so tightly that he looks like a pullet, all trussed up and ready to roast. Only his face is exposed; waxen and crumpled. Nell feels a tugging in her middle, like nothing she has ever felt before. She would do anything for this newborn. Anything.

"All right," she says. "But if them girls of his do taunt me, I'll slap 'em one."

The cunning woman is edging round the pallet, carrying the newborn to his mother.

"You'll do no such thing," she snaps. "Just fetch the minister."

So Nell throws the baby boy one last gentle look, then turns to leave.

The Watchers are blocking the way.

"I'm on a mission," Nell says. "For my granny. So out of my path, if you please."

They shift slowly, one by one, keeping their eyes upon her as they move. The one whose backside she butted treads, heavily, on her toes as she passes. And Nell knows, though no words are exchanged, that these Watchers would have known a horrible satisfaction if that newborn had never drawn breath. And that they would relish it, still, should he die before the minister gets to him. For that, too, would be Nell's fault. Their believing it would make it so.

"Thank'ee," she says to them, flashing the sweetest smile she can manage before rushing through the doorway, down the splintery stairs, and out into the sunshine.

"Old sows," she grumbles. "They can't hurt me." But her heart is thumping as she takes the track leading to the minister's house, and everything, from the beautiful day to the pattern of her own life, seems suddenly less cut-and-dry.

From his place at the forge, the blacksmith's son spies Nell hurrying by. He knows, by now, why she was called away and guesses at once where she is going.

Without thinking twice, he throws down his hammer to follow.

"Oi!" yells his father. "Get back here!"

But Nell isn't the only one with good reason to call on the

minister. Young Sam's long legs catch up with her easily, and he makes a big effort to seem casual, even though his heart is pumping like bellows, and he has only one thought in his head.

"Be the pot lid broken?" he asks.

"Shhh. No. It be good and strong."

"Can I come with you, then? Wherever it is you be going?"

Nell looks sideways at him. "You won't see her," she says. "She'll be shut away somewhere, learnin' the Bible or some such thing."

"I might," he mumbles. "I might see her." And just the hope of it is enough to make him grin.

The minister's house is set apart from, and above, the village. Gabled and turreted, with mullioned windows that reflect every sunset, it looks down upon the church and the forge, the inn and the pond, and the cluster of tumbledown cottages like a great, bleak custodian.

Built by a wealthy merchant during the reign of Queen Bess, no expense was spared on paneling its rooms or filling its garden with sweet-smelling flowers and hedges cut to the shape of birds and beasts. It was rumored, back then, that this house was to be a hideaway for some woman. For a deformed bride, perhaps, or a mad nun. For Queen Bess herself, maybe, should she ever pass this way, with her retinue of servants, a string of fine horses, and trunks full of nightgowns and curly, red wigs.

For years, though, no woman, apart from a housekeeper, raised so much as a spoon in the place, let alone a smile or a brood of children. The merchant lived there alone, like a hermit or a mole. And when he died, he left it to whomsoever came to preach in the church, for so long as this person spoke God's truth and lived.

The last minister to take up residence had been a kindly man, and for a while the house had seemed benevolent. Peddlers selling trinkets and mousetraps had been welcome to put their feet up in the kitchen. The singers of Christmastide had been invited in.

This new minister, though, come recently from a neighboring county, is a right miserable bogger. A Puritan with strict ideas on how the villagers should conduct themselves, and no lenity in him toward any who frolic out of wedlock (or even in it, it sometimes seems); get drunk on the Sabbath (or any other day of the week, come to that); and dabble in Catholicism or the old pagan rituals.

Singers and peddlers get short shrift from this minister, and he is letting brambles grow up the walls.

"We should go round the back," Sam says as he and Nell approach the place. "Don't you think so?"

"No," Nell replies. "I'm on an errand, and I needs be quick about it."

So saying, she uses both hands to shove open the iron gate, with spikes along the top, that leads into the garden and right up to the minister's front door.

"You be asking for trouble, you," mutters Sam. But he follows her eagerly enough, ducking his bright head beneath a stray branch that juts out like a skinny arm, barring the way.

"Ooer," he breathes as more branches slap out to meet him, and the pupils of his eyes dilate in a sudden greeny gloom.

This is like no garden he has ever set foot in. Where are the flowers, for a start? Even the tiniest plots, down in the village, are bursting with color this season—brimming over with gillyflowers, violets, and clots of creamy yellow primroses. But here . . .

The brightness of the afternoon is having trouble getting through to what were once neat borders with gravel paths in between. The trees have gone wild. Great topiary hedges—originally shaped as a griffin, a hare, a cat, a greyhound, and a peacock—are so unkempt now that they all look like sheep. Arbors and tunnels, designed to support roses, are weighed down by a tangle of unpruned stems, seething with greenfly and thorns.

"They'll get piskies living here, if they don't tend to things," declares Sam. "The really bad sort, what need to lie low for a bit."

"Hmmm." Nell is too focused on her mission to care either way.

"I seen one today," he tells her, lowering his voice as they draw close to the house. "'S'truth, I did. A piskie, plain as anything, up in the orchard. What be the meaning of that, do you think? What would your granny say?"

Nell is picking burrs from her hair and the sleeve of her dress, preparing to face the minister. "She'd say you be blinded by love, Sam Towser, and seeing everything slantwise. And don't you be mentioning no piskies in front of the minister. You know he be an unbeliever."

They have reached the studded oak door, with its round knocker the size of a dinner plate. Nell bangs the knocker, hard, and the door swings open.

"Oh," says Sam. "That's good. We can walk straight in, then, can't we?"

"No, you daft beggar," Nell tells him. "We gotter wait. It's manners."

So they wait, on the step. They wait a long time, but nobody appears.

"Come on," Sam says eventually. "Let's go in. You needs be quick, don't you? We can say we knocked. That's manners enough."

Nell thinks of the newborn. If it dies unbaptized, its soul will go straight to the piskies, to flutter forever as a will-o'-the-wisp, lighting up dark places.

"All right," she agrees. "But don't touch nothing. And don't say nothing either. This is my day's business, not yours. Be you listening to me?"

Sam nods. His eyes are as round as the door knocker, and his mouth as dry as a lavender bag. He might see her now; somewhere in there. It all looks extremely promising.

"Come on, then." Nell shoves the door, so that it swings wide open. The great paneled hall is big enough for a family of five to live in. Sam hesitates. There is dung on his left boot, he is sure of it. Dung on his boot, burrs on his shirt, and enough grime on his face to plant carrots in.

"Come *on*, if you be coming," hisses Nell.

Through the entrance and off to the right, Sam can see the sweep of a staircase with carved spindles and newel posts. *She climbs them stairs to bed,* he thinks. *This is her home. This is where she is.* And he jumps the step in one bound.

Nell is peering from left to right, wondering which way to go. Where would he be, the minister? Beside her, on the wall, hangs a long, somber painting of a boy-child dressed in old-fashioned velvets and a plumed hat. He has a sparrow hawk perched on his left wrist. Both boy and bird have yellowish, hooded eyes that seemed fixed on Nell as she stands there, scratching an itch.

"Through here!" Sam tells her. "This way. Through here." He has homed in on a murmur of voices. Girls' voices. Nell hesitates, then taps at the parlor door.

"Enter."

The command is light, but with an edge to it. *Bogger,* thinks Nell. *It's the haughty one.* And she throws Sam Towser a warning glance before stepping into the room.

The minister's daughters are sitting, straight-backed, on low stools, either side of a granite fireplace. They have pieces of linen on their laps, which Nell assumes they are mending. They wear identical black dresses and clean but ugly bonnets. The younger, stupid-looking one gapes in surprise and drops her needle. The older girl regards them coolly, then says: "Does my father know you are here, treading mud in?"

Nell feels her face grow hot. "No," she says. "But he's needed. There be a newborn in the village. A boy-child."

"So?" The girl's eyes are such a deep, dark brown, they look black; yet her brows, and the little tendrils of hair escaping from her bonnet, are as fair as wheat.

"So, he be sickly and a worry to his mother. 'Tis baptizing he needs, and soon."

The younger daughter has turned away. She is hunched, once more, over her needlework; too timid, it seems, or too simple to say a word. Her sister continues to appraise Nell, a contemptuous little smile lifting the corners of her mouth.

"Hmmm," she says eventually. Then she shifts her gaze to Sam.

"Hello," she says, and Nell watches the smile soften and dimple. "You're an apprentice at the forge, aren't you? I've seen you there. And at church, of course."

Sam's voice comes out squeaking. "I am," he gibbers. "I am that. And church. Yes. I do go regular to church."

Nell could have belted him one. And that girl . . . her fingers itch to slap the smile right off her face.

"The minister," she repeats, clenching her grubby fists in the folds of her apron. "Where is he?"

The younger daughter raises her head, startled by such vehemence. The other one ignores it. She is holding up the piece of linen from her lap. It is a sampler, Nell realizes—an intricately worked thing, with a border of strawberries and lizardlike creatures and some words stitched in the center.

"Can you read what it says?" the girl is saying to Sam. "No, I don't suppose you can. I don't suppose you know your letters at all, do you? Well, then, I'll tell you." Her voice is low. Hypnotic. Mischievous. "It says: 'Virtue is the chiefest beauty of the mind. The noblest ornament of womankind.' That's beautiful, isn't it?"

Sam can feel his legs wobbling. He is useless, under that gaze of hers. Totally, utterly useless. "It is," he mumbles "'Tis truly beautiful, that is."

In her mind Nell can see the newborn, all swaddled up and doing its best to keep breathing. She has come here on a mission, to save its soul, and now Sam Towser is stuttering like an idiot. And that sly, hoity maid . . .

Something similar to a growl rises in her throat, and she surges forward, both hands raised.

"Oh! Oh!" The stupid-looking daughter has found her tongue and is squealing like a piglet. "Help!" she yells. And she cringes back against the fire surround, her open mouth drooling as the cunning woman's granddaughter goes hurtling across the room and snatches her sister's sampler straight out of her hands.

"Father! Someone! Help!"

And as the fingers that still tingle from touching damp baby hair prepare to rip straight through an embroidered lizard and the words "Virtue is . . . ," the parlor door crashes open and in strides the minister.

"Ooer," mutters Sam. He had been halfway across the room, preparing to grab Nell by the back of her apron—by the scruff of her neck, if necessary. But one look from the minister sends him scuttling into a corner.

It is the three girls, then, who face the man.

"What devilment is loose in my house?" His voice is soft, but there is danger in it. His eyes flick over each child in turn. Grace. Patience. And . . . ah, yes . . . the scruffy little heathen whose grandmother follows the old ways.

Nell returns his gaze with as much courage as she can muster. His look is like a shadow falling or the brush of cobwebs on a damp day. It makes Nell shiver. She is glad when his eyes return to the curiously flushed face of his older daughter.

"Well?" he says. "Answer me."

Nell opens her mouth, to speak out of turn, but never gets the chance.

"'Twas a bee, Father. It landed on my sampler. Patience feared it might sting her, until this . . . this person shook it off."

What?

Nell swallows, startled by the smoothness of the lie, which is also an unexpected reprieve.

The minister narrows his eyes. He looks across, just for a second, at the blacksmith's red-faced son, then back at his pink-faced daughter. The expression on his own face is grim. He would kill her, Nell realizes. If he thought she had been dallying with some lad, even just *speaking* to one, he would kill her with his bare hands.

"So where is this bee?" the minister says. "For I see it not, nor do I hear its droning."

"It has flown, Father. Through the window."

"Ah. Then you have had a lucky escape, child, have ye not?"

"Yes, Father."

Nell clears her throat. "We knocked," she pipes up. "Me and Sam. But no one came. We been sent to fetch you, if you please, for a newborn in the village. He be . . . he be not right lusty, so they want God's words spoke."

Slowly the minister turns her way.

"I could have you whipped," he says. "Both of you. For trespass."

Nell lowers her eyes. She is still clutching the sampler.

"I could have *you* put in the stocks," he adds. "For your insolence."

Nell flinches. There are spells to turn situations like this around, but she has never needed one, until now, and isn't sure how to begin. Her granny would have managed. This is how:

A SPELL TO MAKE SOMEONE LIKE YOU
Hold the head high, and banish all niggling thoughts.
When the mind be as calm as a millpond,
call silently upon the energy of the southern quarter—
the Power of fire. Visualize thyself wrapped
thrice around by red-gold light. Breathe in the light.
Feel the strength and the warmth of it,
within and without. Know thyself blessed and
worthy of all company. Wait three beats of the heart,
then smile at thine adversary.
So mote it be.

Nell, though, is in no mood to befriend this particular
adversary. She keeps her head down and neither smiles nor
speaks. Her hands feel all sticky. They will leave dirty marks on
the sampler, but she doesn't care about that, either.

Sam is the one who grovels. He does it well—partly because
he is terrified, but mostly because he knows, just as surely as he
knows that "S" is for "Sam" and that the sun rises in the east,
that groveling like an idiot gives him a fighting chance of returning home unwhipped.

And just when Nell thinks she will puke if she has to listen
to another minute of the boy's bootlicking drivel, the minister
sweeps across the room and flings open the door.

"Get out," he orders.

Sam goes, but Nell stands her ground.

"The newborn," she says. "What of him?"

"I will attend to the babe directly."

The girl, Grace, prods her sharply in the ribs.

"My sampler," she says, "if you please."

Nell looks round at her, really looks; and what she sees makes her fearful in a way she cannot fathom. There is no emotion at all in the older girl's eyes, and her face is as blank as her square of linen would have been before she began to embroider it.

Slowly Nell passes her the sampler. Her mouth, as she does so, seems to open of its own accord.

"Beware," she says. "For a bee, when provoked, do sometimes leave its sting behind."

The words are out before she has time to consider them. Later—weeks later—she will remember and regret such boldness, but for now she simply wipes her hands on her apron, turns on her heel, and marches away.

The minister's voice follows her into the hall, the menace of it ringing in her ears as she lets herself out of the house.

"I mislike thee, child. I mislike thee heartily. Mark well what ye do, for the Lord is watching—and so am I."

Miserable old ranter. Sour-faced bogger. Hope the piskies pay a visit. Hope they come by night, slip-sliding down the chimney to curdle the milk and dance widdershins round your table. Hope they pull out every one of that Grace girl's eyelashes while she sleeps. Hope they piss on her sampler. . . .

Sam is waiting for her at the gate.

"She be swooning for me!" he declares, his face shining. "She be wanting me like nothing on earth, don't you think so?"

And Nell pushes him with such unexpected force that he goes sprawling against the gate's iron bars.

"You're a bogging fool, Sam Towser!" she shrieks. "An' you'll keep well away from that hoity maid, if you've any sense at all in that head of yours."

Sam looks at her in total surprise. Her face is all screwed up and dark with rage. She will never be a dainty thing. Not like Grace. His Grace.

"You're just a chit of a girl, you are," he says. "An impudent chit of a girl. Best you get along home to your granny. Go on. Afore the minister hears more of your shrewish tongue or the piskies do stuff petals in your mouth to sweeten it."

Nell needs no more telling. She is already running.

And *husssh* goes the whispering and the rustling through the hedgerows as she passes. *Trouble stirring . . . trouble a-coming . . . oooo yesssssss.*

The Confession of Patience Madden
THE YEAR OF OUR LORD 1692

*Grace was the pretty one. It wasn't supposed to matter, but it
mattered to me. I would lie awake in the dark, feeling my face
with my fingers, hoping my nose might have gotten smaller, by
some miracle, and my cheeks less like dumplings.*

*My wakefulness had grown worse since we had moved
across the border. The new house was on a hill. It was big and
bleak; all covered over with creepers and full of shadows. I knew
it was the Lord's wish that we should make it our home while
Father brought the one true faith to the ignorant and decidedly
scruffy people of the village. But I didn't like the house. It gave
me bad dreams.*

"Stop fidgeting!" Grace would snap at me. "Go to sleep."

*And I would try not to mind that her face, next to mine,
looked like an angel's.*

*Our mother had been beautiful. Beautiful and good. I liked
to think that she had followed, in spirit, from the place where*

she had birthed us. I liked to picture her hovering over our bed at night, a silent, invisible presence. Sometimes, on the edge of sleep, I could have sworn true that her hand came to rest on my brow. I imagine it still, even though I am almost three times the age she was when she died and no longer care that my brow, like the rest of me, is loathsome to behold.

I was a baby when our mother got sick and went away. She went away and never came back because the sickness killed her. Grace and I rarely spoke of her anymore. She was dead, and that was that. But we knew where Father kept some of her things—the precious things she brought to the marriage, before becoming a Puritan—and Grace knew where the key was hidden.

The night it all started we had been in our new home no more than two moons and were still finding it strange. My father had gone down to the village to baptize a baby boy. It was hot for April, and Grace was as restless as a linnet in a cage. She ate next to nothing at supper and seemed distracted during household prayers.

I caught Father watching her as we knelt. I fidgeted to get him to notice me, too, but the looks he threw me were stern, as usual, so I gave all my attention to the Lord.

After Father had departed, and Grace and I had finished our chores, I went, as was becoming my habit, to the window seat of our bedchamber to sit awhile and look out over the garden. I had a whole world of imaginings in my head in which to lose myself. Different family. Different home. Different face. . . . If I sat for long enough, I no longer saw the treetops or the lengthening shades of evening, so lost did I become in

*choosing a dress from my make-believe closet or conversing with
an imaginary brother who adored me.*

*That night I was dragged from both my imaginings and the
seat, by Grace.*

"Come with me," she said. "Quickly."

She had a key in her hand.

*I wanted no part of it. But "Hurry," she said. And she
hustled me out of our chamber and along the passage, her
fingers digging into my arm as we moved. Outside the room
where Father slept, we hesitated.*

*"Quickly," said Grace again, and in we went. The sun had
set, and the room would have been in darkness but for a ripe,
round moon casting silvery beams across the floor. The great oak
chest stood at the foot of Father's bed. It was strangely carved,
with creatures that were neither man nor beast, and it looked, to
me, like a coffin.*

*"Come away," I whispered. But Grace was already down on
her knees, turning the key in the lock. A bittersweet perfume
rose up as she lifted the lid, and for a flicker of time it seemed
the mother I had barely known was right there, about to hug us.*

*"It's here somewhere," my sister muttered. She was pushing
aside brocades and velvets—crushing them, without caring. A
belt like a length of knotted rope, only softer and prettier, fell to
the floor. I wanted to cry out,* Be gentle! Be gentle! *But she
would have laughed in my face. And anyway, I, too, wanted to
rummage.*

*I knelt down beside her. And "Oh . . . ," I murmured, and
"Oh . . ." again as my fingers fastened on one lovely thing after
another. A comfit box, shaped like a scallop shell . . . a silver*

knife strung on a chain of silver acorns . . . a goblet with a rim of jeweled stars.

Such beautiful, beautiful things. My mouth watered as I touched them, as if they were spun from sugar. The comfit box was easy to open. There was something in it—a white substance, hardened to a lump. I couldn't resist a tiny lick. But, ugh—salt. She'd kept salt in there. . . .

I wondered what the knife was for. For peeling fruit, probably, or snipping ribbons.

"Ah," said Grace. And she pulled out my mother's looking glass. It was an object known to us, after all, it was kept hidden away and we possessed no other. Father used it, from time to time, when he preached against vanity. "Woman!" he would thunder, from the pulpit. "Beware the futility of preening and self-love. For thy name is Eve. Thy name is vanity!" And he would raise that glass, in both hands, and tilt it to reflect a face here and a face there. The old, the young, the wrinkled, the pretty . . . nearly every woman in church would lower her eyes then, so revolted did my father look when he caught a flash of them between his hands.

I wasn't interested in the looking glass. The lying glass. Satan's mirror. I had found a cherrywood box full of tiny things—buttons and pins, bodkins and beads, and spools of silken thread. And nestled there, glinting strangely, was a tiny clasp in the likeness of a frog. An exquisite little frog, its warty greenness made of close-set emeralds, with two rubies for the eyes.

Beside me Grace was preening.

"You're vain," I said. "You're like the daughters of Zion who were haughty and walked abroad with wanton eyes. The

Lord will smite you for that, Grace. He will make you stink and go bald."

She paid me no mind, only smiled at her image. Her face, in the moonlight, looked dreamy and far away. She was a girl who was always gazing into darkened windows or pools of water—her only means, ever, of catching her reflection, unless she was lucky enough to see herself in church, when Father swung the glass.

"If you were a boy," she murmured, "a handsome boy, would you fall in love with me? Would you do anything my heart desired? Would you?"

I should have guessed then what was brewing. I should have read the signs. But I was young, and lone, and conscious only of my mother's absence and my father's complete indifference. That desire could be flung out, like a net, went beyond my understanding. And the idea of my sister beguiling someone— anyone—because she was as hungry for affection as I never entered my head.

"I don't know," I said. "Maybe."

It was then we heard the commotion in the yard. A clatter of hooves on cobbles.

"It's Father!" said Grace. "Quick!"

And she slipped the looking glass between the folds of a cambric nightgown and jumped to her feet. I still had the cherrywood box, held open on my lap.

"Come on, you stupid goose. Hurry!"

My fingers touched the emerald frog. It was so perfect. So small. And I wanted it so badly that my hand closed around it and took it away as naturally as a pike's mouth would open and close around a living thing in a small, dark pond.

Then I snapped the box shut and thrust it to the bottom of the chest.

"Hurry." Grace slammed the lid down and turned the key. She hadn't noticed my thieving. She thought I was just being slow. A slow, clumsy goose. "Hurry, hurry, hurry."

I slept badly that night. The emerald frog was hidden beneath my side of the mattress. In my dreams it was choking, and I was to blame. I didn't see Grace get up or hear her lift the window latch. When I woke, with a start, she was leaning out, bending to the dark with her arms outstretched. She looked like a swan or maybe a dove. It seemed to me she was going to fall.

"Grace?" I murmured, unsure, at that second, whether I was truly awake. She whirled round. There was something in her hands; something plucked from the air or from the creeper that grew on thick twisted stems all over the front of the house.

"What is it?" I said. "Is it a bird? Is it a bat? Is it dead?"

"Be quiet," she hissed. "Go back to sleep."

She was about to shut the window. But before she did, she leaned again into the night and made a sound like she was tutting or spitting a mouthful of gruel. I know now that she must have been blowing a kiss. A kiss . . .

I know, also, what it was that she caught. What he threw to her that night. For I found it, long afterward, beneath her side of the mattress. A wooden heart, branded through with the letters "S" and "G." A rough, ugly thing compared to my frog, but equally precious, to her, I dare say. And as dangerous. And as impossible to keep hidden away for long.

MAY
1645

It is still dark on May Morning, when Nell opens her eyes. The cunning woman is talking in her sleep. "Ground ivy," she mutters. "Two drams . . ." and then, "No whitethorn in it . . . No . . . No . . . Leave out the whitethorn."

"Granny!" Nell scolds. "You be blathering again."

The old woman stirs. Her body, beside Nell's, is as small as a child's and as bony as a bird's. "Violets," she mumbles. "For the throat ache . . ."

Nell frowns. Scuttling and nibbling sounds she is used to, because there are mice, starlings, and all sorts sharing this roof space. The rain, too, sometimes wakes her, for there are holes in the rafters where the thatch has fallen in or blown clean away. Her grandmother's nighttime chunterings, though, are a recent thing, and most unnatural.

Wide awake now, Nell rises from the pallet and climbs down a ladder into the bottom room. The fire, with the great cauldron slung over it, has burned to a pile of ashes. The air smells of wood smoke and sour herbs.

"Out of my path!"

A dun-colored chicken with eyes as dark and stupid as currants scuttles heavily away.

May Morning . . . Nell opens the cottage door, pushing hard against damp hinges and a great tangle of honeysuckle. To the east, faint streaks of light and the promise of another fine day.

Not many years ago fires would have been burning throughout the night on hilltops all around. And somewhere there would have been a circle. A circle of green branches, with hay stooks marking the four quarters and flames glowing bright in the center. A circle cast in secret, near oak trees and running water. Nell's granny would have been there, presiding over everything with her wand, her knife, and her platter of salt. There would have been dancing—wild, spiral dancing—and a feast of Sabbat cakes, dripping with honey. Just before dawn the young would have gone whirling away into the woods, and any babies conceived would have been special. Merrybegots. Nature's own.

Nell is a Merrybegot, and proud of it.

Ever since she can remember, she has washed her face in the dew every May Morning and gone with other children to gather flowers for the pole. Today, though, there will be none of that. And what will the piskies make of this sudden break with tradition? Piskies love a bit of revelry, particularly with summer coming to warm their lairs and stir the blood in their stringy veins. The piskies won't think much of the minister for spoiling everyone's fun. Really, someone ought to think about appeasing those piskies, with a bit of cake or a few primroses scattered in the lanes.

Behind her the dun chicken begins to scratch and peck.

"Behave," Nell tells it. "And lay an egg for once. Two eggs, if you please."

Then she snatches her bonnet and shawl from a peg beside the door and goes running through wet cobwebby grass, down the slope that leads to the edge of the village and the dense wood where the best primroses grow.

Meanwhile the cunning woman is dreaming. A strange, troublesome dream; part memory, part prophecy. Her son is there, behind her eyes. Nell's father. Gone for a sailor these many years. Gone . . . gone . . . In her dream he is coming to meet her, with a bundle wrapped in sheepskin clutched to his chest. "Look after her," he says, but his words are whipped away on a bitter, northerly wind.

"Plantain . . . ," moans the cunning woman. "Fresh leaves . . . crushed . . . for wounds."

The image of her son wavers, like a reflection in troubled water. "Look after her," he says again. And the cunning woman knows that he has traveled across some great divide—oceans . . . time . . . even death, maybe—just as surely as he came to her, in the flesh, twelve winters ago, with his newborn daughter wriggling in his arms.

Look after her.

This dream is a sign. Some kind of warning.

There is no rest in sleep nowadays for the cunning woman. She is still dog-tired when she opens her eyes. And her bones, as she clambers down from the roof space, grind in their sockets like pestles in empty mortars.

The girl is nowhere to be seen.

Gone . . . gone . . .

37

The cunning woman bends over her cauldron and gives the dregs at the bottom a bit of a stir. What potion or lotion had she planned to mix today? Was it the meadowsweet and parsley infusion, for Mistress Coombe's cough? Or wormwood steeped in the blood of a hare, to ease the pains in Silas Denby's great windy gut?

Nell will remember. She will wait for Nell before starting anything. Where is the girl? These are strange times. Troublesome times. She must remind the girl to be careful.

Shivering and mumbling, the cunning woman scoops up the dun chicken and settles herself on a rough wooden bench. Her fingers touch crumbs and a few tiny bones, scattered like spillikins upon the seat.

The piskies have been. They have eaten their sparrow and gorged on cake. In return . . . yes . . . they have left the root. The special root that shrieks so piercingly when pulled from the earth that no mortal can dig it up without going mad. Dried and grated, this root is a wonderful tonic, particularly for barren wives. Supplies of it are running low, so the cunning woman is grateful to the piskies for remembering her this day.

"Thank'ee," she croaks, just in case any of the scabby wee things are hanging around. "Thank'ee thrice and thank'ee nice. And thank'ee once again."

Something scrabbles beside the open door—something small, hidden behind the cunning woman's broomstick. The dun chicken stretches out its neck and clucks softly. The cunning woman holds tight to its warm feathery body, so that it cannot launch itself from her lap and go skittering across the room. It would be no contest, a tussle between a piskie and a chicken, for piskies fight dirty when cornered and can see off rats, cats—the occasional dog, even—with no more than their incisors and the razor-sharp ends of their filthy fingernails.

A rustle of twigs, and there it stands—a wizened, cross-eyed, elderly piskie, annoyed at being caught napping and digesting its sparrow meat, when it should have been long gone, back to its ditch, with the others.

"It's all right," the cunning woman tells it. "'Tis only me. Me and this daft chicken."

The piskie grunts, turns, and bends over. It is wearing trousers made from a stolen kerchief, with a flap at the back, which it is about to lift.

"Wait," says the cunning woman. "I see you. You see me. A question asked must be answered free. My granddaughter. The Merrybegot. Be she heading trouble's way?"

The piskie pauses. Then it raises its head—as knobbled as an old potato—and sniffs the air.

Ah. The cunning woman is not so senile that she cannot observe, listen, and learn. The piskie has sniffed the air. It knows, then, just as she herself has always known, that answers to important questions come not from the hollows of the mind, but from beyond the self. From the elements.

Outside a cock is crowing. Smoke begins to rise from chimneys, in soft wavy lines. Down in the village Mistress Bramlow lifts her month-old baby from his crib and frets when he won't feed. The blacksmith stokes the great fire at the forge and curses his absent son for a love-struck scallywag.

Nell, scattering primroses in a quiet lane, feels a shadow at her back and turns to find the minister watching her. He is in the next field, standing among corn like the grim reaper or a particularly dour scarecrow. He is looking for frolickers. Heathens. Merrymakers. A few minutes more, and he will catch sight of the blacksmith's son sauntering out of the woods with bracken fronds stuck to his shirt and a smile like a slice of sunshine lighting up his face. He will put two and two together and come up with the wrong answer.

Meanwhile his elder daughter will have returned home, unnoticed. She will have let herself into the house the same way she left it—hand over hand, one tiny foot after another, seeking and finding a route through the creeper that looks like a shawl, but can serve as a ladder, from bedchamber to earth and back again.

All of this the piskie senses as it lingers in the cunning woman's cottage, sniffing. The distant future, too, is whirling in the air. Tiny signals. Bits of information, dancing around like motes of dust. The piskie snuffs a bit of that up too and tries not to grin too broadly. Piskies love trouble. It is their favorite sport. It is Shakespeare and Greek tragedy rolled into one. It is human life at risk and in the raw.

Ooooo.

"Well?" says the cunning woman.

The piskie licks its lips. Its voice, when it comes, is dry and rasping.

"Oh, merry . . . merry . . . Merrybegots," it caws. "Trouble coming. Shape of the ranter. Shape of the frog. Shape of the heart that cannot love."

The cunning woman shifts on the bench, ruffles the chicken, and sighs.

"I be too old for riddles," she says. "And for shapes. I need things clearer now. But thank'ee anyway. For the warning."

Bending right over, the piskie lifts the flap of its trousers. A flash of its arse—rough as a split log and more clotted with muck than the rear of a sheep—and it is out, into the morning, and away.

Sunday: The little church is full. It always is. There are those who truly believe; some who are trying to; and a few who never will, but need to pretend, for the look of it.

Nearly everyone remembers when there was stained glass in the church window, all lit up on sunny days, like little bits of heaven. There was an altar, too, with a statue of the Virgin Mary, a tall candle always burning, and niches where folk could leave roses, or apples, or locks of hair from a sickly child in need of the Lady's blessing. None of those things are here anymore. They were papist trappings, according to the minister, and no great loss to anyone. There is a plain table now where the altar used to be and nothing at all in the window except a rectangular view of the heavens themselves, be they cloudy, fair, or bucketing rain.

No one knows what has happened to the beautiful statue of Mary. Some claim it was rescued, under cover of darkness, and is standing, still, in some private chapel or secret chamber. Others will tell you it was carted deep into the wood and thrown among brambles, where it lies, facedown, weeping bright blue tears. But those who understand the way of the world say it got smashed to smithereens with a mallet.

Nell misses the Lady. Expecting nothing much from today's sermon, she sits next to her grandmother and drifts into a dream. She is thinking about going later to gather cress beside the old pond. In her mind's eye she can see the play of light on water and the way certain trees lean toward their reflections, dipping and trailing their branches in the shallows like wood nymphs washing their hair. Should the day continue hot, she will leave her clothes and her bundle of cress among the reeds and go into the pond herself. It will be lovely, she thinks, to float there awhile, looking up at the great bowl of the sky and—

"There is lewdness among us, good people. Lust. Lascivious behavior and willful disobedience. . . ."

The minister is in full spate. Nell smothers a yawn. No doubt he has got wind of Silas Denby, and some of the other men, journeying fifteen miles over the moor to get drunk and sing bawdy songs. Perhaps he followed them one night and caught Silas Denby with a strumpet. Perhaps . . .

"A daughter of Eve. Steeped in sin!"

A woman, then. Who could that be? Not Mistress Bramlow, for she loves her husband dearly and, anyway, wouldn't have the energy. Not any of the Watchers, either, for they are so bogging ugly. . . . Maybe Mistress Denby has had enough of her husband's scoundrelly ways and is making a cuckold of him with some farmhand or other. Maybe . . .

"Even now, good people, she feigns innocence. Wide-eyed as a lamb, she sits as if the wrath of our Lord is of no more consequence than a distant roll of thunder or the prickle of a thorn."

Oh, dear. Nell is intrigued now. The whole congregation is intrigued.

Who is it?

Which woman or maid among them has dared be lewd and

lascivious, knowing full well that the minister misses nothing and will label you a trollop simply for wearing a ribbon?

From her place next to her grandmother, Nell can see the minister's daughters holding themselves as still as can be, their hands folded in their laps, their eyes downcast. The older one's cheeks are as pale as milk, but there is something about the set of her profile . . .

Quickly, for it isn't ladylike to gawp in church, Nell swings round, to look at the blacksmith's son. His face is crimson. His face is a beetroot. And he is sweating worse than a spooked stallion.

Nell puts two and two together and comes up with the right answer.

"You!"

The minister raises his right arm, like a mad deity about to hurl a thunderbolt, and points one shaking finger.

Slowly, the whole congregation turns and stares. Nell feels her grandmother's hand steal across her own, to hold it tight.

"Me?" *Me?*

"Do you deny it, child? Do you dare to deny it? Here in the Lord's house? Do you deny that you indulged in wanton pleasures and heathen ritual, at the dawning of the month, against my express command and the teachings of our Lord?"

For several seconds Nell can only gape at her accuser. In the hush of these seconds she finds herself wondering how she could ever have likened his features to a parsnip. For parsnips, when all is said and done, are familiar, wholesome things, and this person is clearly crazed.

"Do. You. Deny it?"

"Yes, I bogging well do!"

The cunning woman's fingers press gently down. It is a warning to her granddaughter to be careful. To accept this humiliation, however unjust, however cruel, rather than rile the minister.

Trouble coming. Shape of the ranter.

Nell snatches her hand away.

"Tell him, Sam Towser!" she cries, wheeling round on the bench. "Tell him it weren't me!"

But the blacksmith's mute and horrified son will not even look at her.

"Tell him, Sam!"

Useless words . . . falling on deaf ears. And no point turning on that Grace one, either, with a mouthful of bitterness and blame. For she is a good girl. A good, pretty, God-fearing girl. And no one would believe it. No one.

Toward the back of the church the baby, Amos Bramlow, begins to cry. It is a weak and weary sound, as if he suddenly understands the kind of place and time he has been born into and cannot bear it.

"Hush now," whispers his mother, but the baby cries on, and the sound of it—the pity of it—dulls Nell's fighting spirit like nothing else and fills her with a kind of despair.

I don't care, she tells herself, slumping against her grandmother with her fists clenched, and her eyes and mouth closed tight, to keep her own wailing in. *I don't care what anyone thinks. They can believe what they like. I don't care.*

The cunning woman places one arm around her shoulders. It is a gesture of solidarity, in front of everyone, but it is not enough. It is nowhere near enough.

• • •

"I didn't do it. It weren't me! It were her—that hoity one. His own daughter! I know it was."

"Be still. Be calm. Everything passes, and so will this."

"No, I won't be calm. It isn't fair. It isn't *fair*. I'm going straight to the big house now, to tell him. I am!"

"No, girl. No. It will do no good. It may even cause more harm. Listen to me. Listen. For I know these things. . . ."

They are back at their cottage, with the door closed. The cunning woman is rummaging among her stone bottles, looking for something soothing. Camomile. Strawberry. Something sweet. With a tincture of poppy, perhaps, so that the girl will sleep.

Nell, meanwhile, is rampaging round the cauldron, butting her head into dangling bunches of rosemary, betony, comfrey, and hyssop, and kicking out at everything—fate, bits of kindling, the dun chicken.

"And why weren't *he* picked on?" she cries, pausing momentarily as this particular piece of injustice hits home. "Why didn't *he* get bawled at for being lewd and disobedient and . . . and steeped in sin?"

The cunning woman considers her granddaughter's face— all crumpled and tearstained now that there is no crowd to enjoy her humiliation.

"'Twas ever thus," she tells her. "Men and boys, they get away with all kinds."

Nell rubs one hand across her snotty cheeks and sighs a great, juddery sigh.

"He should have told the truth," she mutters. "Back there, in front of everyone. He should have said it weren't me."

The cunning woman's sigh is more resigned. "Men and boys," she says. "Some are worthy of us and some aren't."

"We could hex him for that," declares Nell. "We could, Granny. On a waning moon, when the time be right for revenge. We could make it so he never frolics again. Not with anyone. Ever."

"No, girl." The cunning woman is tired now. Tired and strangely pained around her middle. For many years she has felt it in her middle when a local woman is about to drop a pot lid. Usually the ache is dull and low in her abdomen. Only twice before has it been like this—a needling sensation as if tiny feet in pointed shoes are dancing in her womb.

A fairychild. A fairychild is soon to be born, across in the neighboring county. Before long, under cover of darkness, there will be a rapping at the door, and she will be expected to go. It is a rare event, the birth of a fairy, and fraught with significance and danger. Piskies (praise the elements) drop their own litters—one, two, three—among stinging nettles and would spit in the eye of any midwife who tried to interfere. The fairies, though, they do things by ritual—beautifully, precisely, and with dramatic effect.

But, oh, this time . . . this time . . . Just thinking about delivering a fairy makes the cunning woman tremble. She is too old for it. Too jaded. If it happens . . . If the call comes, Nell will have to go in her place.

Only, Nell is so young . . . and not yet fully trained. She will need a particular kind of Knowledge to do this job properly. Harder still, she will need courage and great strength of mind to get home safely after it is done, for the fairies don't always want you to leave. Sometimes they want you to stay with them. Forever.

Beside her Nell is grinding some seeds in a bowl. Grinding and muttering and bashing away, as if the bottom of the bowl needs punishing. She has lit a candle—a dark one—and placed a knife dead center of the table, pointing south. She has found a lardy blob of wax, which she has every intention of melting, in a minute, and fashioning, by guesswork, to the approximate shape of Sam Towser's private parts.

"Where's the hemlock?" she asks.

The cunning woman shakes her head.

"Let it be," she says. "Let it go. There is other Knowledge I must impart to you, and we do not have much time."

The Confession of Patience Madden

THE YEAR OF OUR LORD 1692

*It was toward the middle of May that I began to follow my
sister. The nights were wretched hot by then. Too hot to sleep,
although I always feigned it while I counted the seconds it
would take Grace to cross to the window, then clamber out
and down, to the mess of weeds and stones below. Another few
minutes I would give her before flinging a dark cloak over my
nightgown and going over the sill myself.*

*Some thrill, it was, to be out in the night, like a bat or a
ghost. Yet, to begin with, I was too nervous of shadows and
the strange calls of owls and other things to venture beyond the
garden. It was enough, that first time, to lurk behind the trunk
of an elm, looking up at the stars and waiting.*

*I half tumbled to her secret in the dim hour before dawn.
For he accompanied her home—right up to the gate—and
was in no hurry to let her go. He kept himself in shadow,
so I did not glimpse his face, but from the shiver that*

went through me, I could tell this was no ordinary tryst.

My sister . . . The sound of her simpering brought bile to my throat. In the semidarkness, and from a distance, I could just make out her hair, all loose like a mermaid's, but with burrs as big as snails stuck in it, from lying on the ground.

Part of me wanted to cry out: Grace! Are you mad to behave so? Come away! *It would have driven her to fury, though. She would have struck me right there on the spot and made my days even more of a misery than they already were.*

Instead, I backed away and skittered like some small beast back to the house. My cloak caught as I sought blindly for footholds against the wall—for jutting bricks and thick stems—and I was trembling, scratched, and chilly with dew as I scrambled over the windowsill and back into bed.

Be still, *I told myself.* Be calm. She mustn't know.

And she didn't know. She didn't guess. For I could have been a lumpy old bolster or a warming brick gone cold overnight for all she cared as she slipped beneath the coverlet, some few moments after me, and smiled herself to sleep.

But I—I lay awake long past cockcrow, wondering what to do. Father was away, as he so often was, on the Lord's business. But he would be home in time for the Sunday sermon. Should I tell him? He loathed frolickers with a particular vengeance and would have whipped Grace for sure. And the lad, whoever he was—Father would have whipped the skin right off him and hung it up in church like a stained sheet.

By the time I rose to begin my chores, I had decided to do nothing for the moment; to keep my sister's secret as securely hidden as the emerald frog beneath our mattress, and to bide my time.

Perhaps, *I thought, she will tire of her sweetheart or come to her senses before Father returns. You must remember, I loved my sister and did not want to see her in the worst kind of trouble. I would follow her, I decided. Just to be close at hand, should she fall over in the darkness or find herself in danger and call for help.*

After a few weeks I started to enjoy being out in the night.

My eyes by then were getting used to the gloom, and the moon was ripening. I knew, also, how much time I had before Grace left off steeping herself in sin and returned home. It was several hours at least—long enough, anyway, for me to ramble as far from her as I dared and to know the exhilaration of being as free and as wild as a weasel.

I had no wish, anymore, to waste time spying. Nor was I curious to discover precisely who was dallying with my sister. Just thinking about that made me feel hot and uncomfortable in a way I neither liked nor understood.

I knew frolicking was a sin, but what it involved went beyond my understanding. The word itself put me in mind of lambs, jumping and leaping and butting heads in a meadow, but the other words crowding my head—words like "harlot" and "fornication," "lewdness" and "abomination"—were frightening to me. I understood them least of all.

Fortunately my imagination saved me. What a sweet and powerful force it was. What a friend! In my black cloak, with the hood pulled up, I could have been anyone. I could have been a beggar, an enchantress, or a small thief. Certainly there was much I should have feared. There were vagrants and rebel soldiers up in the hills—rough men who would slip into villages like ours, under cover of darkness, to steal chickens or hay. And there were piskies in the ditches, so I'd heard, capable of all kinds of mischief—particularly at night. I could have had my neck wrung or my senses spellbound at any time. But my imagination wrapped me around as snug as any cloak, and I believed myself untouchable—invisible, even—as I skirted the lanes, haunted the edges of the wood, and watched the moon grow.

The night I met the Devil was one of the hottest of the year, and the moon was as round and pale as a dish. My cloak that night seemed to smother me, so I took it off and left it folded beneath a stone. I felt lighter without it. Daintier. It didn't worry me that I could be spotted more easily, flitting about in a white nightgown. Perhaps I was moonstruck. Perhaps the Devil was already calling from across the moor. Certainly all was not right, for I had a yearning suddenly for something to happen— something outside my own imaginings, which seemed for the first time as stale as old crusts and of no particular comfort.

My usual haunts left me restless. The woods held no mystery, and the narrow lanes hemmed me in. Foxgloves curved like pink scythes from the hedges, shedding pollen into my hair as I pushed them up and away. Over everything lay a thick scent of woodbine, cloying and sweet.

It was a beautiful night, I remember that. It made me want to leap and sing praises. It put me in mind of Solomon's song: "I went down into the garden of nuts to see the fruits of the valley, and to see whether the vine flourished and the pomegranates budded."

There were no pomegranates in this village, though. Only apples and corn.

I had always stayed close to the village before. This time I felt drawn, as if by magic, away from there, along the path that led to the orchard. Perhaps, *I thought,* I will meet a vagrant. Or see a piskie. Perhaps I will help a rebel soldier steal a chicken—or, better still, a horse!

I was thinking exactly that—about stealing a horse—when I heard the muffled thud of hoofbeats approaching from the west. I was next to the orchard and could have taken cover easily enough beneath the trees. I didn't, though. I stayed exactly where I was, beside the stile, my heart drumming in time with whatever I was about to encounter, and my very ears tingling with excitement.

It was only at the last second, when it was too late to run and too late to hide, that I fell on my knees and began to pray.

JUNE
1645

The knock comes, as the cunning woman knew it would, in the dead of a night so humid that the whole of nature seems poised on the brink of ripening, melting, or expiring before dawn.

Nell is the first to hear it. Three sharp raps of a silver hammer—*bang, bang, bang*—on the door. *The fairies,* she tells herself, jerking bolt upright. *The fairies have sent their messenger!*

"Granny!" she hisses. "It's him. It must be. Go answer it."

The cunning woman moves faster than she has done in a long while. Down the ladder she goes, joints clicking, dreams and spells unraveling in her head. On the bottom rung she pauses and calls up a final warning:

"Remember, girl, be not beguiled. Do your job and come straight home. Eat nothing. Drink nothing. And if you hear music, however sweet, do not follow it. All will not be as it seems. Remember that."

Yes, yes, thinks Nell. *A plum will turn to slurry in my mouth. A sip of nectar will shrivel my tongue. And even one or two notes, played on a fiddle, will draw me so deep into the fairy labyrinth, if*

53

I let them, that there will be no getting out this side of doomsday.

"Do you hear me?" her granny calls. "You're a Merrybegot, don't forget. A child sacred to nature. That makes you extra special. They'll keep you if they can."

"I hear you, Granny," Nell calls back. "And I'll be careful. So don't worry."

Still, her fingers tremble as she hurries into her clothes and unhooks a linen bag from the rafters. Does she have all she needs? Is she ready? The things in the bag are the size of marbles, seeds, and toothpicks. Small, magical things for bringing a small, magical being into the world.

Nell takes a deep breath and lets it out. Inside she is terrified. What if she *can't* get home? What if the fairies manage to trick her after all?

Don't dwell on it, she scolds herself. *You have a job to do.*

Leaving the roof space, she lets her eyes rest for a moment on familiar objects: a turnip-shaped hole in the thatch . . . a basin of rose water for washing in . . . the rough pallet where she has slept beside her granny since she was little more than a badly jangled pot lid.

I'll be back, she tells these things. *I won't let no fairy fruit beguile me. Nor no fairy minstrel, neither. Not me.*

The cunning woman is waiting at the foot of the ladder, looking up. To Nell, looking down, that wise, wizened face is the most familiar object of all, and the best loved. The old arms fly out now, like a couple of hinged sticks, ready to wrap her in a bony hug.

"Don't be fussing," Nell grumbles gently as she reaches the ground. "You'll squash the bag. And look . . . Just look at that daft chicken."

The dun chicken is two flaps away from the open door, lit up in a shaft of moonlight, like a fat, feathery performer about to burst into song. All fluffed up it is, like a brushed wig; skittering and bobbing and stretching its silly neck toward the visitor waiting outside.

"Hah!" scolds the cunning woman. "Beguile my chicken, would you? I don't think so."

And she blows her nose, briskly, between finger and thumb, then positions herself between her bird and the cottage door. Nell edges round the cauldron and peers out into the silvery gloom. She is ready now. Ready to go.

But, oh . . . Is that really a horse, sidestepping neatly on the path? It looks like a horse, and a very fine one too—as black as pitch, with rippling muscles and a flowing mane. But the breath flaring from its nostrils twinkles in the air, like powdered stars, and its hooves are striking sparks from the earth.

On its back sits a man, no bigger than a three-year-old child. He wears breeches—nothing else—and his skin gleams, phosphorescent as the scales of a fish. His face, Nell notes, is beautiful. But there is no warmth in it as he leans across the horse's neck to beckon her forward.

"Be thou the Merrybegot?"

Nell nods and hastens her step. She knows what's expected. Jump up quick and be gone. No time for chitchat. No time to check again her midwifery bag or pick a flower for luck. The piskies—who loathe all fairies and would attack on sight—are being kept at bay by the sheer force of her grandmother's will. And her grandmother's will, Nell knows, is not what it used to be.

"Huppa-la!" cries the fairymanchild, in a voice that could shatter glass. And are those roses Nell sees in the bushes as she is whisked off her feet? Newly opened white roses already going brown around their centers? Or a cluster of piskie buttocks raised in outrage as the fairyhorse rears onto its hind legs, peppers the path with a whinny of glitter, and takes off, away from the village?

It takes both seconds and forever to get to where they are going. There is no saddle on the fairyhorse, no stirrups, bridle, or reins; and at first Nell clings like grim death to the sides of the fairymanchild's breeches, digs both her knobbly knees so hard into the horse's flanks that they ache, and silently begs every single Power of earth, air, fire, and water to keep her from falling off.

After a while she realizes that falling is probably the one and only thing she doesn't have to worry about. For although the horse is galloping at breakneck speed, the sensation is more like gliding . . . gliding smoothly, without a bump or a jolt. Like sailing through the air on the back of a thumping great arrow.

"Wheee!" she whoops in the fairymanchild's ear, by way of conversation. "Be we there nearly?"

No answer. Fairymenchildren speak only if necessary, when circumstances force them aboveground. This one's wings are folded so tight against his back, to keep them out of the way, that they look fit to split, like larvae. He is three times his normal size—as big as a fairy gets, when duty calls—but his skin and wings itch from being stretched, and all he wants is to deliver this ugly bug of a mortal to the birthing chamber, shrink into his slippers, and get paralytic on fermented berries.

In something of a temper, he leans into the horse's neck and urges it on.

Loosening her grip on him, just a little, and unscrewing her eyes, Nell senses, rather than sees, trees, hedges, and standing stones zipping past in a dizzying blur of shapes and shadows. They are traveling too fast for her to notice anything in particular.

Until they reach the hill.

The cunning woman has prepared her as thoroughly as possible to face the hill. Fairy magic will get her physically through and in, but to remain self-possessed and unafraid, she must believe, absolutely, that entering solid earth is as natural as stepping from one room into another. This is how:

A SPELL TO ENTER A HILL
AS IF IT WERE MADE OF MIST
Thrice daily, for seven days,
and again in the minute before impact,
call upon the Powers of the east:
"Air whistle, air blow, turn the wheel of magic so.
Wrap me round, from head to toe,
as into the unknown I go."
Visualize every bone in thy body as lighter
than the merest wisps of matter.
As light as a sigh, thou art, yet strong, still, and
sharper, in thy mind, than any digging implement.
Know thyself as much a part of nature as the
highest mound of earth and grass, and as capable
as any mole of entering or leaving it at will.
So mote it be.

This is easier said than done. Particularly in the minute before impact. And as the hill looms larger, then larger still, a shriek as loud as a whistle rises up in Nell's gullet and is out, streaming behind her, before she can stop it. Nor can she keep her eyes wide open as her granny bade her. It is too hard. Too terrifying. Only her mind remains focused—enough, at least, to stop her leaping from the horse and breaking all the bones she is supposed to be thinking of as wisps. And in her mind the words turn frantically: *Oh, Powers of air, please be here now. Please be here now. Please be here now . . .*

Please . . .

BEEEEeeeeeeeeeeee heyeaaaaaaaaaaaaaar.

Ohstopstopstop. OhPowersofbogginganywhereatall

This is . . .

Oh!

It is done.

She is through.

In the end it was a bit like diving into a haystack—a headlong rush into something that prickled and clogged, pressed heavily down, but gave way enough to let her in. In the end it was no trickier than cutting into a green pie. She is through. The horse and its rider have vanished, and she must wait now to be taken farther.

Come, come, come . . .

The inside of the hill resembles a cave. A great, yawning cave, with stalagmites jutting up and stalactites hanging down, each one wreathed around by roots and shining with the same luminescence as fairy skin. From close by comes the sound of splashing, only with a chime to it. At first Nell thinks it is waterfalls making that noise. Then she realizes that the foam cascading down the hill's innards is made up of thousands of tiny white flowers and . . . and faces. Perfect little faces with budlike mouths calling, *Come, come, come* . . . The urgency and resonance of it is like the tinkling of bells summoning small sinners to an illusionary church.

Clutching her bag, Nell steps forward a little way over the rough, sparkling ground. And in a trice they are on her: half a dozen fairyfolk, whirring like dragonflies and tugging at her dress.

Come . . . come . . .

Their cold little hands are pulling her toward a crevice between two vast dangling roots.

"You be jesting, surely?"

The crevice is so narrow that only parchment, fairies, and worms could slip through it with ease. But the hands continue to pull and the wings to whirr, and before she can say another word, or even hold in her breath to make herself thinner, Nell feels her whole body contract, slide, then pull itself together again on the other side of the opening.

"Right," she says, brushing down her apron and blinking rapidly. "I see. I understand." *Granny forgot to warn me of that,* she thinks. *She left that bit out. She . . . she hasn't prepared me properly. Her mind be too spluttery. What else did she forget, I wonder? What else don't I know?*

Too late to worry about that now. She is in an earthen antechamber, ducking to keep from bumping her head. And at her feet is a bed of moss with a laboring fairywoman on it. The bed is little bigger than a bird's nest, and the fairy is thumping it with tiny fists and swearing worse than a pirate. Nearby stands her consort. He shakes his gorgeous head and beckons Nell closer.

"Four years," he chimes. "You took your time."

Time means nothing here, Nell reminds herself. *It's all right. It will all be the same when you get home. No one will be any older.*

Ignoring him she kneels at the foot of the mossy bed and scrabbles in her bag of bits. The light is bad. She will need more light than this, and says so.

"Huppa-la!" commands the fairywoman's consort, and the place is lit, suddenly, by umpteen pinpoints of matter— glowworms, fireflies, fallen stars. Nell cannot tell what they are. Their light has a strange greenish tinge, but it will do.

There is a flat rock beside her left knee, draped with a cloth as fine as a web. On it she places the things she will need. Her fingers hover over each minuscule item: the silver hairpins, the snippets of herbs, the pot of ointment, and the precious stone.

"Tell me," she says to the fairywoman on the bed. "Do you want to twirl this baby out, or shall I use the pincers?"

"**!!!****"

"Twirling it is, then," says Nell. "Come on, up you get."

Standing, the fairywoman is no taller than a wand and so beautiful that Nell could have wasted valuable moments just staring. She is wearing a gauzy gown that clings to the rippling tennis-ball shape of her belly, and her wings, as she unfurls them, seem made of the same delicate material.

Is she the queen of the fairies? Perhaps she is. Or maybe all fairywomen are this lovely, even the ones who cook the dinners, sweep the halls, and empty the thimble-size chamber pots. Maybe they all have gauzy gowns and consorts.

"Right, then," Nell tells her. "Start twirling."

The consort is checking out the bits and pieces on the rock.

"Where's the icicle?" he says.

Nell feels her stomach lurch.

"What icicle?"

"The icicle. For cutting the cord."

Playing for time, Nell picks up the precious stone and makes a big show of polishing it on the hem of her apron. *Granny,* she cries in her mind. *I don't know about no icicle. I don't know what I'm doing. You didn't tell me about no bogging icicle!*

The stone glows, red as blood, in her lap. Plucked from an eagle's nest, it contains another tinier stone, which shakes and sounds within it. Eagles, it is said, will not hatch a single brood without a stone like this lying somewhere among the eggs, like a solid clot. Its magical properties will help draw the fairybaby down and out, when the time comes. But it won't cut the cord. Nell knows that much for sure.

Carefully, professionally, she puts the stone back, next to the herbs. The consort is glaring up at her, arms folded, one foot tapping the ground.

"Well?" he snaps. "Has it melted? Are you such a beginner and a fool that you can't even keep an icicle sharp?"

Nell forces herself to meet his look.

"Times are changing," she tells him. "We midwives don't use icicles with you lot no more. There be other ways—better ways—of doing things."

The consort's eyes glimmer and blink.

"Liar," he says softly.

And Nell could run now. For two pins, she could chuck

61

herself back through the crevice and run, never minding what beguiled or became of her on the way. Let down by her granny, insulted by a tiny man, and minus an icicle, she could happily run for all eternity.

But "Yeeeeow!" and "**!!** ****!!! Get this thing out of me!" shrieks the laboring fairywoman, whose welfare in this chamber is Nell's responsibility—for better or worse.

"Give me herbs. Anything! Only, get it out, get it out, or I'll . . . I'll . . . sting you."

She is twirling madly. Twirling and cursing and whirling above her bed in a frenzy of beating wings and fluttering, flapping gauze.

"Right," snaps Nell, reaching for a snippet of mugwort. "This is it. For when a birthing fairy gets nasty, 'tis time for her to chant."

"But she's always nasty," says the consort, disarmed and distracted now by the speedy turn of events beyond his jurisdiction. "It's her nature."

"Quiet!" Nell orders him. "And get back behind that rock, out of the way."

Mutely he does as he is told.

"Good man."

Nell is calm now. Calm and in control.

The fairywoman's toes touch down on the moss, brace there for a few seconds while she rests, and then lift off again.

"You're doing well," Nell tells her gently. "You be doing really, really well." Without turning her head, she reaches for the eagle stone and balances it on the palm of her right hand. Her knees are cramping from being crouched down, but she must stay like this, as still as can be, holding her outstretched hand with the stone on it midway between the moss and the whirling, cursing fairywoman, ready and waiting to catch . . .

"Now," she breathes. "Start chanting."

It takes both seconds and forever, this final, vital stage. And each moment an eon of time is shot through. For Nell, with a sense of wonder as the sound of chanting swells like a symphony and throbs like a heart. For it isn't just the fairywoman and her consort mouthing the ancient fairybirthing words. The very walls of the chamber echo with them as if hundreds of voices, along with whatever is providing the sparks of greenish light, are lifting and soaring and urging this delivery to a safe and happy conclusion. It is a magical chant, a secret mantra; and the words are blurred together, deliberately fast, so that no human can take them away. The whirl of it, the beauty of it, makes Nell giddy. But she holds her right hand as steady as a cup until . . . until . . . yes . . . *yes* . . .

Here it is. Dropped suddenly and silently, like a winter leaf, into her upturned palm . . . a tiny fairyboybaby encased in a gossamer caul and attached, still, to his limply whirling mother by a silvery thread.

It is seconds that count now. Real seconds. Human seconds.

"Cut the cord!" squeals the consort—beside the moss now, and jumping up and down in a frenzy. "Cut the cord, you great booby!"

And without thinking twice or summoning a single Power from anywhere, Nell bends her head, opens her mouth, and bites through the cord with one open-shut snap of her own front teeth.

"With tooth and tongue, the job is done," she intones for

effect, through a mouthful of saliva and bitter filaments. "So mote it be."

Quickly, with fingers that cannot help but tremble, she eases the thumb-size scrap of fairy-life out of his caul. The fairy-mother, lying in a swoon, raises one little hand. Her consort takes it and presses it to his lips, but his eyes are fixed on Nell, and his face wears a blank expression that will tip into outrage or relief, depending on whether this baby has survived being chewed off at the stem like a dangling cherry.

It is touch and go. It is literally touch and go as Nell begins massaging a smidgen of ointment into the fairybaby's cooling skin. Made from cowslips and quicksilver, mixed with the grease of a white goose, then left for a year and a day where the beams of neither sun nor moon will touch it, this ointment must cover every millimeter of a newborn fairy's skin if it is to be truly fairy and not succumb to old age, smallpox, knife wounds, or any of the umpteen other things that end human lives. And it must be administered by a human hand within seconds of the birth. That is the way of it. That is the reason Nell is here.

The ointment is slippery and smells both sweet and foul by turns. Holding her breath, taking exquisite care not to press too heavily on a rib cage barely big enough to house an acorn, Nell moves her fingertips up and down, then round and round, in tick-size strokes and minute, gentle circles.

Come on, she pleads silently. *Come on, you. Or I'm done for.*

The fairybaby's eyes are closed, beneath bulging lids. When they open, suddenly, to reveal a gaze as blue-green and as fathom-less as the ocean, the relief of it runs like an electrical charge right through Nell and makes her giddy.

"Keep on!" commands the consort. "You've his heels to do still and the soles of his feet. Forget those, and any snakebites, blisters, bunions, or frost-burn will be your fault. Keep on! I'm watching."

The fairybaby is wriggling like a minnow and mewling for its mother. It is a delightful little thing, but becoming stranger and chillier as the ointment does its work. From now on, it will fear nothing. No cut, scald, sting, or fall will harm it. Neither will deeds or words. For the ointment works both outside and in, dulling the emotions and turning the heart, metaphorically speaking, into a hailstone. Like all fairies, this one will live in the present, be utterly ruthless, and never know love. It is a price these beings willingly pay for a chance at immortality. And since they understand no other way, it seems a natural state—superior, even, to the fraught and messy way humans go about things.

"Well now," says the consort, once Nell's job is finally done. "That appears to be all, so be off with you."

With aching, smelly fingers, Nell sweeps her bits and bobs back into their bag. Her knees twinge as she gets to her feet, and her head is swimming. Below her the fairymother taps the top of her newborn's head and smiles dutifully. She will feed it and wash it and give it a pair of boots one day, but she will never feel the awful lurch in the pit of her stomach that human mothers feel when their offspring trip over the grate or are late coming home for their suppers.

Nell turns to the crevice in the wall and wonders how to leave.

"Wait!" orders the consort. He has the caul in which the fairybaby was born between his hands and is offering it up to her. Damp and torn and a lot bigger than you might imagine, it hangs from his fingers like the veil of a drowned bride, its edges drifting a little in the fading greenish light.

Nell hesitates. Then: "Much obliged," she says politely, lifting the caul from his fingers and folding it away in her bag. It is customary, she knows, for a midwife to receive a gift from the fairies once her task is done. But what she or her granny will do with a bit of tatty old membrane, the Powers only know.

The consort stifles a tiny yawn, amused yet bored by her bewilderment.

"'Twill save a human life," he tells her in a tone that says, quite clearly, that she is incredibly stupid and that he is explaining things only because it's no skin off his nose either way.

"Oh," says Nell. "I see. Thank you."

Powdered or boiled? she wonders. *And on a waxing or a waning moon?*

"Any life," he adds. "Howsoever it appears to be ending. But you can use it only once."

"Oh," says Nell again. "Interesting. But I be puzzled by its properties. Be it necessary to soak it awhile? With a pinch of dragon's blood and a bit of myrrh, maybe? And what time of day or month be most favorable to . . . Oh. All right. I see. Never you mind . . . I'll work it out. I'll . . . *Whooooaah.*"

Fairies don't believe in saying good-bye. Not even for the sake of politeness. Maybe they will see you again one day, maybe they won't—it's all one to them. And whether they have known you for moments, months, or years, they will dismiss you suddenly and never think of you again once you have served your purpose.

So back through the crevice Nell goes, her bones loose for a moment, and her innards squashed but then released without damage. It is dark, very dark, on the other side, and there are no fairy hands this time to tug her in the right direction. Far ahead in the distance is an oval of light the size and shape of a rabbit hole. She must reach it alone. She must fix her sights on the way out, hang on to her bag, gather her wits, and walk.

The ground is rough, and the way seems suddenly steep, so she hangs the bag by its string round her neck and uses her hands as well as her feet to clamber along. Seconds and forever . . . seconds and forever . . .

Don't fret, she tells herself. *Time means nothing here.* Still the moments drag, and the blob of light appears no nearer as she scrabbles and crawls toward it.

A drink. How she longs for something to drink. Her mouth is so dry, her tongue so parched, she would lick the stalagmites and stalactites in the hope of finding moisture if she only dared stray from her path.

Come, come, come . . .

Oh . . .

There are three of them blocking the way forward. Three fairypeople from out of nowhere, their hair drifting in aureoles of copper and gold, and their wings gleaming like opals in the dark. How lovely their smiles are. How kind. And they are offering her refreshments—a ripe peach, cut in half . . . a goblet of sweet cider . . . a handful of snow.

"No. No, thank you. I'm not thirsty right now."

Don't give in, she tells herself, over and over in her mind. *Don't give in, or you'll never get home. You'll be here for evermore.*

Still they tempt her, sighing and coaxing and coming so

close that the fruit hovers delectably under her nose and a trickle of melting snow falls just short of her mouth.

"No," she repeats, closing her eyes against them and hurrying blindly on. "No, I said. No, thank you."

Slowly, eventually, the sighs and the summery scent of peach juice fade away.

Safe. Nell is safe now and no longer quite so thirsty. She opens her eyes. The rabbit hole looks closer, so she scrambles with renewed energy.

How silent it is, she thinks after a while. *Silent as the grave.* She listens for her own heartbeat, thinking it might comfort her. But the silence is complete, pressing so hard against her skull that her head aches with it.

"La, la, la, la, la," she sings. "Tra-la, tra-la-la . . ." But the echo of her own voice against the innards of the hill sounds like the faint and useless chirruping of the last bird on earth.

And just when she feels she could weep from loneliness, she hears the rise and fall of music. A rich, haunting sound, spilling and filling the silence the way honey poured from a comb will fill an empty pot.

Come, come, come . . .

"Where? Where are you?"

He is up ahead, just off to the right—a rotund little chappie with a shock of silver curls and eyebrows as bushy and wild as two creatures. He has a flute to his lips, which he plays with such beauty and ease that the instrument itself seems human. Each note is a yearning . . . a calling . . . an enticement to Nell to follow wherever it leads. Each note changes the air, like a wish thrown into a well.

Nell stops moving. Swallows. There are tears in her eyes, which she tries to blink away, but can't.

Come . . . You know you want to . . .

Behind the player a curtain lifts, and through swimming vision, Nell sees a party going on—people grouped in candle-light, eating slices of frosted cake and chattering through the crumbs. They don't look like fairies, for their wings are folded, and some of them are old. They look normal and extremely pleasant. One of them—a gray-bearded fairyman in a waistcoat embroidered with buttercups—beckons to Nell and pats the seat of an empty chair. There is a plate set beside it on a low table and a goblet with a rim of jeweled stars.

Nell shakes her head. She has never felt so alone. Such an outsider. But she mustn't . . . she mustn't . . .

The player changes tempo, the notes of the flute leaping and gliding, leaping and gliding, like invisible fish. Some of the people behind him put down their cake, the better to sway and clap their hands in rhythm. Nell, too, is enchanted.

Remember, girl, be not beguiled. . . . All will not be as it seems.

Oh, Granny! she cries in her mind. *Can't I follow him? Just for two minutes/weeks/month/years? I be in no hurry, really, to get home. Can't I rest for a while and enjoy the music?*

But, no. No. In her mind's eye she sees the cunning woman shake her head. *Life at home can be hard,* says that shake of the head. *Life at home can be sorrow sometimes. But even sorrow keenly felt can be worth knowing. Worth learning from. So you just get yourself back here, back to me and the dun chicken, and leave them pretenders and the music and all that marchpane behind.*

I will, thinks Nell. *I will.* And she starts to run.

The player unfurls his wings as if to follow her, but cannot get them up.

Tutting he lays aside his flute, produces a blue pill, and swallows it. He is still trying for liftoff as Nell passes in a cloud of glittering dirt.

"Bye-bye," she calls in passing. "And a dose of powdered bark, taken from a lusty oak, will solve your little problem. Bye-bye."

The hole in the hill is so close now that she is sure she can see the time of day through it. Dawn. It looks like dawn out there, all pale and misty.

Nearly through, she tells herself. *Almost safe.*

She can smell the air—a tang of grasses and fresh-fallen dew. She can feel a breeze wafting in. And she can hear, both far away and right behind her, the piercing cries of the fairyboybaby and the whirling of hundreds of wings beating in apparent distress.

Come back, come back, come back . . .

Nell pauses. What now? What's happened? What can possibly have happened to make that newborn shriek so? It sounds like he has been abandoned or dropped on his head. It sounds like he's in terrible pain. Only, he can't be. He can't possibly be in pain unless . . . unless she missed a bit of him, by mistake, with the ointment. Could she have done? She is almost certain she covered every pore of him, every dimple, fold, and follicle. But she is only human, after all, so maybe . . .

She is on the point of turning round, of being drawn back, to check. But another sound, a thudding sound, distracts her. And out in the real world, framed by the rough edges of the hole, she sees a hare. It is looking right in at her and thumping its back legs. *Danger,* says each thump. *Danger. Danger. Danger.*

It is supposed to be bad luck to encounter a hare—like having a toad hop over your foot or a bat fly three times around your house. But this one has something about it. This one seems incredibly bright—and completely focused on Nell.

The baby-wailing rises a tone. It has an angry edge to it that wasn't there a minute ago. And the fairies are growing impatient.

Listen! Listen! Listen! Come back! Turn round!

They really do sound like wasps. And they are swarming.

Thump goes the hare, so hard that a trickle of soil spills into the hill and down over Nell's fingers. It feels solid and real, that bit of earth, and it definitely does the trick.

"My job is finished!" Nell screams, without looking round. "And I did it well. That baby be as cold and safe as a beetle in an icehouse, and this is all a deception."

And so saying, she launches herself at and through the rabbit hole, swimming and plunging and hauling herself to what feels like a second birth . . . a shivery yet triumphant delivering of her own body from the belly of the hill onto a broad green lap of sheep-nibbled turf and old bunny droppings.

The hare has gone. Above her rears the fairyhorse, its rider slipping a little on its back. The fairymanchild is completely sozzled on six acorn-cups of blackberry wine and none too pleased at having been summoned from a snooze to take this midwife home.

"Hulp-hic-ala," he drawls, reaching down with an unsteady, glimmering hand.

"You be as drunk as a fish," Nell tells him sternly. "You be as

71

tipsy as a lord and in no fit state to ride." But she gets to her feet anyway, a little light-headed herself in the cool sweet air, and allows him to haul her up onto the horse's back.

The animal skitters and turns. The fairymanchild burps and spurs it on. Even in the state he is, he will have Nell home before cockcrow. She can relax—even doze a little—as they reel back past trees and valleys, standing stones and fields of wheat. But before she does, she reaches into her bag, curious to know whether the caul she put into it seconds and forever ago will still be there.

It is.

The Confession of Patience Madden

THE YEAR OF OUR LORD 1692

I told no one at first about meeting the Devil. No one. I just thanked the Lord that he hadn't harmed me or taken me with him after all. Then I went home. I even remembered to collect my cloak. But I knew full well that I would never venture out at night again—and in all these years, I tell you true, I never have. Except that one other time . . . the time my sister made me. But that came later. . . .

Meanwhile, as June turned to July, I was like a cat that jumps from its own shadow. Even the sound of our housekeeper beating eggs and milk to make a batter put me in mind of hoofbeats and upset my concentration.

"What's the matter?" snapped Grace after a week of watching me tremble and start at the slightest noise. "Are you sick?"

I said nothing. And anyway, she was the one who looked sick.

The heat had led to thunderstorms, which gave way, eventually, to days of steady rainfall. The lanes were a quagmire; the sky, a pile of dirty clouds. My father returned from doing the Lord's business looking strangely animated despite a grueling journey and a dripping hat. He had been to a place called Essex to meet with a man who, he informed us, was routing Satan from his community in a most impressive way.

The man's name was Matthew Hopkins. That was all I knew about him, which was a mercy, really, for had I understood the precise nature of his business so soon after meeting the Devil, I might have panicked and run away. As it was, I was just glad to have my father home and pleased that he was so busy and involved with the Lord, our protector.

For a short while I felt better. I embroidered a lily on my sampler and said my prayers with renewed interest. Grace left me alone. She, too, had ceased her nocturnal wanderings, but that was no surprise. It wasn't the weather for frolicking. And if she looked paler than usual and left most of her breakfast, I assumed she was pining for her sweetheart, whoever he was, and wishing the rain would ease. Serves her right, *I thought.* She's a sinner. Serves her right.

On the second Sunday in July my father preached the sermon that turned everything upside down. The one that set the villagers whispering, and wondering, and scared me so much that I had to grip the edge of the bench to keep from fainting dead away.

We knew, Grace and I, that this sermon was going to be particularly important, since Father had spent all week

*preparing it and strode so fast down the slope to church that
we had to run to keep up. Grace had been ill in her stomach
upon rising and was still rather green-looking as we took our
places and bowed our heads in prayer. I half hoped she would
vomit again and be shamed—and half hoped she wouldn't.*

*My father's face, as he began to praise the Lord, seemed lit
from within, so intent was he on keeping evil at bay and so
utterly certain of the way to do it. He looked glorious, like
Moses, as he gazed down upon his congregation and asked for
our help.*

*We were to be vigilant, he told us in his most solemn voice.
On our guard, morning, noon, and night. For he had it on the
highest authority that Satan was abroad in villages just like
ours and that women in particular were being drawn straight to
him, like midges to foul water.*

*Since the spring, he informed us, thirty-six women had
come under suspicion in the place called Essex. And of those, a
goodly number had already been tried and found guilty of doing
wicked deeds in the Devil's name.*

*"Witches," he breathed, as if the word hurt his mouth.
"Witches, all."*

*He had no need to tell us their fate. We could imagine it well
enough. The rope. The drop. The jeering crowds. I've no doubt I
was looking as sickly as my sister by this time, and with sound
reason.*

*With thumping heart, I cast over in my mind the things
the Devil had said to me before galloping away from the orchard
in a shower of sparks. He lied, I told myself. He surely lied.
Because that is what the Devil does best. He lies. And anyway,*

I was not the one he sought that night. He did not take me with him, so despite what he told me, I was as safe as anyone else. Safe in body and soul.

All around and behind me: the sound of people breathing carefully as if the simple act of exhaling or coughing might somehow dislodge their own precious souls, leaving them vulnerable to wickedness.

My father had his eyes closed, and his arms raised toward heaven.

"The Devil is nobody's fool," he declared after a long and weighty silence. "The Devil will seduce your soul from you so swiftly that you will miss it no more than if he had stolen a button. And the Devil, good people, knows that England is divided. He knows full well that the King and his Parliament are too deep in conflict to notice the wheedling away of a soul here, a soul there . . . until it is too late! Too late! In a month . . . two months . . . a year . . . How many of us will remain to fight the great fight of righteousness? How many will be left to pit themselves against the loathsome, swelling ranks of Satan's army?"

Not many, *I worried to myself.* Not many. *Gone for witches, every one.*

I could feel Father's eyes scanning the church. Resting, probing, lingering. You could have heard a pin drop.

Then: "Beware one who wishes you ill!" Father thundered. "Beware the sickening of a child, the curdling of milk, or the failing of a crop. Beware a sudden ache in your bones. Beware all these things and more. And should ill health or luck befall you, look around. Look around! Seek out the witch who has

cursed thee, in the Devil's name, and have her answer for her
sins!"

All day and into the evening those words of my father's
echoed in my head, mingling with those of the Devil, until they
seemed like a single warning. It was too confusing for me. Too
frightening. I had to speak. I had to tell someone.

And so I told my sister.

She was peaky still, and as subdued as I, as we retired to
bed. For a while both of us lay there, lost in silence.

Then "Grace," I whispered.

And out it all tumbled, in a great tearful rush. How I'd
woken one night to find myself alone and had been drawn from
the house all the way to the orchard. How the Devil had
appeared to me as a small man with horrible sulfur-colored skin
and made as if to lift me onto his horse and gallop me off to
Hell. How I had slapped his nasty, shining hands away and
clung to the stile for dear life.

"He said he had come for me and that we had to be quick,"
I told her, a sob catching in my throat. "He said he was glad I
was ready and waiting, for he so hated unnecessary talk or
hanging around at cottage doors, where filthy little piskies might
be. I told him I was waiting for no one, least of all him. And . . .
and . . . he glared at me, Grace, while his black horse stamped
fire and brimstone, and he said, 'Aren't you the Mary by God,
then?'"

"The what?" said Grace.

"The Mary by God. That's what he said. And . . . and I
told him I was no such thing. That I was Patience Madden, the
minister's daughter, and he wasn't to take me."

My sister took both my wrists in her cold hands and dug her nails in, hard. "You're lying," she said. "This is one of your stories, isn't it?"

"Grace," I cried. "'Tis the truth, I swear it. He went away in the end, but he said he'd been certain sure I was this Mary by God, all ready . . . and . . . waiting. He . . . he . . ." I was blubbering hard by then. Too hard to speak properly.

"Be quiet!" Grace hissed. "Be silent before Father hears. You and your stupid, stupid fancies. I could kill you sometimes."

And she kicked me on the shins and turned her back to me.

I continued to cry softly until I could cry no more. She didn't believe me, it seemed, and in truth, I could scarcely blame her. Still, I felt better for having unburdened myself, for having shared the horror of it with someone.

After a while I began drifting toward sleep.

"That night," Grace asked suddenly. "When you woke up. Did you wonder where I was?"

"No," I fibbed, for fear of being slapped. "I didn't think."

"Because I was here all the time," she lied. "All the time. Which just goes to show that you had a bad dream. That's all. That's all it was."

"Maybe," I fibbed again.

"And if you so much as breathe a word of this nonsense to Father, I will make you wish yourself away with your Devil, truly and for all time," she said. "Do you hear me?"

I said I did, and she spoke no more.

And I thought, as I pressed my tearstained face against the bolster, that if I pretended hard enough that I really had met the Devil in a dream, I might start to believe it.

JULY
1645

The rain has stopped. The sun is blazing again, and gardens are choked with roses, hollyhocks, and beans. There are no pot lids to worry about, and no one's bones are aching. So for now, there are no mutterings or finger-pointings and the whole village seems to have sunk into a doze, beneath a blanket of pollen and heat.

Even Mistress Denby, upon finding a jug of milk gone sour, merely shrugs and mutters: "'Tis what happens, when it be hot enough to roast the skin off a piskie's arse. There be no witch ill-wishing me and mine. That minister be making too much of faraway doings, if you asks me."

Her husband grunts through a mouthful of cold beef and shifts his great buttocks on the household bench. He is not the healthiest of men—but no sane countrywoman would blame witchcraft for what is clearly the result of a lifetime of sloth and the gobbling and glugging of too much food and ale.

"Be you troubled again by bad wind?" Mistress Denby

inquires. "Because if so, get you straight to the cunning woman for a nip of tansy and wormwood. Go on."

Silas Denby swallows a lump of meat the size of a fist, winces, and reaches for his hat. It is as hot as Hell out there and a fair old walk to the cunning woman's cottage. But he has had enough, for one day, of his wife's nagging. And anyway, his guts are in turmoil, and wind as noxious as his is no joke.

Tee-hee-hee goes something in the ditch as he waddles and farts his way along the dusty lanes. *Old Fatty Flatfeet. Tee-hee-hee.*

Before turning off along a narrow track of beaten corn, he spies the minister's daughter—the older one, the beauty—making her own way somewhere. She has a basket over one arm, covered by a cloth. Their paths do not cross, but he holds an explosion of wind in anyway and raises his hat in her direction before plodding onward.

Grace sees but ignores the greeting. Her father believes she is visiting Mistress Bramlow, to see how the baby fares. Her father believes she is a good girl, taking a different path and doing the Lord's work.

In truth she has no interest in the Bramlows and no desire whatsoever to converse with the stout, evil-smelling Silas Denby. There is only one villager she wants—needs—to see, but he has been avoiding her for weeks. Perhaps he has grown tired of her. Perhaps he has decided she is not worth getting a whipping for, should her father find out. Who is to say?

She knows, for he once told her, that he heads for the orchard whenever there is a lull at the forge and his lungs are bursting for a breath of fresh air. And that is where she finds him now, lying in the long grass and gazing up at the sky. His face is quite untroubled, until he sees her standing there. Then it clouds.

"I be with child," she tells him. "By you."

He says nothing. Only stares at and through her as if trying to remember her name.

Difficulty of breath, she tells herself. *He is having difficulty of breath for the moment but will comfort me soon, and all will be well. Father will see us married before the harvest is in, and I . . . I will teach him his letters . . . I will always be kind.*

"It will be born in the dead of winter, I believe," she says.

He clears his throat—a small, nervous sound, like something about to be netted and kept in a cage. Otherwise he gives her nothing. Not a word or a hug or any further hint of how he might be feeling, in case she takes it for some kind of promise.

"Will you stand by me?"

He looks away. He looks up at some branches, across at the stile, then back at the sky again. Anywhere except at her. She could be anyone, she realizes. She could be any thing. She could be the church's lost statue of the Lady, weeping blue tears, and he would have looked away just the same.

"In the winter, is it?" he says at last. "A long time off still?"

"Yes." Her voice is subdued; a whisper almost as she waits for all to be well.

"Then you could go to the cunning woman, couldn't you? She could give you something. Some potion to get rid of it."

Above his head there are apples growing. Cider apples ripening and reddening in the heat. They will grow bigger and redder and be picked when the time is right. The tree is not yet weighed down by them, but it will be soon.

It is Grace's turn to clear her throat. The sun is hot on her head and against the back of her dress. She feels faint but remains rooted to the spot. This is worse than she imagined it would be, but she cannot believe it is hopeless. Not yet.

"Please," she hears herself saying. "Don't utter such things. I want you to stand by me. You must."

She is too proud to walk over the grass to him, if he will not come to her. Too proud, and too conscious still, of the power she had over him not so long ago, when he wanted her more than anything and she still belonged to herself.

"If you don't," she adds, testing her power one last time, "I will despise you. I will think you a coward and beneath contempt."

That gets to him. She can tell by his face that he doesn't want to be considered beneath contempt. Not by anybody. Not even by her. And for a moment she—

"All right." He is up on one elbow suddenly, giving her his full attention. "All right. I'll stand by you. Only . . . I've been thinking, I have. There's a garrison of the King's soldiers two days' walk away, and they be desperate needy, so 'tis said, for men and boys to join up. I been thinking of going. I were going to say to you, about me going . . ."

Hot and faint, Grace listens to what he is telling her. She hears the words "I'll stand by you" with relief, but the rest of it . . . surely, the rest of it is no comfort at all?

"I'll send for you," he continues. "Or I'll come back before the winter. But them traitorous Roundheads are laying siege over the border, and I'd be some coward, don't you think, if I didn't do my duty like other men?"

He is smiling at her now. And he would kiss her, too, if she wanted.

And she does want. She wants, more than anything, to believe in what he says. To see herself as the wife of a soldier and the mother of a little thing to love. She is no fool, though. Standing there, hot and horrified, the core of her remains as clear-sighted as ever.

He is lying, and she knows it. He is offering her a sop. Something to be going on with. Perhaps he even believes, for the time being, that he *will* send for her or come marching back to the village before the snow falls.

Perhaps.

Some moments pass.

Grace looks at the big old apple tree as if it might help her. There are piskies in it, so she has heard, but if they are up there now, she cannot see them.

The blacksmith's son is still smiling. It would be easy enough to go to him—to pretend to have swallowed his lies and then try to bind him to her, properly, with cunning and sweetness. But, no. She cannot do it. For he would go anyway; she knows he would, leaving her all the more wretched for having beggared herself in order to be wed.

"Will you kiss me, then?" says the blacksmith's son.

"No," she replies. "I will not."

And she turns, feeling cold right through under the bright summer sky, and walks toward the stile.

The door to the cunning woman's cottage is closed and half hidden behind a tumble of leaves and spidery honeysuckle. From inside comes the drone of female voices, singsong soft and intent on some kind of lesson.

"Two drams of lupine and thirteen grains of savin, mixed with peony and fennel . . . Ragweed, bruised and boiled in old hog suet with a pinch of saffron . . . The juice of barberries and licorice, made thick."

"Good girl. That's right. I believe that's right. I think that's right. And the living creatures most beneficial to sick bodies are . . . ?"

"Wood lice, silkworms, crabs of the river, larks, tortoise of the woods, hedgehogs, vipers, earthworms, foxes, and . . . and . . . what's the last one, Granny? Can you remind me?"

"Grasshoppers."

"And grasshoppers."

"Yes. Good."

Silas Denby clears his throat, thumps what he can see of the door, and since he reckons himself far enough away from a village full of pricked-up ears and clacking tongues, shouts: "Pardon me! May I enter? I be in need of a purge summat desperate."

Too late, he spares a thought for those other sharp-eared pests, the piskies.

"Just a little purge," he adds quickly. "For a slight gurgling in the belly."

He gets no reply, but the door creaks open and in he goes.

The inside of the cunning woman's cottage is as cool and dark as a priest hole, and just as cramped.

"Thank'ee," grunts Silas Denby, plonking himself down on the only bench. He could do with a mug of strong cider after his long walk, but he knows all he'll get here is something the color of piss that tastes vaguely of elderflowers and fizzes like a mean joke on his tongue.

"Thank'ee," he says again as the granddaughter pours him a

cup of exactly that, then retreats into the shadows without a word.

The cunning woman is looking him over with something of a twinkle in her mad old eyes. "Another purge, is it, Silas Denby?" she cackles. "Well, I'm afraid I don't think so. A good purge will do a body mischief if constantly taken, and you have already taken more than is prudent for a man of your age and girth. Go home. Eat raisins of the sun. Be kind to your wife and be at peace with thyself. Go."

Silas Denby blinks. What's this? Has he trudged all the way here, through piskie-infested cornfields and the midday heat, for nothing? Nothing, that is, except a sip of fizzy piddle and a lecture on how to behave?

He doesn't think so.

"I need a purge," he growls. "And not just for the wind. I be all out of sorts and in right bad spirits."

The cunning woman flaps her hand at him, for the big nuisance that he is, and turns to her granddaughter. "Signs of melancholy in a man of advancing years?" she asks.

Nell, perched small and thin on a three-legged stool, considers the man on the bench. He shifts a little under her gaze, for it makes him feel like a wet cowpat that she has trodden in accidentally.

"Fearfulness and foolish imaginings," she says. "The skin rough and swarthy, and the pulse very weak. Stinking breath. Thin, clear urine. Chronic impatience and a waning of lust."

Silas Denby isn't sure where to look. He would like to go home now, with or without a purge.

"Have you any of those signs, Silas?" the cunning woman asks him.

"One or two," he mumbles. "The imaginings. The pulse, perhaps."

Out of the corner of his eye he sees the granddaughter raise a hand to cover her mouth. She is laughing at him, the little vixen. There is a thumping great chicken on her lap, which, given the size of it, should have been in the pot with a few onions long ago. It is clucking softly as if it, too, finds the signs of melancholy in a man of advancing years unbearably funny.

That does it.

"A purge!" he roars. "That's what I need, so don't either of you hussies be telling me otherwise!"

The cunning woman shrugs.

"So be it," she says. "Nell, fetch the bottle. The one I prepared on the last new moon."

Nell hesitates.

"Maybe I should make up a fresh one," she says, keeping her voice low. "Or we should do it together."

The cunning woman looks puzzled.

"What?" she says loudly. "What's that you're saying?"

Nell feels her face grow warm as she repeats every word.

The cunning woman wrinkles her brow.

"Make up a fresh one? Why?"

It is getting harder and harder, Nell thinks, to deal with the slipping and sliding of her granny's mind.

"So I can watch what goes into it," she explains. "I wasn't with you when you mixed the last one. Remember? And I should have been, shouldn't I? I should have been watching. To see what goes in."

The cunning woman still doesn't grasp what she is getting at.

"Pshaw!" she snorts. "You know what goes into a purge, girl. We've studied purges. Now fetch the bottle, so this man can go empty himself out, since he be so mule-minded and set upon it."

Slowly, reluctantly, Nell puts the dun chicken down and goes to find the bottle marked with a brown smudge. She knows better than to run through its contents in front of Silas Denby, for no healer, or one in training, would ever knowingly give away her recipes. All she can hope is that her granny got all the ingredients right on the last new moon, and in the correct measures.

"Here it be," she says, handing the bottle to Silas. "Take two swallows at sunset and three more upon rising. Payment by Friday, as usual. A pound of cheese, a sack of flour, and a rabbit fresh-skinned should do it. Or a dozen eggs would be welcome, in place of the cheese."

Silas Denby eyes the dun chicken.

"She's family," Nell informs him. "She doesn't have to work."

With the door firmly closed and the big man gone, she turns to her granny.

"Remind me," she says. "What went into that purge?"

The wrinkles on the cunning woman's face seem to smooth themselves out as she considers the question, only to deepen and furrow when she cannot answer.

"Prunes?" Nell prompts.

"Yes." The cunning woman nods. "Forty of those, pulped and strained. And carrot, parsley, and anise seeds, ground fine." She pauses. "Half an ounce," she adds. "Of each."

"All right," says Nell. "And what else? What else is in that bottle?"

The old woman reaches for her broom and starts sweeping the floor.

"Oh . . . this and that," she mumbles. "A peck of this and a smidgen of that."

Nell grabs the broom handle. "It's important. Think hard. Senna. Did you add any senna?"

It is like wringing milk from a stone, drawing facts from the cunning woman on mornings or afternoons when her memory is particularly addled. Such mornings or afternoons are becoming more frequent, Nell realizes. Before long there will be whole days like it.

"I did!" declares the cunning woman, her voice triumphant yet scarily girlish. "I did, yes. And garlic. That's the other thing. Senna and garlic. Both powdered. Now let me be, girl. I'm in the middle of something . . . some task or other."

There is a little pile of sweepings between them—cinders, chicken droppings, petals from a mallow flower, and little bits of lavender. The cunning woman stares at it as if wondering how it got there.

"How much of each ingredient?" Nell presses her.

The cunning woman blinks rapidly.

"Have we fed the chicken today?" she wonders.

"How much, Granny? How much powdered senna and garlic went into Silas Denby's purge?"

The cogs and wheels of the cunning woman's mind are spinning and flying now. Spinning and flying and all out of time as she remembers . . . and realizes . . . and knows herself lost.

"Forty," she mumbles. "Of each."

"Specks?" Nell says hopefully.

"Ounces."

"*Ounces!?* Granny, it's forty *prunes* in a purge and just *four* ounces of senna and garlic. That's enough to turn a bogging giant inside out! I'll go after him."

"No, girl." The cunning woman clutches her sleeve, holding her back. She is lucid now—for the time being—and well aware that Silas Denby is more than likely to down every drop of his purge on the spot, turning all his vital organs to goo, if some chit of a lass asks for it back. "I'll go. I'll explain. He'll listen to me."

Nell isn't at all sure. "It's a long walk," she says. "And it's still hot out there."

But the cunning woman is already tying her bonnet strings.

"I'll be home before nightfall," she tells her granddaughter. "Start drying the next batch of earthworms for me. And be sure to cleanse them first, of all impurities. At moon's light we'll make a syrup of roses with hellebore, so you'll need to make up the fire and get started. Six parts rose water to four parts sweet syrup. And purify the cauldron first. There be traces of fox fat in it still."

She is all briskness as she pushes open the door and making enough sense for Nell to feel less apprehensive about her going. Left alone, she finishes sweeping the floor before turning her attention to the worms. It is a tricksy job, slitting earthworms up the middle and flushing out the dirt, and she is only on her third when she hears another knocking, through the honeysuckle.

"Who's this now?" she grumbles to the dun chicken. "Who be this, tapping at our door?" She half hopes it will be Silas Denby, come back of his own accord to get a gentler remedy for his gut. The very last person she expects to see, wilting like a lily on the step, is Grace Madden.

For a few moments she is too surprised to speak. Then: "My granny be out," she scowls. "If that's who you be wanting. You must have passed her, surely?"

"Well, I didn't," Grace tells her. "Because I didn't take the path. I came another way, around the back."

She is telling the truth. There are burrs snagged on her clothing and in her hair, and her hands are scratched from parting brambles. The tricksiness of cutting and cleaning earthworms pales in comparison to struggling through the dense scrub behind the cunning woman's cottage. Quite apart from the difficulty of making a path, there are snakes out there. And they bite.

Whatever brings Grace Madden here, the long way round and in secret, is clearly serious. Still, Nell can't resist this chance to get her own back on the sly, hoity maid.

"You'd better call again tomorrow," she says. "Bye-bye." And she begins to close the door.

"I can't," Grace replies. And she looks so pale and desperate, leaning against the door to stop it shutting, that Nell feels curious, suddenly, and just a little sorry.

"All right," she relents. "You can wait. I'm busy, though, so don't talk to me. And don't touch our chicken. She won't like you."

Meanwhile, in a spot where no one ever walks and the corn grows tall, something small and pesky is jolted from a doze by the sound of a human voice. ("Sweet marjoram. Lovely . . . lovely. An herb of Mercury under Aries . . . good for the brain and diseases of the chest.") Squinting up from its nest, it spies the old one picking long, flowering stems less than a spit away and almost right above its face.

Ooooo, it chunters. But it won't attack or torment, because the old one is known to be harmless and going rapidly to seed in the head region. And anyway, it is a female piskie, this one, so it bites only when provoked or threatened beyond endurance.

The sound if its squeaking attracts some neighbors—all females, three with offspring attached to their chests and one so ancient that the lichens sprouting from its head and clumped beneath its armpits are as white as frost. Their menfolk are either dead or off scavenging.

Budge! Budge! they squeak, settling down to watch, listen, and learn.

"Marjoram," croons the cunning woman, "made into a powder and mixed with honey, takes away the marks of blows and bruises."

Oooooo.

Before long the cunning woman's arms are full of flowers, but she is in no hurry to be on her way. The sun is warming her old bones like a big hug, and the yellow of the corn and the blue of the sky are like medicine to her ragged senses.

Moving dreamily she makes her way farther into the field. And as she walks she remembers the rituals performed long ago, in this very place, to mark the Summer Solstice. Wrens' nests on an altar . . . goblets with rims of jeweled stars marking the four quarters . . . libations to the Corn King . . . the drawing down of the sun.

She feels almost young again as she pats out a space among the stalks, places her heap of marjoram at one end, for a sweet-scented pillow, and lies down for a bit of a rest.

Ahhhh. No memory of any mission now. No nagging scraps of thought at all. Only the Powers of earth and air, as familiar as lifelong friends, keeping her company while she nods. On impulse, she unties her bonnet and lays it aside. It is good, very good, to feel the sun on her face and the ground beneath her head as she drifts easily into sleep and begins to snore.

Yippeee! Woooohooooooo!

The piskies won't harm the cunning woman. But they will swipe her bonnet—and anything else they can filch from her person or pockets while she snoozes.

Nyingy ding ding! Oooo yes! And up they scamper and away they go—all but one, that is—dragging the bonnet among them, deep into the corn. Even their offspring are excited. *Nyit!* they squeak, showing tiny teeth already as green and crusty as tombstones.

It is the elderly piskie who lingers. Not that there is anything else to steal, for the cunning woman wears no jewelry or lace and her pockets contain only fluff. No. It is something else that prompts this rickety twig of a creature to kneel down beside the old woman's right ear.

Sympathy.

Sniff. Sniff.

Sympathy, unlike malice, glee, and spite, doesn't come naturally to most piskies—at least where humans are concerned—but this one has mellowed with age. And the information it gleans through the clat in its nostrils as it snuffles and sniffs around the cunning woman's head, is making it sad in the heart and mind regions.

Nyeeeear, it rasps softly, the sound of it like paper tearing. *O nyear, nyeeear . . .* And it reaches out with shriveled fingers to lift a strand of silvery hair away from the old one's mouth region, so it won't tickle or bother her or give her bad dreams.

Then it hobbles off after its neighbors, to claim its share of the bonnet.

There is no timepiece in the cunning woman's cottage, but Grace can tell from the way a puddle of sunlight has moved across the floor that she has been here long enough.

She doesn't like this pokey hovel. It is too dark and strange. There is a bittersweet scent in the air that disturbs her. It seems familiar, although she cannot place it. The dun chicken has just tried to land on her basket. She slapped the fat, smelly thing away as roughly as she dared, but it is still fussing around the bench, aiming inquisitive pecks at her boots.

The cunning woman's granddaughter is crouched beside a cauldron, doing something horrible with a pile of dead worms. *Perhaps it is supper,* thinks Grace, drumming her fingers restlessly on the bench. These people are very poor, after all.

"I can't wait much longer," she says, doing her best to sound calm—friendly, even. "Why isn't she home yet, your granny?"

Nell shrugs and throws a clean earthworm into a bowl.

"None of your concern," she replies. "But I'm expecting her back by sunset."

"Sunset? But that's hours off still. Why didn't you say so before?"

Nell shrugs again. She is enjoying herself. "You didn't ask," she says. "And anyway, I said 'by' sunset, not 'at' sunset. She could walk in any minute . . . or not for ages and ages."

Grace can feel sweat breaking out on her forehead.

"Then *you'll* have to help me," she says. "It will have to be you. And don't pretend that you can't, because I know full well that you can. That you know enough about . . . about the right plants and things to be able to help."

Nell wipes her fingers on her apron. Torn between disliking this girl so much that she begrudges giving her so much as a spoon to lick and a natural inclination to be of service—to do her job—she isn't quite sure which impulse to follow.

"All right," she says eventually. "What is it you need? What's the matter with you?"

She suspects, from the older girl's fidgety manner and the unhealthy pallor of her skin, that this is a stupid love thing. Maybe she wants a charm or a spell to attract some lad. Maybe Sam Towser spurned her after that awful sermon about frolicking, and she wants him back.

If so, there are all kinds of spells Nell could whisper to her. This is one:

A SPELL TO MAKE A LAD
SWOON WITH DESIRE

On a spring or summer's morning—
and best it be a Friday, on a waxing moon—
follow the one your heart is fixed upon
until he maketh a clear footprint in the earth.
Dig out the earth and bury it beneath a willow tree
with a lock of thine own hair and a sprinkle of petals
from a pink geranium. Tilt thy face toward the sky,
and declare, in utter certainty:
"As many earths on earth there art,
so shall I win my true love's heart."
So mote it be.

"I be with child," says Grace. "And I need something—a potion—to be rid of it."

"Oh . . ."

Nell stares, openmouthed, over the rim of the cauldron, too surprised and alarmed to say more. *A bit late for charms, then,* she thinks. Too late for pink petals, waxing moons, and pretty words. This is a grave and troubling matter—and dangerous, too.

"I think you'd better wait for my granny," she says eventually. "I really do. Or come back another day."

"No!" Grace jumps to her feet, clutching her still-flat belly with both hands as if whatever it contains is hurting her. She looks almost deranged—no longer serene, anyway—and Nell does not know what to do.

The minister, she thinks. The minister will surely kill this daughter of his, now that virtue is no longer her chiefest beauty and noblest ornament And the lad . . .

"Be it Sam Towser's?" she asks quietly.

"Yes," Grace replies, in a voice so bitter and low that Nell needs ask no more. Sam Towser, she realizes, will be unable to drivel-talk his way out of this one, in front of the minister. Both he and Grace Madden are in the worst possible trouble unless what is done can be undone.

Behind Nell's back the dun chicken has pinched an earthworm and is clucking and bobbing with glee—too stupid to simply keep quiet and eat it. Nell picks up the bowl of clean ones, so it cannot get at those, then returns her attention to Grace.

"So you won't be wedded, then." It is a statement of fact

rather than a question, since the answer seems blindingly obvious.

Grace swallows and looks away. The worms in the bowl look like a mess of entrails. The sight of them is turning her stomach.

"No. He's going for a soldier. He may already be gone."

Nell sighs. "Men and boys," she says kindly. "Some are worthy of us and some aren't."

Studying the older girl's tragic profile, she feels an even stronger rush of concern. It isn't right that Sam Towser should get clean away, leaving someone he has saddled with a pot lid to suffer the consequences alone. And Grace, Nell knows, will be very much alone. For if the minister doesn't kill her, he will surely take her way out onto the moors, or into a forest, and leave her there to survive as best she can. Death or vagrancy, that's all Grace Madden can look forward to now unless . . .

Moved at last to sympathy, Nell sets the bowl of worms at her feet, leans forward, and touches Grace on the arm. "There is something . . . ," she falters. "A syrup you can take, to bring on the courses. So long as you be no more than a couple of moons gone."

"Fetch it."

Nell moves slowly. She is feeling sorrier by the moment for this beautiful, foolish girl. Still, something stays her hand as she reaches for the bottle marked with a splash of red.

"This . . . this unborn," she says, turning suddenly. "Might it have started up in you on May Morning? On the first day of May—the day sacred to nature?"

Grace frowns. "It might," she says, annoyed and embarrassed by such a personal question. "But what of it? Give me the syrup. Hurry up."

Nell shakes her head. "A Merrybegot . . . ," she whispers. "A child sacred to nature."

Grace doesn't understand. She hears the word—"Merrybegot"—and, like the bittersweet smell, it reminds her of something.

"I don't know what you're talking about," she cries. "And what does it matter anyway? Just let me have the syrup."

But Nell has turned away from the collection of stone bottles, without even touching the one that would change everything.

"I can't help you," she says sadly. "And nor will my granny or anyone else with the Knowledge. 'Twould be a sin against nature . . . against every Power there is. This unborn is meant to be, to know its life and be special."

She is opening the door.

Stunned, Grace picks up her basket. There is a feather from the dun chicken's hindquarters stuck to the handle. *It is the same color as the basket,* Grace thinks mechanically.

She stands very still beside the cauldron, just in case the cunning woman's granddaughter is toying with her for the pleasure of it before fetching the syrup after all.

But, no. There is no pleasure or guile in the younger girl's face as she holds the door ajar. She is sorry. Very sorry. But she means what she says—every word of it. "I will help you any other way I can," she promises. "And so will my granny. And we will see you safely delivered, when the time comes, wherever you may be."

"Pah!" A great wave of fury rises up in Grace Madden and gets her moving. Just a minute ago she thought she might cry. Now she knows she never will. Not over this. Not now or ever.

Holding her head high and clutching her basket, she pushes past the cunning woman's granddaughter, resisting the urge to slap her on the way.

"It will be all right," Nell tells her, at a loss to know what else to say as she flattens herself against the door. "The Powers look after their own."

Grace wheels round then, almost spitting. "How would you know?" she mocks. "How would you know anything at all, you . . . you . . . *simpleton,* you ugly *worm!*"

Nell stares back at her, round-eyed. She can afford to be charitable now and ignore such an insult. But her stubborn streak insists she gets the last word. "Because *I'm* a Merrybegot myself," she replies, with more than a hint of pride. "So I *know.*"

Something clicks in Grace's memory. She lets it settle before her eyes harden and her mouth curves in a sneer.

"Then know this, *Merrybegot,*" she hisses before turning away. "You are bound for Hell, one way or another. Trust me. I *know!*"

The piskie women are pleased with their bonnet. They have torn it into equal parts and made neckerchiefs and nappies out of it. One of them is in a ditch now, feasting on nettles while its offspring chunters and slobbers on its back.

The bits of information hanging in the air are making it sneeze.

Trouble of the worst kind. Ooooo! Chaos in two people's gut regions. Turmoil and panic and revenge. Nyingydingy ding!

It is too busy sneezing to notice the blacksmith's son loitering in the lane. Nor does it see whom he meets there or pick up on the few words that pass between them before the blacksmith's son hands this other person a bottle that gets hidden, quickly, in a basket covered by a cloth.

Only after they have gone their separate ways do snatches of their conversation filter through the ditch-mess to tickle the piskie's itchy nasal passages like invisible, potent snuff.

"I've been waiting for you. Have you been to the cunning woman? Did she give you something?"

"No. Let me pass."

"Then take this."

"What? What is it?"

"It's a drench. 'Tis what my father did give to a thorough-bred mare to drink after she got jumped by a donkey."

"I . . . I don't know. Is it safe? And will it work?"

"I don't see why not. It worked for the mare. There be only a drop or two left, but for a person I'd say that's enough. More than enough. You don't have to drink it. 'Tis up to you. But I thought you might want to have something in case . . . in case I be killed in battle and cannot stand by you, like I promised."

A-a-tishoooo! Oooo, what taradiddle! What falseness in the tongue region! Achoo! Achoo! Achoo!

But what's this now, seeping through the echoes? The piskie sniffs, hard, between sneezes, and knows it to be the shattering sound and acrid smell of a single musket shot—a shot yet to be fired, by one of Cromwell's men, but destined to hit its target smack bang in the heart region.

Oh, oh . . .

Nudging its offspring to hang on tight, it scrabbles and

claws up the side of the ditch and peers with bright, inquisitive eyes through a clump of dirty-yellow loosestrife, hoping for a chance to flash its arse at the doomed fool who dared mention battles in the same breath as promises and thoroughbred mares. As if these things were all the same. All much of a muchness and under his control . . .

Too late. The lane is empty. The great, golden ball of the sun is slipping, slowly but surely, behind the rise and dip of cornfields. And there is nothing else, for now, to sniff; no other clues about the exact time and place of the foolish one's untimely death.

Nyit, grumbles the piskie before sliding down to the foulest, greenest parts of the ditch, where the best suppers spawn and grow.

Meanwhile the cunning woman has woken up and wandered home, refreshed by her nap on the ground. She hasn't missed her bonnet, but remembered to pick up the great pile of marjoram, which she presents to her granddaughter with a flourish.

"We were running out of this," she declares. "So I'm glad I found some. You've done the worms, I see. Good girl. We'll have our supper now, and then start shredding the hellebore."

Nell sits her down on the bench. She needs to talk. She needs to know if she has done the right thing by Grace Madden. She speaks slowly, taking her time, so that her granny will absorb it all and, she hopes, understand.

When she has finished, she begins to cry. It is too much being both a Merrybegot and the cunning woman's granddaughter. Too heavy a responsibility. Too *hard.*

"There now," murmurs the cunning woman. "You did the right thing. I'm proud of you. There now. . . ."

And Nell is so relieved, yet so worried still about what is to become of Grace Madden and her unborn, that she forgets to ask about Silas Denby's purge. It is only later, with the bottom of the cauldron burning white-hot above a nest of blazing sticks and the air full of rose-scented steam, that she remembers. But by then the sun has set, and the big man's innards are already bubbling.

The Confession of Patience Madden

THE YEAR OF OUR LORD 1692

"We're not getting up," Grace announced one morning. She said it so calm and matter-of-fact that I had to tell myself twice that this was not a usual thing to agree upon.

"Why not?" I said cautiously.

"Because I say so," she snapped back. "That's all you need to know for now. Just do as I tell you. Exactly as I tell you. All right?"

Father was away, but our housekeeper would expect us to behave as usual—and would, I knew, report anything amiss to Father the very moment he returned.

"Are you ill?" I asked, turning to stare at her.

"I have what feels like the beginnings of something," she replied carefully.

I did not see why I had to remain languishing in bed just because she was poorly. And it seemed peculiar that she should wish it so.

"Well, there's nothing wrong with me," I told her. "So I think I ought to get up and do my chores."

She pinched me then. Hard.

"You will stay right here," she hissed. "Right here, or I will see you in the worst kind of trouble. Do you understand?"

I understood nothing. But she looked so odd—her face all gray and sweating—that I felt compelled to do her bidding.

By the time the housekeeper came, she was holding her stomach and biting her lips as if in mortal pain. But she kept her eyes closed, feigning sleep, while I said, exactly as she'd told me to, that we both felt "strange" (not ill, but "strange") and in urgent need of bed rest, in a darkened room, with no fuss or bother.

The housekeeper—a simple soul—knew us to be good, obedient girls who would never dream of telling falsehoods. It worried her greatly that the two of us felt strange. Perhaps, she suggested, our father should be sent for. Or a physician.

I anticipated, then immediately felt, a sharp kick in my leg.

So, no, I assured the housekeeper. There was no need to bother anyone, least of all my father, who was so very, very busy doing the Lord's work. All we needed, I said—remembering, just in time, that Grace wanted these things—was a pail, in case one of us should vomit; fresh linen, in case one of us should vomit and miss the pail; and a large pitcher of water to ease our thirst.

Grace kicked me a second time.

"Oh," I added, "and the Bible, if you please, so that we may consider a psalm or two and keep our minds fixed upon the Lord until this strangeness passes."

The housekeeper bustled away, returning some moments

later with the pitcher in one hand, the pail in the other, and a bundle of fresh linen slung over one arm. Behind her came her daughter, a mute slip of a thing who helped in the kitchen sometimes, holding the household Bible reverently in both hands.

This child's face, as she approached the bed, would have been level with Grace's. And I can only assume that she saw something terrible in my sister's expression—something tormented—for she jumped back with a mighty start and dropped the Lord's book on the floor. It made a terrible thud, and our housekeeper was appalled.

"Goodness me, girl," she cried. "Whatever made you do such a thing? Pick it up at once, and place it on the chair!"

The child did so, her hands all a-tremble and her eyes badly startled.

"Thank you," I said. "You may leave now. We will call if we need you."

We never did consider the psalms, Grace and I, although as the hours passed I myself prayed earnestly, then beseechingly, for an end to my sister's violent affliction.

First, the sweats grew worse. Then she began to vomit. She vomited until it seemed her very heart would come up next in the pail.

"Grace!" I begged. "Let me call the housekeeper. Let Father come. Let us send for the physician. Grace, you frighten me!"

But in between bouts of dreadful sickness and pains that doubled her up, she just clung to the sheet, with her eyes tightly closed, and muttered through gritted teeth: "No! Call no one. Tell no one. It will soon pass, soon be over."

And then, after what seemed like an eternity, it did seem to be over. The pains and the sickness eased. The sweat cooled on her brow. The sip of water she took from the pitcher stayed down, and she sank back against the bolster with a groan of what I took to be relief.

"Are you better?" I whispered after a while. "Is it over now?"
She turned her face to the wall.

"I don't know," she answered me. "I really cannot say."

For both our sakes I hoped it was over. The smell in the room had grown very bad, and I was running out of sympathy.

"We'll get up in a minute, then, shall we?" I ventured. "We'll tell the housekeeper that we're better now and would like our suppers, shall we? Shall we do that?"

"Shhh. Shut up." She had not regained enough strength to kick, but she could still nip. And her mind, I sensed, was busy.

"Your hair's all clumped together," I said. "And your face has blotches. You look like Job afflicted with sore boils. You might have to go and scrape yourself and sit among ashes."

"Shut. Up."

She was thinking so fast I could almost hear her head ticking, like a clock.

"No," I protested, when she finally spoke her mind. "No, no, no, no, no. I won't do it. Why should I? What for? It's a sin to lie. You can't make me."

"You must do as I say," she insisted. "We might have no choice."

And then she took one of my hands in hers and began, very gently, to stroke it.

"Let me explain," she said. "For a start, I believe you now."

"About what?" I replied, startled by the unexpected change in her.

"About being drawn from sleep and out to the orchard by the Devil."

"Good," I said. "Because I do not lie. I am not a liar."

"I know," she soothed. "I know you are not. You are my sister and the only living person I can really talk to and trust."

I didn't know what to say to that. She continued to stroke my hand. I didn't like it. My fingers remained clenched as her voice murmured on.

The Devil, she declared, had no claim on me—yet. He had made a mistake. It was another girl he had arranged to meet that night. A girl already known to us—and to everyone else—as a lewd, foul-tempered little heathen.

The cunning woman's granddaughter.

"But her name is Nell," I said. "And the Devil was looking for a Mary. A Mary by God."

"No," Grace insisted, keeping her voice low and pleasant. "A Merrybegot. The cunning woman's granddaughter is a Merrybegot. A . . . a person with special powers. Dangerous powers. She came to the Bramlows' cottage while I was visiting the baby, and she told me so."

"Oh," I said. "A Merrybegot. I see. That sounds pretty."

I felt my sister's hand tighten and knew she itched to slap me.

"It's not 'pretty.' I've just told you. It's . . . it's ungodly. She is ungodly. And if Satan has her, she will be doing his work. She put this strange sickness upon me, Patience, I know she did."

"How? How could she do that?"

"Listen. Listen to me properly!" She was really angry with

me now. Her voice was weak still, from the sickness, but she pressed urgently on: "You heard what Father said, in church. You heard him: 'Beware the sickening of a child, the curdling of milk, or the failing of a crop.' The sickening of a child, Patience. That's me. And 'Beware one who wishes you ill.' That's her, isn't it? You remember how she flew at me, the day she came into our house? You remember what she said, about a bee leaving its sting behind? She is a witch, that girl. She is in league with the Devil and wants my soul. And you will be next. Imagine it, sister. Imagine the two of us burning forever in the fires of Hell. Imagine—"

"Stop!" I cried. "Stop it."

It was too much. My head was spinning with images of bee stings, curdled milk, and hellfire.

"It's your choice," sneered Grace, throwing my hand aside as if it bored or disgusted her. "I'm only trying to help. For you are probably in far more danger than I, anyway. Far more, since you have conversed with the Devil already—had quite a cozy chat, in fact. For all we know, your stupid . . . little . . . soul is already half wheedled, and all it will take is a little tug."

My soul, I can assure you, was never in the slightest bit of danger. But I did not know that then, and I was frightened.

"I'll do it," I moaned. "If what you tell me is truly so, I will do whatever you say."

"Good," she said. "Then listen carefully."

AUGUST

1645

It is spawning time for the piskies. In ditches, hedgerows, and hollow trees they make temporary nests of nettles and grass and drop their litters—one, two, three. Newborn piskies look like something you would scrape off your shoe, holding your nose while you did so. But their mothers love them, fiercely.

"Never pick early blackberries in the lanes," the villagers warn their children. "For them piskie mothers will bite off your fingers should you get too close to their offspring."

Normally this would be a tranquil time in the village. For the harvest is approaching, the apples are almost ripe for the picking, and days of fine weather are as mellow and golden as days in England ever get.

But *nyit, nyit, nyit* squeak scores of wizened little turd-shapes, turning still-blind eyes toward the light and sniffing, with learner-nostrils, at the barrage of information hanging in the air—information so troubled and dangerous that it tingles their newborn senses like a slight electric shock.

The blacksmith's son has gone to do his duty by the King.

He strode away early one morning, with a sprig of mugwort in his shoe to prevent weariness while walking and a fresh borage flower in his pocket for courage. Had he found the nerve to show his face at the cunning woman's cottage before leaving, she might, perhaps, have given him a charm—a snippet of vervain, charged by the Powers of the south to enable a soldier to escape his enemies. It might even have saved his life.

Ordinarily people would have wondered why the lad went so suddenly—or even at all. For he had never expressed Royalist sympathies before or shown a particular inclination toward anything much besides idleness and frolicking.

But there is something else going on that makes Sam Towser's departure hardly worth remarking on. Something truly sinister, which the villagers are trying hard to comprehend.

Silas Denby has barely touched his food since that fateful night when his guts erupted like molten lava and he believed himself as good as dead.

"'Twas like the cavorting of devils in my belly," he tells anyone who will listen. "The worst kind of torment. The very worst." He will never be a shadow of his former self, this man, but his face is no longer ruddy, and his skin hangs that bit looser on his bones, like a badly fitted suit.

His wife is worried about him.

"Eat!" she commands, banging roasted rabbits, bowls of whey, and a cheese the size of her own head down in front of him.

"No," he growls. "For if there be devils in my belly, best I starve the boggers out."

Mistress Denby does not like this kind of talk.

"The cunning woman's purge," she confides to a neighbor, "has done my man no good at all. He be all of a rumble still and uneasy in his mind. It troubles me, neighbor, it troubles me greatly."

The neighbor is a Watcher. Gravely, she leans across the gate to whisper in Mistress Denby's ear.

"Never!" exclaims Mistress Denby. "The minister's daughters? Never!"

The Watcher nods.

"What does it mean, neighbor?" Mistress Denby's voice is low. This is gossip of the first order, and no piskie must overhear it. If one does, it will summon its friends, and her garden will be thick with the wretched things—all eating her cabbages and tormenting her hens while they listen out for further bulletins.

The Watcher's eyes gleam moistly.

She leans forward again, to whisper some more.

Mistress Denby's face turns as pale as parchment. "If this be so," she murmurs, "then we must be vigilant. We must all be Watchers, neighbor. Our very souls may depend upon it."

It is Mistress Bramlow who brings the gossip to the cunning woman's cottage. She also brings baby Amos, for he is ailing still and so listless that he seems more like a tired old man than a four-month child.

Nell answers the door.

"Sweetling!" she beams, holding out her arms to take the baby from his mother. He goes to her happily, as if he too remains aware of their tingling moment of connection, before he fell into the world.

Mistress Bramlow is glad to give him up for a moment and to sit quietly in the cool, bittersweet-scented shadows, resting her feet.

There are mounds of flowers and grasses on the floor, waiting to be sorted and dried. It is the month for picking dill,
mustard, larksfoot, and angelica. Mistress Bramlow knows that
much and can recognize what is there. It is the art that trans-
forms these things into magical charms and potions that is
beyond her understanding. And the way things are going, that
is probably just as well.

"Where's your granny, Nell?" she asks.

Nell looks up from rocking the baby. "Up there," she says,
jerking her head toward the roof space. "Asleep. She be . . . she
be tired after a long night herb-gathering."

Mistress Bramlow nods. Her face is both sweet and serious.

I wish I could tell you, Nell thinks to herself. *I wish I could let you
know that my granny's mind be so wispy nowadays that the simplest
spell or remedy be like something spilled in her head—all spilled and
spoiled and trickling away. But I cannot tell you. I cannot tell anyone.
Not yet. For without payment for what we do, we would not survive.
And I do not know enough, just yet—I have not practiced enough—to
do everything alone. I am too young. It is too soon. I don't want to.*

"Nell," says Mistress Bramlow. "There is talk in the village.
Talk of . . . ill-wishing."

Nell keeps her eyes on the baby's small, trusting face. "If 'tis
Silas Denby spreading such talk," she answers slowly, "then no
one should pay him any mind. My granny warned him. She
warned him clear as day that too much purging can do a body
mischief. I know. For I was here when she said it."

Mistress Bramlow sighs. Not Silas Denby. No. Although his
grumblings and grouchings are certainly adding fuel to the gos-
sips' fire.

"It isn't Silas Denby," she tells Nell. "'Tis the minister's daughters. Have you not heard what is happening up at the big house?"

Nell holds Amos Bramlow a little tighter and rests her cheek on the soft down of his head. She has heard nothing—nothing at all—but a shiver passes through her, a premonition of something bad.

"What is it?" she says. "What?"

So Mistress Bramlow tells her about the minister's daughters, afflicted by some strange malady that confines them to bed and has them shrieking and writhing like demented things. About the pins they are spitting and the terrible words that they bark, like dogs, at the sight of visitors or holy water.

"'Tis said the minister be half mad with anxiety," she whispers. "'Tis said he believes his daughters are being drawn to Satan. That someone—a witch—has cursed them, in the Devil's name, and that they be battling with all their strength to keep possession of their souls."

Nell keeps her face blank.

"Those be troublesome, foolish girls," she says. "And it will all turn out to be nonsense."

Up in the roof space the cunning woman turns in her sleep and starts to babble.

"Starchwort . . . with vinegar . . . and dung of the ox . . . laid upon a plague sore . . . or a filthy ulcer . . ."

"She's dreaming," Nell says quickly. "Only dreaming."

Mistress Bramlow looks anxiously up, then back to where Nell sits, her thin arms cradling the baby. She opens her mouth, then closes it again, although there is plenty more she could say.

She could speak of the sheep's heart stuck full of gooseberry prickles that Mistress Denby has hung above her door—a gory yet potent charm to protect her home from witchcraft.

She could tell how the Watchers spent the whole of last night in a dark huddle under the stars, watching and waiting to see if anyone came to the churchyard. For after twelve of the clock, as everyone knows, a witch may summon the Devil by walking widdershins round hallowed ground, chanting the Lord's Prayer backward.

She could warn the cunning woman's granddaughter that there is an ill wind blowing and that both she and her granny are slap bang in its path.

But Mistress Bramlow is a person who always hopes for the best. How could she not, when her little son seems to hover constantly between this world and the next? So she tells herself that Nell is probably right. It will all turn out to be nonsense. And she drinks a glass of cordial, gathers her shawl and her baby, and goes home.

Left alone, Nell sinks onto the bench, scoops up the dun chicken, and wonders what to do. *Maybe,* she thinks, *Grace Madden has confessed to the minister that she is with child, and he, in his wrath, has banished her to her chamber with instructions to stay abed until her time comes.* Maybe all this is playacting and scaremongering, a ploy to keep the truth from getting out. But why involve the sister? The stupid one? And why not act out a duller, more acceptable affliction? Why draw so much attention to the house, the room, the girl, and—before long—her belly?

It is a puzzle. It needs sorting. *Above all,* thinks Nell, *there is the unborn to consider.* The other Merrybegot. Too much excitement in an expectant mother is not good for the one growing inside her. Not healthy. Grace Madden should be looking after herself now, not spitting pins and behaving like a lunatic.

No.

The dun chicken has fallen asleep. Its heart pulses through its feathers against Nell's hand, and its stupid head lolls against the crook of her arm. As living things go, it is pretty much a waste of space, but here it is—and Nell loves it.

Grace Madden's unborn, she tells herself, *is at least as deserving as a daft chicken of a bit of love and care.* And as a midwife, a healer, *and* a fellow Merrybegot, it is up to her to make sure it survives.

Resolved now, she plonks the sleeping chicken under the bench and reaches for the pestle and mortar. Cinnamon, nutmeg, honeycomb, and tansy . . . that is what she must pound together, then mix in milk with a fresh egg for nourishment. And then she will take this concoction herself to give to the minister's daughter.

And something else . . .

Now where is it?

Leaving the container of half-bashed nutmeg for a moment, Nell crosses the room, stands on tiptoe, and reaches high into the sooty throat of the fireplace.

There.

A frog. Very dead, very dry, and very, very flat.

A wizened yet potent charm to keep an unborn from harm.

It ought to be enough, Nell thinks. *It* should *be enough.* But all the same, just in case, she goes to the place—the secret place—where the most powerful charm of all is kept hidden away, wrapped in dock leaves and weighted by a magical stone found in the maw of a swallow.

Light as half a feather. As transparent as water-smoke. The fairybaby's caul.

The minister's housekeeper answers the front door and steps back in alarm when she sees the cunning woman's granddaughter standing bold as brass on the step, with her bag of bits.

"You'll do no good here, with your potions and powders," she snaps at her. "Go away home, child. Quick before the minister catches you, calling at the front door like any highborn lady. Whatever next . . ."

Nell stands her ground.

"I have to see them girls," she insists. "The older one— Grace—would wish it so. Let me pass."

The housekeeper wrings her big chapped hands in her apron and darts an anxious look behind her, toward the room where the minister has been closeted away, writing furiously for hours.

There is a bowl of red roses and the white flower called "baby's breath" on a table beside the stairs. They are all shedding their petals—big red ones, like gouts of blood, and tiny white ones, like snowflakes; yet they were picked only this morning. It is but another bad sign in a house already buzzing with strange portents.

"Well?" says the cunning woman's granddaughter. And she seems so sure of herself and of whatever she has in her bag that the housekeeper decides it can do no harm to let her see the minister's daughters. Who knows? It might even help where all else has so far failed.

And if it does, the minister will surely thank her for having let the brat in. He might even smile, and how lovely that would be.

"All right, then," she says. "The first door you come to, at the top of the stairs."

Quickly Nell slips into the hall and up the wide polished staircase.

She thinks about knocking at the bedchamber door but decides it will put her at a disadvantage to appear so timid and polite. She is on a mission, after all, and must maintain the upper hand.

"Good day," she says, barging straight in. "It's me. What be the matter here?"

The girls in the bed are too startled at first to react. Their faces and their hair are so pale that they, the bolster, and the coverlet drawn up to their necks seem composed of the same stuff. There are drapes across the window, blocking the light, and the room is all musty, like an animal's lair.

Grace is the first to move. Up out of the bed she leaps, staggering a little on weakened legs.

"Out!" she hisses. "Out, out, out!" And before she knows it, Nell finds herself bundled from the room and into a window seat jutting from the passageway.

Grace Madden smells bad, and her eyes are wild.

"I've brought you a potion," Nell tells her. "Not that kind," she adds as the older girl's eyes light up in desperate hope. "A cordial, to nourish you and make you easier in your mind."

The light fades immediately from Grace Madden's eyes. "A pox on your cordials!" Her fingers tighten on Nell's arms. "Tell me this and only this. If . . . if the thing inside me be no more . . . if I be rid of it for good and all, how would I know?"

Nell gapes at her.

"Tell me!"

"Well . . ."

"Tell me!"

Nell braces herself and shrugs the pinching fingers away.

"You'd know," she says grimly. "There would be pain. Then a great gushing of blood, like the courses, only worse. It would come away from you, like being born. Believe me, you'd know."

Slowly Grace Madden steps away, moving backward from the window seat as smoothly and listlessly as a ghost. And Nell can tell, just by looking at her, that whatever damage she has wished for, or tried to do to her unborn, the Powers are watching over their own. The Merrybegot is safe. At least for now.

The closing of the bedchamber door has something very final about it.

"Wait!" Nell leaps from the window seat, bangs that door wide open, and hurries to the side of the bed. Grace is climbing back into it in slow motion. Without a word, she pulls the coverlet up over her body and lies there, like something strange and lovely made of alabaster. Her sister's face beside hers is a gargoyle in comparison.

Nell wonders how much the younger sister knows. Decides it doesn't matter. For everyone will know soon enough about Grace Madden's pregnancy. In a month or so there will be no hiding it.

She takes the bottle of nourishing cordial from her bag and sets it down on the bed, in a dip between the two bodies.

"I'll leave this here for you," she tells Grace. "And I suggest you take it. I suggest you look after yourself and your Merrybegot from now on."

The beautiful face remains expressionless. The ugly one looks puzzled.

It is a pivotal moment. Had there been a piskie in the room, it would be jumping up and down, frothing at the mouth in its excitement. For moments like these hold catastrophe within them, like an invisible egg that could crack at any second, releasing something that will seep, and spread, and have all kinds of consequences. Just a few words . . . a little string of words will do it.

"Your sister be with child," Nell tells the ugly face. "By Sam Towser, the blacksmith's son. She—"

"Noooooo. Father! Father! God in heaven! She burns me! She burns me! Aaargh!"

Nell is horrified, so appalled she can neither speak nor run. For the sound spilling from Grace Madden's mouth is so far removed from ordinary speech that it hardly seems real. It is beyond anger, beyond spite, beyond the worst emotion you could ever imagine a good Puritan girl might feel. It is harsh. It is frenzied. It is *demonic*. And she is thrashing around like a thing possessed; arching her spine, tearing at the coverlet, baring her teeth like a rabid dog.

Appalled Nell turns back to the younger sister.

"We must help her," she cries. "Her mind . . . her mind be all but unhinged. 'Tis fear, I believe. But she mustn't be afeared. And she must hush up, before your father—"

In the hallway below: a flurry of voices, the banging of a door.

Grace is holding herself rigid now, her arms flung wide, her eyes rolling back in their sockets.

"I burn!" she howls again. *"She burns me!"*

Nell is waiting still for some sign from the younger sister. Some flash of understanding—a little empathy. It isn't happening.

Is this girl really so dim-witted, Nell wonders, that she hasn't understood?

But, no. Patience Madden is simply mulling the information over.

"We must calm your sister," Nell appeals to her. "We must think clearly, before the minister—your father—comes."

For an instant it seems as if Patience Madden is about to say something wise. But then her eyes narrow, her pinched lips open. And: *"Father!"* she screams, in a voice every bit as frenzied as her sister's. "Come quickly. *Save us!"*

And there are footsteps thudding up the stairs. And—

Nothing. With all of them against her, there is nothing Nell can really do. Still, as a last resort, she scrabbles in the cloth bag with a trembling hand. *The caul,* she thinks wildly. She could rip the coverlet back—she might just have time—and fling that caul across Grace Madden's belly. Would it work? Would it save a human life before it is full-formed? Before it draws its first breath, even?

She hesitates. She doesn't know. She has no idea. And it would be a terrible shame to waste such a valuable charm . . .

The frog, then. The frog-charm will have to do.

So as the door crashes open and the minister bursts in, Nell flings wide her right hand and throws the wizened gray-green amphibian onto the bed. Dead and flat as it is, it looks like it is leaping, for its dried-up legs are still perfectly formed, like a diver's. Through the air it goes, in a neat curve, before landing skull-down on Grace's stomach.

The sisters' screams leave their mouths in one great, ear-splitting wave. The bottle of cordial strikes the floor as they flounder and kick and throw their arms around as if fending off a plague of locusts.

The minister appears to be dithering. Ashen-faced and halfway across the room, he seems torn between rushing to the aid of his stricken daughters, or calling upon the Lord, or grabbing Nell by the scruff and hurling her down the stairwell.

Seizing her only chance, Nell makes a dash for the door. The minister whirls round, his black cloak billowing, one hand reaching out like a claw.

But Nell is too quick for him.

The housekeeper is at the top of the stairs. She had just started plucking songbirds to make a pie, and the hand she raises to cross herself as Nell pushes past leaves a smear of red on her forehead.

"Grace Madden be with child!" Nell shrieks as she clatters blindly down the stairs. "She be with child by Sam Towser, the blacksmith's son!"

There. It is out. Loud enough for the minister and the housekeeper to hear, even through the girls' screams. *It is surely for the best,* Nell tells herself as she half runs, half staggers out of the house, down the steps, and into the tunnel of briars and vines that weave and trail and snag on her clothes as she stumbles, with knocking heart, toward the open gate.

It is surely for the best that they know the honest truth.

All around her the frenzied babble of little mouths sounds for all the world like the scraping of crickets' wings in the heat. And the *sniff, sniff* of hundreds of one-, two-, three-day-old nostrils is fainter than the faintest snuffling of a mole, far underground.

Shape of the ranter, shape of the frog . . .

Wheeeeeeee!

I had no choice, really I didn't, Nell thinks, slowing to a walk once the great iron bars of the gate have clanged shut behind her. But her ears still ring with the girls' cries, and she can only hope and trust that the minister will do the right thing by his ruined daughter.

By the time she turns into the cornfield, she has convinced herself that the minister will probably send Grace away. To a nunnery, perhaps, or a strict aunt—somewhere far from the village, anyhow—until the Merrybegot is born. He cannot abandon her. Not now that the other daughter knows. And the housekeeper too. It would reflect badly on him. Surely, as a God-fearing man, the minister will see to it that this special pot lid—his very own grandchild—survives somewhere and wants for nothing? Surely he will?

Won't he?

The cunning woman cannot say what the minister will or will not do. It doesn't seem important to her—or even all that real. She has made some broth and swept the floor, but her eyes have a faraway look, and whatever Nell says is sparking odd connections in her mind with things that happened a long time ago.

She doesn't mention—because she has already forgotten— that she went for a walk herself this afternoon and that some unruly lads threw stones at her. She delivered those lads, all three of them, and saw them safely weaned. She cured one of the whooping cough by rubbing his back with a concoction of lily roots, peony, and the fat of a fox. Yet he taunted her today from a distance as she wandered down one of the lanes, muttering to herself as she tried to remember what quarter the moon was in and the types of plants she ought to be gathering.

They had called her names, those boys. They had called her "witch" and "Satan's drab," and then they had thrown their stones and bolted.

"*You* were born a Merrybegot," she tells her granddaughter, gazing dreamily over the cauldron's rim. "You can be proud of that."

Nell is crouched on the floor, feeding bits of corn to the dun chicken.

"Tell me again," she says, stretching her palm as flat as it will go while the chicken picks and pecks. "About my mother. Tell me everything you remember."

"You know all there is to know," the cunning woman replies. "It is little enough, I grant you, but what more there was I was never privy to."

Nell sits back on her haunches and lets what's left of the corn sieve through her fingers onto the floor. The events of her day seem less threatening now that she has shared them with her granny. She is extremely worried still about Grace Madden and her unborn, but she is more inclined to trust in the Powers and let the future unfold as it will.

It is cozy tonight in the cottage, with a fire burning and the chicken eating its supper. And Nell is content to follow her granny's mind as it meanders into the past, alighting on one bright memory here and another there, like an old butterfly doing one last round of a garden.

"She was beautiful, wasn't she?" Nell says, resting the point of her chin on her knees and gazing wistfully into the leaping flames.

"She was," crows the cunning woman. "Oh, she was, she was. As lovely as a rose in June."

Nell sighs. "But wedded, though. Already spoken for."

"Yes."

A log shifts and settles in the hearth. Nell prods it with a poker, to make it flare again. She knows her birth story by heart, but likes to be reminded of it once in a while.

The cunning woman's hands flutter like crippled spiders as she sifts her memory for the right connection. Then a smile crinkles her face as she discovers what there is to remember— events as fresh and real as if they were happening right here, right now. All over again.

Her voice, when she speaks, sounds almost young:

"It never mattered, in the circle, what your earthly ties were—or even *who* you were. Once we were all gathered together—like-minded souls holding hands in a ring—we were between the worlds, beyond the bounds of time. She came from over the border to celebrate the summer solstice. I could tell at once that she was one of us. I could see it in her eyes. She brought flowers for the Corn King and cakes and wine to share. She had her own goblet, as we all did, with a rim of jeweled stars. And a silver box of salt for protection against evil. And the cord around her robe had forty knots—long enough to mark out a nine-step circle."

She pauses for breath and for the pleasure of her own remembering.

"And then," Nell prompts. "She came again . . . for Yule."

"Yes. To the Standing Stones this time. Your father, for all he was no longer a lad, had been chosen to play the young god— he who fights and triumphs over the old one, that light may return to the earth. As I watched him leaping like a stag, I knew full well that it was not just in honor of the ritual that he pranced and preened so. It was for her. And when, as victor, he tore off his mask and shook the sweat from his brow, a look passed between them that none could mistake."

"A look of love," murmurs Nell.

"A look of longing, girl. No need to pretty it up."

Nell lifts the dun chicken onto her lap and buries her face in its feathers. *Love,* she tells herself. *It was love that sparked between my mother and father that winter's night, while a great fire warmed the ancient stones and the other man—the old god—played dead on the ground, his antlers ripped off and his face chalked and sooted, to resemble a skeleton.*

Love . . .

"I said nothing afterward to your father—my son," the cunning woman continues. "For whatever is set in motion once a circle has been cast and the Powers summoned is meant to be. It cannot be stopped any more than a wave poised to crash can be sent rearing back on itself as if it never started. As winter turned to spring and we prepared for the May Eve ritual, I knew that your coming was inevitable. And so it was."

The next part of the story is vague and sad. Yet it is the part Nell likes best, since it surely proves that her father truly loved the mysterious woman from over the border and that she loved him back. For her father, like Sam Towser, could have denied all responsibility for his frolicking. He could have run away. As for the woman . . .

"Did you really never know her name, Granny? Did my father never tell you?"

"No, girl. 'Twas best I never knew, for then if anyone had asked me, I would not have had to lie. All I learned—all your father ever said—was that no one in her family was aware that she followed the Old Ways. To them, it would have been unforgivable—even worse, perhaps, than her getting with child, the way she was."

"She could have got rid me, Granny, couldn't she? She had the Knowledge."

"Ah, yes. But you were a Merrybegot. Nature's own. She understood what that meant. She knew how special it made you."

"So why didn't she pretend that I was her husband's?"

It is a new question, one she has never thought to ask until now.

"I don't know, girl. Perhaps they had not lain together in a long time, so he knew it could not be."

That made sense.

"So she got sent away?"

"Yes."

"And my father went to her?"

"Yes."

"He should have brought her here. You could have delivered me, Granny. I would have liked that. And you might have saved my mother. She might have known more of her life, and Father would not have pined so, and then gone away to sea. We could have lived here all together and been happy. Couldn't we?"

The cunning woman's eyelids are beginning to droop. She is losing the thread of her story. It doesn't really matter. For Nell already knows that the ending in her head is not the one that would have come to pass had her mother survived her birthing.

"Bryony roots, saffron, and syrup of wormwood . . ." The cunning woman's head is nodding sleepily. ". . . helps bring away what a careless midwife has left behind . . . Might have saved her. Might not. Who's to say?"

This tale is unraveling now, like a piece of bright knitting. In the maze of the cunning woman's mind, the enchanting visitor from over the border is fading fast. Running away. Had she lived, she would have disappeared just the same—back to her husband as if Nell had never been. It was all arranged. The husband, whoever he was, had been prepared to forgive her for lying with another man. Perhaps he was spellbound . . . she was so beautiful. Perhaps there were other younglings to consider. Who's to say?

Nell is rocking the chicken in her arms. "But she held me, didn't she?" she half asks, half remembers. "Before she died? She knew me for a little while?"

"Mmm? A newborn . . . safely delivered. Dance it daily, to keep it from the rickets, and lullaby it often . . . and suffer it to howl, for howling be good for its brain and lungs."

"Granny?"

It is too late. The cunning woman is exhausted. Both the fire and her tale have flickered briefly, then gone out. The last bit of the story—the bit about Nell's father struggling through snowdrifts to bring his Merrybegot home—will have to go unsaid.

Unrecalled.

The Confession of Patience Madden

THE YEAR OF OUR LORD 1692

The cunning woman's granddaughter came on the fourth day. She burst into our bedchamber as if someone—something—had spat her in, and it fair scared the breath out of me to see her there.

Grace had convinced me, you see, convinced me beyond a shadow of a doubt, that this girl was in league with Satan. That she had fixed Grace already with her evil eye and that I was to be next. She carried a cloth bag with something in it, and her hair, which was red and cut short, like a lad's, was sticking from her head in hedgehog spikes.

I wanted to yell for help, but a whole morning's shouting had left me barely able to whisper.

So much shouting. My throat was raw from it, and my tongue all pricked and cut about by the pins I had been squirrelling away, at Grace's insistence, to sputter out at visitors.

The villagers had been easily fooled. They came in twos and threes, once word got around. The housekeeper let them in through the kitchen. So far I'd done exactly what Grace had told me to, and I'd done it well—so well that I was beginning to wonder whether my soul was half wheedled after all.

My behavior, though, was nothing compared to my sister's. The lowest sailor would have blushed to hear the language that came spewing from her lips. Her mouth frothed as she heaved up pins, fingernails—little bits of coal, even—and her limbs arched to such shapes and degrees that they really should have snapped.

Faced with such terrible strangeness, most of the villagers had backed away, crossing themselves as they went. Only some older women—great ugly people, with faces like slabs of lard—had come closer, to stare. They would have pulled up a bench, those women, had there been one in the room.

"Grace," I'd whimpered once they had finally gone. "Speak to me. Speak to me properly. You frighten me when you behave so, for it is as if you are truly possessed."

"Perhaps I am," she had rasped, her voice as spent as mine. "Yet trust me. For Satan and his witch cannot get a proper hold of me while I rest here with you. Your pretense confuses them, Patience, and weakens their grip on my senses. Trust me. It will not be for much longer."

We had not yet faced my father. He had been summoned on the second day but had only just got home, traveling as fast as humanly possible from wherever the Lord's business had taken him. He had come straight to our bedchamber, but since Grace had seemed to be dozing, I, too, had feigned sleep, so he had looked briefly upon us and gone away.

*I was not looking forward to spitting pins at my father—
even if it was to save Grace's soul. I was not looking forward to
that at all.*

*When the door to our chamber crashed open, I assumed it
was Father, come back to check on us. I was relieved to see it
wasn't, but Grace's agitation knew no bounds when she
realized it was the cunning woman's granddaughter standing
there. Some words were exchanged over the bed—nothing of
any great consequence, but enough to set my sister weeping
and howling at such a pitch that my father came flying up the
stairs just in time to catch the cunning woman's granddaughter
throwing something on the coverlet.*

A frog. A dead frog.

*Of all the things she could have tossed through the air, with
good intent or bad, she threw a frog.*

*And in my alarm and confusion I was sure I felt the other
frog—my mother's jeweled clasp—shift beneath the mattress,
like a living thing.*

*How I screamed then, at what seemed to me beyond mere
coincidence and too frightening for words. She could have
thrown anything, anything at all, yet she threw a frog. . . .*

*Father tried to grab her, but she was too quick for him.
Down the stairs she ran and out of the house, leaving Grace
and me shrieking and Father in a whirl.*

*Grace was the first to fall silent. Her mouth snapped shut
like a trap, and she began to tremble. I looked at Father and
he looked at me, and the sounds I was making stopped at
once.*

I could tell from his face that he was trying—and failing—

*to understand what was happening. For the first time in my
life I felt akin to him. I wanted to cry out:* Father, I don't
understand either. I don't know if it is Grace, or Satan,
or the cunning woman's granddaughter making me behave
this way. Father, I'm scared.

*But beside me Grace was shivering like a beggar in winter,
and it was to her that he turned, his face as stern as Judgment
Day.*

*I waited for her to do something. To spit pebbles or say
dreadful words. For then I would have known for certain that
Satan had her against her will, for she would never in her right
mind have dared so much as scowl in Father's presence.*

I waited a long time. And so did Father.

*And eventually, after many moments, my sister opened her
mouth.*

*"Take it away," she whispered. "Take it off me. For it
burns . . . it burns. And I feel . . . I feel . . . He is here! Satan
is here! She brought him to me! The witch brought him to me!
He's right here, right here! He's with me, Father! Stop him!
Please stop him! Noooooooooo!"*

*Appalled I cringed away from her. And for an instant I saw
the dried-up frog perched on her belly before Father, with a great
yell, snatched it up like a burning coal, flung it onto the floor,
and began stamping and stamping and stamping.*

*Outside the door our housekeeper was making a din of her
own, crying, "Let me fetch someone! Let me call someone!"*

*And then the dried-up frog was nothing but a scatter of
dust-colored fragments—not even enough to fill an ashpan.
And Grace was lying beside me as if in a swoon. And Father*

had dragged the housekeeper into the room and was speaking in his harshest voice to all of us.

"Not a word! Not a word of this to anyone, do you hear me? Do you hear me?"

We did, we all said. We heard him. Not a word. Not to anyone. Not a single word.

And then we prayed. All four of us—Grace and I, rigid where we lay, and Father and our housekeeper, down on their knees, getting specks of frog on themselves. Father led us, his voice growing stronger and more sure of itself by the second.

Our housekeeper was all of a shudder, but Grace and I lay good as gold, while Father begged the Lord to deliver us from evil, to give us the strength to keep witchcraft at bay.

After a good long while he fell silent and simply stood with his eyes closed and his arms raised. Listening. The rest of us stayed quiet and respectful while he communed thus. For the Lord, if He had any answers, would hardly have shared them with a lowly housekeeper or two troublesome girls.

By the time Father opened his eyes, he had answers writ all over his face. First, he sent the housekeeper away, with instructions to continue preparing supper as if nothing were amiss. Then he turned to my sister and me, leaning so close over the bed that I thought he might kiss us.

"You must get up now," he commanded. "Both of you."

I felt Grace stiffen beside me. She was as tense as a doe that hears a strange noise and realizes it might have to run for its life. I thought she might speak, but she didn't.

I looked up at my father's face, daring to hope it would turn to me. But his mind, I realized, was full of whatever the Lord had imparted to him. And it was directly to Grace that he spoke.

"You must act as usual," he told her. "You must go about your chores and attend to your prayers as if none of this had been. As for she who does the Devil's work . . . the one who brought evil here this day . . . Vengeance will be mine, saith the Lord, and so it will come to pass. But Satan is a cunning foe, and only guile of the sharpest order will see him vanquished and his witch with him. You must leave this matter to me now, daughter. Do you understand?"

"Yes," Grace murmured.

"Do you understand?"

"Yes," Grace repeated, more loudly.

"Then get up!"

And he swept from the room without another word to either of us, banging the door behind him.

For a moment I continued to lie there, fretting over my own fears—all of them still unanswered, in the darkness of my head. I should have felt relief. Father was going to take care of everything. I could get up now and act as usual.

And yet . . .

My thoughts returned to the jeweled frog. I had stolen it. And that was a sin. Not as bad as being a witch and throwing evil charms, but still enough to set you on the path to Hell. Father did not know I was a thief. But the Lord, who sees everything, probably did. And Satan too. Maybe the dried-up frog had been a warning to me—a sign that Satan could claim my wicked soul at any time. Maybe it had landed on Grace by mistake.

*And so I confessed to my sister. I withdrew the clasp from
its hiding place, and I showed it to her.*

*"Should I tell Father?" I whispered, close to tears. "Or shall
I just put it back in the chest?"*

*I had placed the precious thing on the coverlet. It sparkled
there, all glinty and green, while Grace looked from it to me, the
dullness in her eyes sharpening into something else.*

"Don't tell Father, and don't put it back," she said eventually.

*"But I must. I can't keep it. It was our mother's, and I
stole it."*

*She reached out one finger and began thoughtfully stroking
the ridge of emeralds along the frog's back.*

*"I believe you were meant to take it," she said softly. "I
believe the Lord guided your hand, Patience, so that you and I
would have something . . . some object with enough power to
keep that witch away."*

I didn't understand her. I didn't understand her at all.

*"So what shall I do with it? What are you saying?"
I said.*

She picked the clasp up then and handed it back to me.

*"Let me think about it later," she said. "I feel too strange
still to think about it now. Strange . . . and somehow altered.
The cunning woman's granddaughter has sullied me with her
charm and the terrible things she said. I need to compose
myself. I need to pray. I will think more on this by and by."*

*And so I slid our mother's clasp back under the mattress.
And we got out of bed, on weak and tottering legs. And we
washed and dressed ourselves and tied each other's bonnet
strings. And we ate our suppers and did our chores, like good,*

obedient girls. And the only things to fall from our mouths all evening were words of prayer and a "please" and a "thank you" for the passing of a jug of cream.

And that night, after returning to our bed, Grace told me what she believed I was meant to do with our mother's clasp.

At first I would not hear of it.

"I can't," I said. "What if the Devil is waiting for me again out there on his horrible horse?"

"The Lord will protect you," she replied. "For you will be doing His work—helping Him to rid our village of a filthy witch."

"And Father? What if he catches me? What if I'm seen and someone tells him?"

"Then we will say that you were drawn from this house against your will. By the witch. After everything he witnessed here today, he surely will not doubt it."

It needed more consideration than that. I should have known better than to follow my sister's lead. I should not have trusted her. But I was tired. And anyway, it all seemed to fit. The cunning woman's granddaughter had thrown us a nasty dead frog, so it seemed entirely sensible to use a charm of our own to keep her malevolence at bay.

"It must be planted in secret, after dark," Grace told me. "Or it won't work. Hide it in their garden, in a place only you and I will know of. You were meant to do this, Patience. You know you were. For you are not a thief. You stole mother's clasp for a reason, and this is surely it."

"All right," I said. "But not tonight. Later. When the moon is full, and I can see where I'm going. I'll do it then."

And so I did.

SEPTEMBER
1645

On the second Sunday in September the cunning woman gets out of bed, climbs down the ladder, and promptly forgets where she is. Nell finds her huddled beside the cauldron, mouthing a garbled spell of protection and glaring at the chicken.

"Go back to bed, Granny," she coaxes her. "Go on, and I'll bring you up a cordial."

"Who are you?" the old woman replies. "And where are my scarlet slippers?"

It is forty years, at least, since the cunning woman has worn anything on her feet except clogs or broken boots.

It takes a great deal of persuading to get her up the ladder and back under the coverlet, and still she isn't sure whether Nell is her sister, a neighbor, or some daft maid come from miles away for a love potion.

"Those love potions . . . ," she murmurs. "They don't always work."

Nell tucks her up like a poorly child and goes back

down the ladder to rake the hearth and feed the chicken.

It is time, she realizes, to let everyone know that her granny is sick in her mind. It is time to stand alone as the village healer and midwife—that is, if folk will let her.

Her own mind, she is sure, contains enough of the Knowledge now to conjure a remedy for just about everything from itchy scalps to gouty toes. The properties of every herb, root, flower, seed, gum, bark, and berry she is ever likely to use are clear in her head. She can distill, infuse, and preserve as necessary. And she understands the significance of adding magical things—the skin of a snake, flakes of iron, foam from the sea, or wine in which a ruby has been swirled seven times.

The cunning woman has taught her well, for as long as she has been able. She might not have covered everything, but it is enough to get by on, and the rest will come with experience. There can be no more lessons. For her granny's moments of clarity are so rare nowadays that when they happen, it doesn't seem kind to press for more Knowledge. The past . . . that's all the cunning woman wants to dwell on now. Little bits of the past, as bright and precious as the lozenges of glass that once formed a picture in the window of the church.

It is weeks since Nell and her granny last showed their faces at church. A Sunday in the village might as well be Tuesday on the moon, for all the cunning woman knows or cares anymore. Even if Nell were to get her ready this morning and down through the fields in time, it is doubtful she would sit still for the sermon. She would dance a jig, more than likely. Or rattle off various ways to pull a tooth without pain. Or loudly accuse the minister of never smiling or of stealing gooseberries from someone's garden. She would behave, anyway, in an odd and unacceptable manner. People would get annoyed. Children would take fright. No one would understand.

And so Nell stays home and lets her granny sleep. She is in no great hurry herself to meet with the minister and his daughters—not after their last encounter. *Best let the dust settle on that one,* she thinks. "I don't suppose we'll miss much," she tells the dun chicken. "'Twill be the usual rant about hellfire, I imagine. No more sermons on frolicking, though, I reckon—not now. Hah!"

She has a pile of purple flowers with dangling roots to sort through. Saffron: a powerful herb, to be used sparingly lest it cause convulsive laughter and too rapid a pulse. An excellent remedy for yellow jaundice, so long as no more than a pinch of the grated root be taken, in a syrup of honey and white-wine vinegar.

Nell feels peaceful—happy, even—as she takes the large heap of flowers and roots onto her lap and reaches for her knife. The villagers have always respected her granny. Once they know how things stand, they are bound to feel compassion. And if they doubt Nell's ability to tend to their ills alone—well, it will be up to her to prove herself. She can do that. She knows she can. She no longer doubts it. Then she and her granny will be all right. They will have enough to eat over the winter, and her granny will not have to worry about a thing. Not a single thing.

Who knows? she tells herself, flicking petals as dark as bruised thumbnails from the edge of her knife. Who knows, if she earns everyone's trust and respect quickly enough, she might even get to deliver Grace Madden's Merrybegot—wherever it ends up being born. If it has to be birthed in secret, then is she not the only midwife suited to the task? The only one they can trust? The minister might even send her by carriage. What a thrill that would be.

At her feet the dun chicken makes a lunge for something.

"Off!" commands Nell, nudging it away with her bare feet and reaching down to retrieve a dropped root. "It may look safe, but it isn't. 'Twould probably make you puke until your feathers fell out, so don't touch it. Don't be fooled."

The minister's daughters cannot tell who is present in church and who is not. They cannot tell because they dare not look round. They have perfected the art of stillness, these two, as they sit on their usual bench right up at the front, with their heads bent and their hands already steepled in prayer.

Behind them the villagers shuffle and cough and peer expectantly at the door. For the minister is not preaching the sermon today. Somebody else is. An important visitor, from far away.

And he is late.

Patience Madden grows restless. She tugs her sister's sleeve.

"I'll tell you a story," she whispers. "About the daughter of Herodias, who was given the head of John the Baptist, served up on a platter like a mess of brawn."

"Shhh!"

It was murky, first thing, and although the mist has cleared, there is a mushroomy smell of autumn in the air that sneaks into the church whenever the door opens.

It wafts in now as the big door bangs, and the congregation turns, like one body, to gawp at the person just arrived.

Matthew Hopkins. Witch-finder General. Come all the

way from the place called Essex to rout Satan from their midst.

The congregation gasps, for although he is a small person, his style gives him height and a regal presence. His expensive broad-brimmed hat tilts disdainfully as he takes stock of his surroundings, and his Geneva cloak swishes like a king's mantle as he strides toward the pulpit.

He used to be a lawyer, this man, so he knows full well how to mesmerize an audience—how to put the fear of God into them.

Already, before he has opened his mouth or even reached the pulpit, the villagers are falling silent. Coughs are being smothered, and little boys are nudged hard to make them behave.

For who knows whether a coughing fit or too much fidgeting might turn out to be proof of Satanic possession? Who's to say? This witch-finder has already drawn confessions from dozens of folk in the place called Essex. Ordinary folk, probably. And good folk, too—until the Devil sweet-talked their souls away.

At the back of the church a little girl gets the hiccups. Her mother presses a hand over her mouth as if to stop her screaming.

Matthew Hopkins holds a gold-topped cane in his right fist, which he taps, deliberately, as he mounts the pulpit steps. The sound has a menacing ring to it, like carefully timed slaps.

Towering now over everybody else, he leans forward and scans the rows of heads and faces intently. No one dares meet his eye. Even the Watchers look away.

The minister is standing apart from the congregation, the better to oversee the proceedings.

The witch-finder nods to him briefly, grips the pulpit rail, and unleashes, with all the subtlety and eloquence he can muster, enough fear of God to frighten twenty saints.

Afterward . . . after he has swept from the church, with the minister and his daughters trotting in his wake, the villagers glance at one another in stunned silence. *Is it you?* their glances wonder. *Can it be you? For it isn't me, I swear it.* Then they look round, as the witch-finder suggested they should, to see who is missing . . . who dared not show themselves in the Lord's house this day.

And then they gather in huddles outside, to murmur, then to argue, as suspicion feeds on rumor and spreads from group to group.

Four people were not in church: Mistress Bramlow and her baby boy, the cunning woman, and the cunning woman's granddaughter. Mistress Bramlow has a reasonable excuse. She also has a husband to defend and protect her.

"Never!" he shouts now, so all can hear. "Never would my Jenny dabble in Satan's doings. The baby's ailing, 'tis all, and ailing bad."

His usually frank and pleasant face becomes troubled, then grim, as he realizes how this situation could put those he loves in danger. Those women, the ones the witch-finder told of, the ones hanged as witches—Margaret Moore, who showered vermin on spotlessly clean houses; the servant girl Rebecca Jones, who willingly gave two drops of blood to the Devil; Elizabeth Clarke, the one-legged crone who suckled imps in the form of a white kitten, a fat spaniel, and a long-legged greyhound—they are nothing like his Jenny. And no one must believe it. Not even for an instant.

"The cunning woman!" he blurts out, without really thinking. "Where is she?"

And the muttering groups come together to form one crowd, and everyone looks to Jack Bramlow for further guidance. He hesitates then, knowing in his heart that he has no proof whatsoever that the cunning woman is a witch.

He opens his mouth, prepared to soften such a wild accusation, but Silas Denby interrupts.

"That purge she gave me weren't right," he whines. "She put the worst torment into me with that purge, and I be all out of sorts still and badly feared in my mind."

"'Tis true," declares his wife. "'Tis true what he says. The cunning woman did him great harm with that purge. She's the one—the witch among us."

Half a dozen voices rise up in agreement, recalling how a love potion did nothing but bring on heartburn or a tonic for the liver caused a rash of boils bad enough to scare the crows.

No, someone argues. The cunning woman has birthed our children and cured our ills for many years. She is no witch. She cannot be.

But then a young lad chimes in, recalling how the cunning woman met him and some others in the lane, just a few weeks back; how she looked at him slantwise and muttered a curse.

"That's right!" his father yells. "And you heard what that witch-finder said. A sly wench will keep up appearances while serving Satan all the while. 'Tis only by testing her the way he tested them witches in Ezlix that we will know for sure."

"Aye!" bellows Silas Denby. "Let's float her! Let's throw the cunning woman in the pond, neighbors, and see if she sinks or swims!"

And "Aye! I'm with 'ee, Silas!" calls out the blacksmith, for no better reason than he cannot understand why his lazy scamp of a son went for a soldier, and he needs someone to blame.

There are those who protest still, but their words are drowned out by ugly shouts of "Let's do it!" "Let's fetch her!" "Float the witch!"

"Wait!"

A woman's voice, high-pitched and determined, cuts through the rest. Everyone swivels round. It is the minister's housekeeper, hovering there on the edge of the crowd—with them, yet slightly apart.

"What about the girl?" she says, blinking fast. "The cunning woman's granddaughter? For did I not see her with my own two eyes enter the bedchamber of Grace and Patience Madden? And did I not hear her ill-wishing them until they howled to be released from her hexing?"

Silas Denby pounds his fist in the air and stamps one foot upon the ground. "Aye!" he roars. "Let's float the brat as well."

But Jack Bramlow shakes his head. "Not Nell," he calls decisively. "Not the child." He frowns over people's heads, directly at the minister's housekeeper. "Those girls howled at all and sundry, so I hear," he says. "Would you duck every woman and maid who went to gawp at them, Mistress? Just to be on the safe side?"

The housekeeper looks flustered. She cannot answer that.

"The cunning woman, then!" she shouts out quickly. "We needs must float the cunning woman. For she had a hand, I'll wager, in whatever ailed those innocent, God-fearing girls."

Silas Denby, the blacksmith, and some of the bigger lads are already shifting impatiently and flexing their big hands as if preparing to wrestle with an ogre or storm a whole battalion of Cromwell's army.

"What are we waiting for?" shrills the housekeeper. "For if the old crone be a witch, best we find her out. And if she be innocent, what needs she fear from a bit of a drenching? We can always pull her out if she sinks."

Other women, silent up to now, find their voices and agree. They could not go along with the men's rough talk, but what the housekeeper says sounds both fair and reasonable.

"Fetch her!" they shout. "Fetch the cunning woman!"

The men cannot change their minds. Not now. Not with womenfolk urging them on. Only Jack Bramlow hangs back as the blacksmith and Silas Denby lead other, rougher men away from the church, heading for the fields that lead to the cunning woman's cottage.

At the last minute he decides to follow on.

"Go home," he tells his daughters. "Let your mother know the way of things. Tell her I will be back directly."

"I want to watch the ducking," says the middle one. "I want to see the old woman go splash in the pond. The others are going. Can't we?"

She is jumping up and down in her eagerness to follow the stream of women and children making for the wood where the pond lies in its circlet of rushes as still and as charmed-looking as a dish of mint tea.

Jack Bramlow places a restraining hand on this daughter's shoulder.

"No," he tells her. "This is no revelry, child. This is not for you to witness. Go straight home. Now."

With his children scuffling reluctantly away, he prepares to follow the men. Before he does so, he turns to the one other person still lingering beside the church and gives her a long, searching look. The minister's housekeeper flushes, but she meets his stare defiantly. Then she turns and flounces off—not in the direction of the pond, like most of the other women, but back to the big house, where the minister and the witch-finder will be waiting for her.

She hopes this pair of very important men will not be disappointed by the turn of events. After all, if the cunning woman is found to be a witch, it surely won't be long before the granddaughter is suspected too.

At the crest of the hill she stops to catch her breath and looks back down. She cannot see the other women, for the wood has swallowed them up, and they are already gathered beside the pond. Waiting.

Away to her right she can just make out the men, drawing closer to the cunning woman's cottage. From this distance, they look like animals moving slowly but surely from one stubbled field to another. What she cannot see is that the ringleaders have torn thick branches from trees and are waving them like cudgels. Jack Bramlow, walking many strides behind the others, just looks like a straggler—an animal that cannot keep up with the herd.

The minister's housekeeper pictures the cunning woman sitting unawares at her fireside. She feels a thrill of malice, which she stifles quickly, knowing it to be wrong. Still, who knows? The old crone might well be entertaining Satan this very minute. The men might burst in on all manner of evil doings, in which case she herself need have no qualms about the things she has said this day.

Turning, she walks the last few steps to the gate of the big house. There will be a meal to prepare after she has reported back to the minister and the Witch-finder General. A fine meal, with sauces and sorbets. Perhaps Miss Grace will manage something light. She needs to eat, in her condition.

No mention has been made of Miss Grace's state since the cunning woman's granddaughter let the cat out of the bag some weeks ago. The girl's belly does not yet show, but the housekeeper is no fool. All the other signs are there. Still, she has given the minister her solemn oath—sworn on the Holy Bible, in his presence—that she will not breathe a word of it to anyone.

"Whatever ails my elder daughter is the Devil's work," the minister told her, pressing his own gloved hand over her work-reddened fingers where they rested, like five sausages, on the Lord's book. "Satan's trickery! The result of witchcraft!"

It had made her blush to feel his hand upon hers. It had made her go all of a flutter. So she had kept her own suspicions to herself, while the minister murmured on:

"With the Lord's help, we will trap the witch—the cunning woman's granddaughter. But we must tread carefully, matching the Devil's stealth with our own. In the meantime, Mistress, you must remain silent on the subject of my daughter Grace's health. Do you understand my meaning?"

"I do, sir," she had replied.

He had reached for his purse then, producing a sovereign.

Keeping her gaze lowered, she took it. She appears to be in the minister's confidence now, and it feels like a thrilling place to be. He is a devout man, after all, and a clever one. And if *he* believes the cunning woman's granddaughter hexed Miss Grace, why then surely his faithful servant has a duty to join him in his fight against such witchery.

Knowing herself so privileged, so *special* to the minister, brings a smile to the housekeeper's face as she hurries through the briars, scattering stones and breaking cobwebs with her great big feet.

She has no more thought for the cunning woman's fate than for the spiders that scuttle from their broken homes and the heavy tread of her boots. Nor does she see the thing that scrambles from the undergrowth, until it has lifted the hem of her skirt, grabbed the top of her right boot for leverage, and bitten her hard on the back of her leg.

Snake, she thinks, whirling round in a panic. *Or rat. Where? Where is it? Whatwasitandwherediditgo?*

And it is only because the piskie that attacked her is too old to move fast—or even to flash its arse anymore—that she spies it disappearing into a clump of thistles . . . a rickety, rheumy female, in a skirt made from a patch of sacking and belted with the strings of a stolen bonnet.

"May the Lord and all His saints protect me!" moans the housekeeper. "A piskie. A piskie went for me, all unprovoked!"

But she has enough of her wits about her, despite the pain in her leg, to remember the age-old line.

"I see you. You see me. A question asked must be answered free."

Slowly, grudgingly, the ancient piskie parts the thistles and steps out, a scowl deepening the pits and wrinkles of its face.

"Quickety-quick," it rasps. "Traitor. Judas-person. Causer of harm."

The housekeeper flinches. Then she swallows and clears her throat.

What to ask?

The piskie, she knows, won't linger long. So:

"Will I be better off one day?" she wonders. "Will . . . will my situation improve?"

The old piskie woman is sniffing and snarling and snorting and glaring all at the same time. Its nose is all bunged up still, with the memory that compelled it to bite this traitor-woman on the leg region in the first place—a memory of the old one asleep in the corn, unaware of the cruelty . . . the indignity . . . the terrible dishonor in store for her. And now the air is humming with the kind of information that most old piskie women would prefer to ignore as they live out their last decades in a rambling, toothless stupor.

"Bah!" this one spits, shaking fists like rotten apples in the general direction of the housekeeper's face region.

"Answer the question," insists the housekeeper. "As you be honor-bound to. Will I be rich by and by?"

"Honor-bound, my arse!" snarls the piskie woman, swatting away more bits of unwanted information like invisible flies. "And better ye be a witch than a bitch getting rich any day, any era, any lifetime. Eh? Eh? Throw that in your purse and clink it. Stick that in a pie and bake it. Snitch. Traitor. Causer of sorrow."

And with a final defiant wave of its arms and a stamp of one gnarled and filthy foot, it is gone—deep into the rotting, seeding mess of thistles and back to its nest.

Well, thinks the housekeeper, staring crossly at the place where the nasty little thing had been. *Thanks be for nothing. Thanks be for no answer at all.*

There is no time to summon it back. The minister and the witch-finder will be wondering where she has got to. So she hurries on, wincing a little from the pain in her leg. She might need a salve, she realizes, if the skin is broken. A special salve, a magical salve, to heal a piskie bite. Only the cunning woman or her granddaughter would know how to mix such a thing. The irony of that is not entirely lost on the minister's housekeeper, so she smiles, a little ruefully, as she limps round to the back of the house, to the door used by servants and other lowly people.

Nell is not at home when the men burst in and take her granny away. She is up in the orchard, picking the last few apples from the oldest tree. For as long as she or anyone else can remember, it has been customary for the village healer and midwife to take these last fruits of summer to use for spells and potions. So she has left her granny dozing and come by herself to perform the necessary ritual.

If she is honest, she is glad to be out of the cottage for a while. It can get very stuffy in there, with the air full of smoke and the acrid pong of boiling leaves—and lonely, too, now that her granny's mind is all but gone.

Up here in the orchard she feels cheerier, even though there is nobody else around. She has spent a while just dreaming, with her back against the oldest tree and the autumn sunshine warming her kindly. Now the tree itself seems to lean toward her, in a generous mood, as she reaches for its remaining fruits.

"Thank'ee," she murmurs before twisting each apple from the knobble of its stem and placing it carefully in her basket. Higher up she can see a great globe of mistletoe. She will come back for some of that, she thinks, when the moon is right, and twist it into pocket-size charms for keeping lightning, the pox, or bitter imaginings away.

Higher still, among the tree's topmost branches, there is something else. A little knot of palest pink at the tip of a twig. Blossom. Unseasonal yet unmistakable.

Nell frowns. It is a bad omen for a tree to bear flowers and fruit at the same time. It tells of death—and untimely death, at that. Nell shivers and decides to go home.

She is over the stile and halfway down the lane when she sees Mistress Bramlow staggering toward her, her dark skirts bunched up in her hands to make running easier.

Amos, Nell supposes wildly.

And as she cries out the baby's name she drops her basket—she can't help it—sending apples rolling in all directions, bumping and rolling and bruising their skins, so they will be completely useless after all for healing or magical purposes.

Mistress Bramlow has reached her now and is grabbing at her hands, saying, "No . . . no . . . not Amos. Not the baby. It's your granny, Nell. Something bad . . . Jack tried to stop it. He told them . . ."

She is gasping and gabbling in distress, so that Nell cannot tell . . . cannot understand . . .

"Tell me," she wails. "What's happened? Is she . . . is she . . . ?"

Mistress Bramlow moans softly and shakes her head. She was not there for the dunking. She didn't see, but her Jack has told her everything, so she can picture it clear enough. Those men, the roughest louts in the village, dragging the cunning woman through the fields and into the thick of the wood . . . The catcalls of mothers and the shrill echoes of children as the blacksmith slung a rope around the old woman's middle and tied her the correct way—left thumb to right toe, right thumb to left toe, so that her arms formed the shape of the holy cross.

And then the splash as they threw her into the pond . . . ripples of green scum and just a few bubbles breaking the surface as she sank.

She can picture the Watchers, clumped among the bulrushes, their eyes fixed greedily on the water . . . and other faces, craning and peering, waiting for the cunning woman's trussed and broken body to bob up, so they could shriek at her, and jab her with sticks, and hand her over to the witch-finder.

She can imagine the silence—charged, at first, with a shared and vicious excitement, but altering, as time passed, and one or two folk began shifting their feet in the smelly mud, and a child's voice, sweet as a bird's, cried out: "Where is she?"

Then: "Enough!" her Jack had dared to shout, grabbing the rope from the blacksmith's fist and bracing himself to pull.

And nobody had argued, or shoved him away, or spoken any more about devils in their bellies or young girls spitting pins. Shame-faced at last, the very men who had hauled the cunning woman from her bed and bullied her to the brink of the pond had caught hold of the rope themselves and tugged and strained as if the love of their lives lay submerged at the end of it.

And just when it had seemed, to horrified onlookers, that

the cunning woman must surely be wedged down there, whatever was holding her fast had given way and let her rise.

Splashing and wading, making as much noise as possible to cover their guilt and their shame, the men had gone into the pond and brought her out. No one had thought to bring a blanket. No one had thought of anything much beyond the thrill of trapping a witch.

So they had just landed her, like some ancient mermaid; cut the thongs from her broken thumbs and toes and prodded her nervously for signs of life.

At first they had thought her as dead as a fish. But . . .

"She lives, Nell. She lives. Only . . . the shock of it . . . and all the water that she swallowed . . . and her already frail—"

Mistress Bramlow is holding Nell like one of her own daughters, soothing her as best she can, while preparing her at the same time for what will surely come to pass as a result of such a terrible day's business.

But the instant she hears that her granny is not dead, not drowned at the end of the blacksmith's rope, not killed or murdered after all . . . as soon as she can be certain of that, at least, Nell snaps out of her stupefied stillness and runs like the Power of the wind straight down the hill and—bang—in through the cottage door, beneath the quivering mass of honeysuckle, across to the ladder, and up.

Granny . . . Oh, my granny.

The cunning woman, brought home in a wheelbarrow and bundled quickly, expediently, up the ladder and back into bed, is lying on her side, staring, just staring at the turnip-shaped hole in the thatch.

Someone—Mistress Bramlow, perhaps—has peeled off her wet, stinking clothes, wrapped her in the coverlet, and bandaged her broken thumbs. But one look is all it takes for Nell to understand that what has been done to her granny may never be healed. For it has broken her spirit as well as her bones, and it has blown the few remaining threads of her sanity clean away.

Standing there unrecognized, Nell waits to feel something—pain, rage, anything. But all she feels, for now, is numb. It is nature's way, she knows, of protecting the heart and mind from great despair. And in truth, she is relieved to feel so little, for it enables her to think more clearly about what to do, which herbs and spells to use to try to make her granny better.

Quietly, methodically, for the remainder of the day she does what she can, using all the skills at her fingertips and every magical word in her head. But all the while the cunning woman continues to stare vacantly upward, her breathing growing more and more labored as the turnip-shaped piece of sky turns from blue to mauve and then to night.

And as the air grows chillier and the roof space dark, Nell lights a candle, climbs stiffly down the ladder, and calls to the dun chicken. It waddles obediently from under the bench, hoping for a worm.

"You daft thing," Nell murmurs, picking it up. The familiar warmth of it and the noise of its clucking weaken whatever it is that is keeping her going. But just as she fears she might break down and cry, the sound of someone outside—someone trying not to be heard—stiffens her spine. It will be another villager, leaving something at the door. A honeycomb . . . a dish of plums . . . a peace offering, anyway, to ease a troubled conscience. They have been coming all afternoon, the villagers, and well into the evening—too ashamed to knock or to talk, but sorry, deeply sorry, for what they have done.

Nell waits, holding the chicken close to her heart, until whoever it is has gone away. The piskies can take whatever has been left, and welcome. She herself would only spit on it and leave it to rot.

Back under the roof space she kneels down beside the pallet and tucks the dun chicken under the coverlet. It doesn't wriggle or protest. It seems to understand. And after a moment or two the cunning woman turns her cold cheek to rest upon its feathers, and Nell feels her own pulse quicken with hope.

"Granny?" she whispers.

Slowly, the cunning woman focuses, and recognizes, and smiles something like her old smile, and Nell knows one moment of blessed relief.

Until: "Fetch . . . my . . . box," the cunning woman rasps, in a voice so small, it can barely be heard.

No.

Nell doesn't have to ask which box her granny means or where it is kept. She knows. She has always known. But she stays where she is, as if she hasn't heard properly or doesn't understand. Only a jutting of her lower lip and a flash of hurt in her eyes show she understood precisely.

No.

"Fetch . . . it," the cunning woman rasps again. Her breathing is dreadful, but her mind has rallied itself for this one last task, and she is not to be argued with.

All right.

There is a big lump in Nell's throat, like a lodged crust, and a tightness in her chest as she reels blindly down the ladder again and across to the secret place. Sorrow and fury bubble and swill in her, like two potent ingredients that don't mix, and her fingers feel like a bunch of traitors as they fasten on the box.

It shouldn't be this way, she thinks, her heart bumping, her hands dithering. One day, inevitably, her granny will die. But not now. Not like this. Not because a group of cruel, ignorant boggers have wished it so. Not broken and shamed, with the stench of the pond still about her and smears of weed lodged deep in her ears and lungs.

No.

It shouldn't be this way. It doesn't have to be this way.

And Nell's fingers pass over the box. And when she returns to the roof space, she is holding the fairybaby's caul in its wrapper of leaves and silently thanking the Powers that she didn't use it after all for Grace Madden's unborn.

The cunning woman recognizes the package in her granddaughter's hands and grins weakly, to know herself so greatly loved. Nell is thrilled and relieved to see her granny's face light up so. For it surely means that her mind is working enough to understand and take pleasure in this amazing piece of fairy magic—in this incredible piece of stuff that is going to save her life.

"I think it just needs to be laid on you, like a plaster," she whispers. "I'll spread it on your forehead, shall I? And call on the Powers for good measure. It never hurts to call on the Powers for good measure, does it? Or maybe just the Powers of earth will be enough . . . enough to ground you, I mean. To keep you here—"

No.

There is no need for the cunning woman to speak the word. It is written in every line of her face, in the stubborn set of her jaw and the stillness of her bandaged hands upon the coverlet. It is hanging in the air, that word, like an obstinate moth.

And Nell realizes that she has misread her granny's response. This act—this extraordinary, lifesaving act—is not welcome after all.

"I'm not listening to you," she mutters, plucking hastily at the leafy packaging that's keeping the caul intact. "I'm in charge here. I'm the healer now, and I know what's best. So you just lie there, and let me do my job, all right? You taught me, Granny. You taught me to do everything I can to make a body well again. So that's what I'm doing. I'm just doing my job."

The caul is out of its wrappings and drifting between her fingers, so wispy, so fragile, she fears it might disintegrate before it can be used.

All she has to do is lean forward and place it on her granny's cooling skin. That's all she has to do.

But the cunning woman's mouth is working. "No," it croaks. "Save it . . . save the caul . . . Not right . . . for me. I'm ready to go . . . girl. You mustn't—"

"I'm not listening," Nell sobs. But her fingers are shaking so much that she cannot—dare not—lift the caul from her lap, in case it tears. And the cunning woman's will is like a force field between them, keeping the magic away. And the stupid, stupid chicken is craning its head from under the coverlet and going peck, peck, peck, as if the caul were some tasty morsel that it would shred in a trice, given half a chance and a better angle.

155

"I'll rip it up, then!" Nell shrieks. "I mean it, Granny. There's no one else will ever deserve it so. No one!"

But even as she raves, she knows she will do no such thing. Already the caul feels useless in her hands, and the moment for it has passed.

The cunning woman waits while she weeps, allows her as long as she needs to let go of the hope she had pinned on the power of the caul and to accept that the wish of a tired, hurt, old woman to drift away with dignity must be respected.

Then: "Fetch . . . the . . . box," she says for a third and final time.

And the urge to rant and wail goes away. Nell actually feels it lift as she does as she is told. Later she will give in to a great pile of anger and more tears than she ever thought two eyes could hold. But she knows enough about time and about magic to understand that the next few hours—the last she will ever spend with her granny—can be made fleeting or endless, ordinary or incredible, depending on how she shapes them.

And so it is that with the candlelight flickering and the dun chicken pulling a loose thread from the coverlet—too stupid to realize it isn't a worm—Nell snuggles close enough to her granny to make her feel warm and loved, without clinging or imposing her own desperate wish to keep her near forever, and waits for her own mind to be quiet.

And eventually, it is. And as the cunning woman slips in and out of different stages of drifting away, the hour, the year, and whatever is or isn't happening beyond the walls of the tumble-down cottage no longer matter.

It's like a birth, Nell thinks. *A birth in reverse.*

And just as she would anticipate the final stage of labor, she instinctively knows when the time has come to let go of her granny's hand and open the box.

The lid is stiff, but when it gives, Nell can see that the things inside have neither rusted nor mildewed nor been eaten by insects, for all they have been hidden away for so long.

She holds a warning hand out to keep the dun chicken from investigating, but it is roosting quietly in the crook between the cunning woman's neck and shoulder and doesn't even turn its stupid head.

"Yours now, girl," the cunning woman murmurs. "Only, keep . . . box . . . hidden . . . Dangerous times still . . . Keep . . . safe."

"I will," Nell replies gently. "I promise." And she touches her granny's things—her things now—with a mixture of sadness and awe. The knotted cord for measuring an enchanted circle. The goblet with the rim of jeweled stars. The silver knife for drawing down the moon. The box of salt, to keep powers of evil away.

And something else. Something she did not expect to find, since her granny has never mentioned it to her.

"What's this for, Granny?" she asks, not wanting to misuse it one day, out of ignorance.

The cunning woman has drifted a long way off now. It is a struggle to come back, but she hears and remembers.

"Found it," she whispers. "In the . . . garden."

Nell is turning the object in her fingers, close to the candle flame so that it sparkles and glints.

"It's beautiful," she sighs. "But how did it get into our garden? Someone must have dropped it."

And the cunning woman holds on, although the patterns in her head and what feels very much like the powers of the air are pulling her to go. And in a swirl of images, scents, and sounds she sees again the woman from over the border, dancing in the May Eve circle. Dancing, laughing, then whirling away, away, the clasp on her cloak flashing vivid green in the firelight.

Dropped it. Yes. Must have done. Long ago, though . . . a long, long time ago.

And far away—from far away now—she watches her granddaughter's wise little face recede . . . sees emeralds flash as if the jeweled frog Nell holds in her hand is about to leap.

Important . . . something important . . . still to say . . .

But how did it get into our garden?

Precious, precious girl . . .

And as everything fades . . . as the Powers move her gently onward, the cunning woman clings for just a few seconds more to the time and the place she has known, and she says:

"Hers . . . Nell . . . The clasp. It belonged . . . to . . . your mother."

The Confession of Patience Madden

THE YEAR OF OUR LORD 1692

It was easier said than done, acting as usual, while we waited to see how Father and the Lord intended to trap the witch. I might have managed better had I not been so worried about the change in Grace—a change I truly believed to be the result of some wicked enchantment.

You have to remember, I was only a child. An innocent girl. I had no idea . . . no idea at all that the bloating of my sister's belly and the tiredness that came upon her in the middle of the day were the results of her frolicking. She continued to insist that the cunning woman's granddaughter had hexed her with her evil frog-charm, and I continued to believe it so.

As summer turned to autumn I dreamed most nights of creatures that hopped and croaked and came to me for sustenance. In my dreams I hid from them—under the bed, mostly, or behind a velvet curtain. Once I dreamed I hid in a tree, but a fierce wind came to blow the leaves away, and the creatures swarmed around the trunk, looking up at me with wet, red eyes. Waiting.

Awake, my thoughts turned often to the cunning woman's garden and the place where I had hidden my mother's clasp. I had not buried it in the end—only placed it on a stone, beneath a bush with leaves that smelled of lemons. I couldn't bury it. It was too beautiful to be stuck in the earth like a seed or something dead.

"Fool!" Grace had hissed when I'd told her exactly where it was. "You should have concealed it better than that. You'll have to go back."

But I wouldn't. For the moon was waning and nothing would persuade me to walk those lanes again on dark nights. Nothing. And anyway, I liked to think of the jeweled frog sunning itself on a stone after it had been so long shut away in a box or squashed beneath our mattress.

Then, as days turned into weeks, I dared to wonder whether we should fetch it home.

"It's not working, is it?" I said to Grace. "You're still hexed, aren't you? Let's get the clasp back and leave everything to Father, like he said."

"Shut up, fool," she replied.

And then the Witch-finder General came from Essex to speak in our church. And the villagers threw the cunning woman in the pond to see if she would float. And she didn't, but she died anyway and got put in the churchyard, since no one could say for certain that she was a witch and should therefore be buried facedown at a crossroads with nothing to mark the place.

Father went round the house after that with a face like a thunderclap. And Grace grew mopier and even lumpier around the middle. And I began to wonder why Father and the Lord were taking so long to trap the cunning woman's granddaughter, when she was so much in thrall to Satan that she would let suspicion—even death—fall upon her own granny rather than confess.

October came, damp and dismal, and I hated to think of the jeweled frog getting rained upon. What if it rusted? What if the wet and the cold loosened its ruby eyes or set a mold on its emerald skin that no cloth would ever remove?

"I'm going back to get that clasp," I told Grace as the moon ripened and the first frosts silvered the grass.

"You'll do no such thing," she insisted, wringing my left wrist between both her cold hands until it stung. "You'll leave it exactly where it is and say nothing about it to Father until I tell you."

"Oh, we mustn't tell Father!" I squeaked. "Why must we tell Father? I thought this was our secret. We can't tell Father, Grace. He would know then that I stole it. And that I went out alone at night. He would be furious!"

"No, he won't," she replied. "He won't. You don't understand. Trust me."

Truly, she was far more privy than I to the workings of Father's mind. And though I tried not to care, it rankled me more and more, to be so left out.

The witch-finder paid us a second visit two days before All Hallows' Eve.

"What is happening?" I said to Grace as we bent over our samplers in the parlor. "Is he here to trap the witch at last?"

"Ask no questions, and you'll hear no lies," she snapped. "Just pass me the blue thread."

It was chilly in the parlor, for no fire had been lit. Our

housekeeper was busy in the kitchen, fashioning a chessboard from marchpane (the witch-finder had both a sweet tooth and a fondness for chess). There would be roast swan for supper, with a sauce pressed from oranges, and a pie stuffed with carp, salmon, and hard eggs. Grace and I would dine alone, though. We had been told to keep out of sight.

"I'm using the blue thread for my unicorn's eye," I told my sister. "You'll have to wait."

She didn't argue or hurt me, as once she would. She just sat there in a lumpen huddle, with her hair draggling over her face and her hands idle.

"There," I said after a while. "I've finished. I'm going to the kitchen now, to see about lighting our fire."

She said nothing, just took the thread and began unwinding it round one finger.

"I'll bring you back a slice of orange," I added in an effort to be pleasant. "If there is one to spare."

"Don't trouble yourself," she answered me. "Just go."

In the hallway I hesitated, hearing the drone of men's voices in my father's study. There was no one to see me, so I crept closer and pressed my ear to the closed door. It was a sin to listen at doors. I knew that. But I had my dear sister's best interests at heart.

My father was pacing the floor. I could hear his feet treading the boards. His speech was rapid and impatient.

"We need more proof," he was saying. "Firm evidence."

The witch-finder's reply was little more than a murmur. I had to strain to hear it.

"Your daughter's . . . affliction," he said with a slight cough. "Won't that be seen as proof enough?"

"Perhaps," my father replied. "Perhaps not."

He paused, and I held my breath. Could they hear my heart, thumping through the wood of the door?

"Well then," said the witch-finder. "The death of the infant. Might not that have been caused by witchcraft? For its mother, I understand, has made much of the girl—ill-advisedly, you might say—since that bungled business with the old crone."

He meant Amos Bramlow. The dead infant was Amos Bramlow, a village brat.

"I don't know," my father replied. "The babe had been ailing since birth. He was never going to make old bones."

I heard a clinking of glass as if something was being poured.

"Well then," the witch-finder continued, a note of impatience in his voice. "Let us take a different tack. Might the girl have a familiar? Think, man. A cat or a goat. A pet piglet, perhaps? Any living creature that might conceivably be one of Satan's imps in disguise?"

And then the parlor door swung open, and there stood my sister, holding her sampler over her stomach.

"Patience Madden," she called out, her voice pealing and echoing round the hallway. "What is the meaning of your lingering outside father's study, with your ears flapping like a rabbit's?"

And the study door flew open so fast, I all but fell into the room.

I am in trouble, I thought. Of the worst kind.

Father was glowering in the doorway as if he wished me several counties away, in somebody else's family. I thought fleetingly of the marchpane chessboard. I had hoped for a taste *of it, once a game had been played and the board partially eaten—a sugared pawn, perhaps, maybe even a castle. Not a bishop, though. It would have seemed sinful indeed to bite the head off a bishop—even one made of almond paste. But it would be crusts and water for me after this, I was sure of it.*

To my confusion, things took a very different turn.

The witch-finder was sitting in Father's chair with his boots up on a footstool. He wore splendid boots, trooper's boots with silver spurs, like big spiky insects, fastened to the heels. He was looking past Father and me at Grace, as if she were a statue or a painting that wasn't quite to his taste but interested him all the same, and delicately twirling a point of his mustache between finger and thumb. He didn't appear to care that I had been caught eavesdropping. It didn't seem to bother him in the slightest.

"Well, well," he said. "Good evening, ladies." And I watched Father move aside as the witch-finder surged to his feet and strode across the room, his spurs jangling.

"Come in, come in," he bade us, "and allow me to shut the door, for I cannot bear a draft."

Cautiously I sidled into Father's study with Grace close behind me, like a fat shadow. The room smelled of spices, tobacco smoke, and claret. A good fire burned in the grate.

The witch-finder returned to Father's chair, sat back down, and poured himself another drink. There was paper, pen, and ink beside him on a low table.

"Stand here, girls, where I can see you," he said. It seemed wanting in manners, his behaving with such authority in another man's study, but it was not my place to say so. And Father did not seem to mind. Indeed I sensed relief in the way he kept to the

shadows while Grace and I stood politely in front of our guest, waiting to be conversed with or ordered away as he wished.

"Now, then." The witch-finder leaned back in Father's chair and regarded us with eyes like ice and honey mixed. "Tell me again. When the cunning woman's granddaughter came to your bedchamber, what did she do?"

He was looking at me, but it was Grace who answered.

"She cursed me, sir, in the Devil's name. She caused me to burn. Then she threw an evil charm that did land upon my belly and cause a strangeness that persists and has yet to leave me."

Slowly the witch-finder reached for the pen, dipped it in the ink, and began to scratch words on a piece of paper.

"And you witnessed this?" he said to me, his pen poised.

"Yes, sir," I replied, since it was truly so.

"And you understand, child, what has come to pass as a result of this evil deed?"

"Yes, sir," I said again, although I understood only that my sister was afflicted with a bloated middle that rippled occasionally in the night as if there were waves in it.

"And there is no doubt in your mind that your sister's— ahem—condition was brought about by witchcraft?"

"No, sir."

How innocent I was. How stupid.

The witch-finder could not fault me. He wrote some more.

"If we trap the witch, will Grace's belly go down?" I dared to ask.

He cocked his head then and allowed himself a tight-lipped smile.

My sister's hand moved with all its old stealth and purpose.

"Oh!" I yelped, feeling the nip through my clothes. "Why did you—?"

But she interrupted me, her voice shrill and scared as if she were the one being hurt.

"There is something else," she cried. "Something I hardly dare speak of, for I fear the witch's power so. Patience knows of it. She was there. She will vouch for it."

The witch-finder stopped writing. He laid down his pen and gave my sister his full attention. I stared at her too—in complete surprise.

"Tell me," the witch-finder bade her.

"A jeweled clasp," Grace continued. "A precious thing that belonged to our dear mother. She stole it. The cunning woman's granddaughter stole our mother's clasp. She was wearing it beneath her apron when she threw her evil charm. I glimpsed it as she moved. So did Patience."

I watched the witch-finder's face grow more animated as he listened to my sister lie. He turned excitedly to where my father stood.

"Can this be verified?"

"It can indeed."

And Father left the room, his face grim.

We waited in silence for him to return. The witch-finder was writing so fast that he had knocked his claret cup over. Luckily it was empty.

I pictured Father unlocking the carved wooden chest and lifting the lid. I imagined him delving among my mother's gowns, bodices, and mantles to find the small box hidden beneath them, like a heart. I tried to picture his face the exact instant he discovered that our mother's secret, hidden treasures had indeed been plundered and that the jeweled frog was missing.

I tried to still the panic that rose in me, knowing that it was I, Patience Madden, who had taken the jeweled frog and should by rights be punished. And now here was my sister, lying through her teeth—shifting all blame for the theft onto the cunning woman's granddaughter.

I could have confessed right there on the spot. I could have burst into tears and trusted my superiors to show mercy: the witch-finder, the Lord, my God; and the minister, my father. But the witch-finder was smiling as he blotted his page of evidence; the Lord seemed very far away; and child as I was, something told me that my father would not welcome the truth being spilled abroad. For didn't he want to trap the witch? Didn't we all?

The cunning woman's granddaughter, I told myself, deserved to be trapped, by fair means or foul, for bewitching my sister with this strange bloating disorder. I could not blame poor Grace for seizing this chance to get back at her tormentor, nor could I expose her for a liar when she was clearly possessed still and desperate for an end to her torment. The witch-finder and Father, I decided, were best left in ignorance of the part I had played in bringing the witch to justice. And the Lord, who sees everything, would surely understand.

Then Father returned. His arrival made me jump, for it seemed only an instant since he had left—hardly long enough for him to have gone upstairs, unlocked the chest, and located the box.

"It's gone," he announced. "My wife's emerald and ruby clasp. The one shaped like a frog—shaped like the very creature the witch hurled at my daughter."

The witch-finder poured two cups of claret—poured them so merrily that they slopped.

"We have her!" he declared. "For the likeness between the charm and the stolen item falls not by chance. And 'tis part of a witch's trickery to draw power from a stolen ring, a locket, or even the paring of a fingernail, the better to possess her victim. This clasp. It would, I presume, have formed part of your elder daughter's dowry by and by?"

"Indeed," Father replied. "Undoubtedly."

"Then it is as good as hers already, and the witch knew it."

This was news to me, about Grace's dowry. What would I have got, I wondered. The pins?

"And there is something else," Father was saying excitedly. "Something left by the witch, among my wife's possessions. Look!" And he held up a feather. A big brown feather.

Beside me Grace began to shake and to roll her eyes.

"Her imp," she moaned. "I've seen it with her, out in the lanes. She talks to it and coddles it like it were a child newborn."

The witch-finder grabbed the pen.

"What manner of creature is this?" he asked.

"A chicken," Grace replied, clutching my arm and staring in horror at the feather as if the very sight of it caused her pain. "A great, ugly chicken."

"Her familiar," the witch-finder declared, his voice thick with contempt as he licked his lips, bloodred from the claret.

And so they had her.

She was trapped.

OCTOBER
1645

With her granny gone, Nell feels too numb to work. Luckily she doesn't have to, for the villagers place so much food and kindling on the cottage step that she knows she will neither freeze nor go hungry for as long as she needs to mourn.

The piskies leave these offerings alone, out of respect, even though they are filching whatever scraps they can before bedding down for the winter, with plugs of beeswax in their nostrils, to block out the awakening call of too much information.

At first Mistress Bramlow visits every day, to light the fire and make sure Nell is eating.

"Come stay with us," she offers. "Let me look after you."

But Nell prefers to be alone. And anyway, the dun chicken is miserable too and would only molt and refuse its corn in a strange environment. It follows Nell wherever she goes, which for several weeks isn't far. At night it roosts beside her up in the roof space, blinking up at the hole in the thatch as if it expects something—a tasty worm . . . the cunning woman's spirit . . . who knows?—to suddenly appear there.

On the day of the first frost Mistress Bramlow doesn't come. A Watcher trudges up the path instead, to let Nell know that baby Amos died in his sleep without so much as a fever or a cough to warn of his passing. It is not wholly unexpected, this little death, but the Watcher crosses herself before stepping over the cunning woman's threshold and will not take the cup of cordial or the piece of apple pie that Nell offers out of politeness.

There is no room in Nell for more sorrow.

"Tell Mistress Bramlow that my feelings are with her," she says dully.

And the Watcher's eyes gleam back at her suspiciously.

Wretched little unwed, those eyes say. *This is all your fault.*

That night Nell dreams of her granny for the first time since she died, and she wakes with tears trickling over her cheeks and pooling in her ears. It is another frosty morning, with the stars only just fading. And whether because of the dream or because the death of baby Amos has shown that things still happen, that events continue to unfold with or without the cunning woman there, Nell feels like getting up and going out. Just for a while. Just to breathe some fresh air and get her thoughts in order.

"Stay here," she tells the dun chicken as it cranes its stupid head above the pallet, waiting to be carried down the ladder.

"I mean it," she adds as it half flutters, half dives across the roof space, preparing to launch itself down the rungs rather than be left alone. "I won't be long."

At the door she hesitates. She has her basket with her out of habit, just in case she finds a clump of something worth picking and using, and a small knife for cutting stems or digging up roots. What else might she need? Nothing, really.

Still, she pauses, knowing only that leaving the cottage, even for a short while, is making her feel like a tortoise of the woods stepping out of its shell or a fledgling about to quit the safety of its nest. *A charm,* she thinks. *I will take a charm of protection with me. Nettle and yarrow to allay fear and two rowan twigs, bound with red thread to the shape of a solar cross. Or the caul. The strongest charm of all. Yes, I will take the caul. In fact I will keep that caul close by me all the time from now on, and then I will feel safe.*

Ready, finally, she pushes open the cottage door.

The garden is threaded with cobwebs that sparkle like fairy lace in the frost. There is a bag of walnuts on the step and a loaf of barley bread. Nell adds them to her basket in case the fresh air restores her appetite. She doubts it will. She doubts anything will. Everything tastes of nothing since her granny died.

Through the gate she goes, along ruts and bumps of frozen mud toward the orchard. The oldest apple tree has lost most of its leaves and all of its fruit. Nell looks for the sinister knot of blossom, but it, too, has gone, fallen off, vanished, or eaten for pudding by a piskie.

All the trees look very dead. The ball of mistletoe is flourishing, though, high up in the oldest tree's branches. Nell knows she ought to gather some, but she hasn't the heart to try. And anyway, she has lost track of what the moon is doing. It has to be six days old, for the picking of mistletoe. No more, no less, or the stuff will be as useless as a handful of grass pissed upon by piskies.

Oh, Granny, I miss you.

She turns her back on the orchard and heads west, away from the village. There is nothing for miles in this direction, except open moorland and tracks that meander to nowhere. You can get lost if you're not careful. Or step into a bog and be sucked down and swallowed like a dinner, with no one ever knowing what became of you.

Nell walks until her ankles ache, until the frost has melted and a pale sun has risen behind her. She has a vague notion to keep right on going until she reaches the fairy hill. Common sense tells her that she will never find it again and that even if she did, and tried to get in, she would only bounce right off its surface with a bruised nose for her trouble.

I could try, though, she thinks to herself. *I could search for a while.*

She has no idea, really, why she would want to return to a place where time means nothing and emotions don't count. All she knows is that she cannot stay huddled away in the roof space forever, with only a daft chicken for company. The fairies, for all their strangeness, might give her something—a piece of advice, a challenge, a surprise . . . something, anyway, to get her thinking properly again. Something to move her on.

Trudging farther, she turns over in her mind the various spells her granny taught her for summoning different beings. Each one is different, depending on whom or what you want to see. There's one for goblins, another for unicorns, and a complicated one for water nymphs involving three cups of seawater, a lily root, and the beams of a spring moon. The one for fairies is pretty straightforward. This is it:

A SPELL TO SUMMON A FAIRY
**Find thyself a gallitrap (fairy ring),
and lay down within it, with thy feet pointing north.
Best this be when the moon is full and the hour late.
Wear thy coat inside out, and have a four-leaf clover
in the pocket, to prevent mischief being wrought upon
thy limbs or senses. Take three swallows of sleeping draft,
place wild thyme upon thine eyelids, and recite,
over and over, until sleep claims thee: "In peace I come,
in peace I lie. Come forth in peace and round me fly."
So mote it be.**

Since she has no thyme, four-leaf clover, or sleeping draft, and since it is early morning, and anyway, the moon could have turned hexagonal or exploded like a cannonshot for all the notice she has been taking of it recently, Nell can have no real intention of trying to summon a fairy this day.

Still, she keeps half an eye out for gallitraps as she walks and thinks about what she would do or say should she ever meet the fairyfolk again.

So deep she goes into her imaginings that she doesn't see the lad, sprawled among bracken with his back against a boulder, until she practically trips over his outstretched legs.

"Oh!" she cries, jumping away. And because her mind is all taken up with spells and conjurings, she truly believes, for a few startled moments, that she has summoned this boy from the land of fairies by the sheer force of her will.

But, no. There is blood seeping through the front his shirt and pain all over his face. This is a human being, all right. A soldier. One of the King's, by the look of him, and so glassy-eyed and blue around the mouth that Nell can tell that he is going to die.

Where's the battle? she wonders. *I don't hear one. I don't see one. How did he get here? Who shot him?*

No point asking, for the boy has drifted beyond all reason. If Nell is to do what she can to save him, there is no time to lose.

Flinging aside her basket, she kneels down, grasps the front of the bloodied shirt between both hands, and rips right through the blossoming stain. The boy winces but does not cry out.

"Yell if you want to," Nell tells him. "I won't think you a coward for it. Now . . ."

The shot has missed his heart but made a mess of his rib cage. Frowning, Nell forces him to lean forward while she feels rapidly along his back. No exit wound, so the ball must still be lodged somewhere in the smashed pulp of his body. He has lost a lot of blood and is sinking deeper.

Moss.

Peat moss.

Packed close to a wound, it will staunch the bleeding and aid recovery.

There is plenty of moss around. But will it do the trick?

'Tis worth trying, thinks Nell. *Particularly if I summon the Powers, for good measure.* And she leans past the boy's shoulder, gathers up two great clumps of spongy greenstuff, and slaps them against the open, seeping hole in his chest.

The boy's cry rises in agony, like the wail of a martyr being weighted with stones or stretched on a rack.

"Beggin' your pardon," Nell tells him. "But if I'd warned you first, you might have clenched up, and then it wouldn't work."

It isn't working anyway.

Powers or no Powers, it is doing absolutely no good at all. In fact it is making what was already looking like a very nasty death ten times worse.

Nell is thinking fast.

An injured man's dressing, sprinkled with oil of rue, then hidden inside a hollow oak, will transfer the injury from person to tree and thence into the earth. . . . A plaster made from ship's pitch, white wax, oil of juniper berries, the fat of a heron, and a dozen leaves of plantain, crushed, be good for wounds caused by shootings. . . . Carnation oil will speed healing, but only if applied during a waxing moon.

"Oh, bogger it!"

There is only one thing left for Nell to try, and it has nothing to do with waxing moons or heron fat.

She doesn't want to do it. She doesn't *have* to do it. She could stand up right now and walk away—on toward the fairy hill, if she feels like it, or back to the village. It would be easy enough to simply go. There are no Watchers around—no one to know or care that she left a fellow human being to bleed to death on the moor.

And the caul, the most valuable piece of magic she owns, would still be hers, to use at a time and on a person of her own choosing.

She looks down at the useless wad of moss, soaking up red gore like a sea sponge, then away down the hill toward home.

She doesn't even know this soldier's name. He could stride away from here as fit as a ferret and get shot again tomorrow. He could walk straight into a bog and get swallowed. And what a waste of good magic that would be.

The boy is watching her with glazing eyes. Another moment, and even the mightiest of spells will be useless.

Now, Nell tells herself. *Run away from here. Go on. Go.*

But her legs won't move.

What would Granny have said? she wonders. *What would she have wanted me to do?*

And the answer is right there in her head.

You're a healer, girl. You do all you can, for as long as you can, with whatever you have to hand. It's your calling.

"You'd better be worth it," she tells the dying boy as she reaches for her basket. "You'd better be deserving, that's all I can say."

The boy can barely focus, through the blurring of his eyes that goes with dying. When the girl first appeared, he thought she was a ghost, come to guide his spirit to wherever spirits go. When she ripped his shirt away, he had a moment's fear that she was going to pluck his still-beating heart straight out of his injured body, to hasten him on.

Fetch help, he wants to say. *Bring me a horse. Get word to my father.* But it is too late for any of that, and he knows it.

He has no idea what it is she has slapped against the open wound in his chest. No idea . . . only that the agony of it is worse than anything . . . anything . . .

Through the mist in front of his eyes, he sees the girl throwing things from a basket. A knife, a loaf of bread. What? Is she going to feed him now? Is she mad?

This is not the way my life should end, he panics. *Not lost in this godless part of the kingdom with none but a brain-addled maid to bear witness.*

He struggles to speak, but a great wash of pain takes him, and it is as much as he can do to keep his eyes open, to fight the pain and the mist and the fading.

And now the girl has flung aside whatever infernal weights she had pressed to his chest and is coming at him again, with upraised hands. Her face is a pale oval, looming closer, and she is muttering something about water and air.

What now, for pity's sake?

What is it she holds?

The knife? A bandage? A slice of bread?

He cannot see. He cannot tell.

Such pain . . . too much pain . . . too much to bear . . .

Oh!

Nell isn't sure what she feels as she watches the fairybaby's caul work its spell. Regret? Awe? Pride? Relief? They're all there, crowding her head, as the boy's torn flesh and mangled innards begin to heal. First, the blood disappears, sucked back into the body as if the hole in the chest was a mouth. Then the edges of the wound knit together, forming a livid line that gradually pinkens, then lightens, then vanishes completely.

She had expected the caul to change color; to fizz, perhaps, or emit sparks. She had thought the air might fill with fairies and glowworms, all chanting and watching and willing the magic to work. She had hoped for high drama. Some pomp and ceremony. A bit of a show.

But the caul simply settles, to the right of the boy's heart, as if it just happened to land on him, like an autumn leaf, while this incredible thing took place. And when the spell is complete, when the boy is whole again, as if the wound had never been, the caul looks just the same. No flimsier or smaller or paler or darker. Nothing to show that its power has been all used up or that it has done something quite miraculous.

Maybe it will *work again,* Nell dares to think. *If I charge it by moonlight and say the right words.*

But: "What happened?" shouts the boy, sitting bolt upright and staring goggle-eyed at the place where he is entirely certain he recently got shot. "What in the name of heaven did you do?" There is what looks to him like a cobweb sticking to his skin. Quickly, impatiently, he brushes it away.

"What manner of creature are you?" he adds, uncertain for the moment whether to be grateful or afeared of this skinny being with the solemn eyes and hair so short and ragged, it looks nibbled.

Nell considers the fairybaby's caul, all ripped and crumpled on the ground and definitely no use anymore to man nor beast.

"My name is Nell," she replies, without shifting her gaze. "And I be a healer. A cunning woman."

The boy inspects her face, her small hands, her grubby clothes.

"Well, Mistress Nell, healer and cunning woman, I owe you my life," he says eventually. "And I thank you for it."

She looks back at him then, mildly curious. He is not from

hereabouts, for his voice is refined. A gentleman's. He has dark eyes and a tumble of brown hair, and his hands, she notes, are as smooth and white as a lady's.

She does not ask how he came to be dying alone with no comrades to aid him and no sign of a skirmish, for it no longer matters. He expects her to ask and is relieved when she doesn't, for had she known he was shot by a landowner for frolicking in a hayloft with his apple-cheeked daughter, he suspects she might not have been so ready to save his life—by whatever miraculous means she has managed to do so.

She doesn't ask his name, either, so he keeps that quiet too.

In return, as seems only fair, he does not press for further details about her incredible healing powers.

"I'll never be able to do it again," she snaps as if reading his mind. "So don't go spreading tales around the bogging garrison, or they'll say I be a witch and come after me for it. I won't be telling no one about this day's business, and nor must you."

"You have my word on that," he declares. "It will be our secret. Always."

"Good," she says.

He smiles at her then, a charming, easy smile.

"I must get back," he tells her. "Before I'm missed."

"Me too," she says briskly. "I've a chicken to feed."

He holds out his hand, and she takes it, thinking he wants help getting to his feet. When he raises her fingers to his mouth and kisses them, she grows flustered and embarrassed.

"You really are human, aren't you?" he laughs. "Not an apparition haunting the moor or an angel sent to save me?"

"I told you," she splutters, pulling her hand away. "I told you what I am." And she jumps up quickly, brushing bits of moss and dirt from her apron with her kissed fingers. Her empty basket is beside the boulder. She retrieves her knife and flings it in.

"Take the bread," she tells the boy. "You might need it for strength. Really, you could do with a cordial."

"I am as good as new," he reassures her. "Truly!" And to prove it, he leaps to his feet, flinging wide both his arms as if he wants to dance or be hugged.

"Go carefully anyway," Nell tells him warily. "Mind the bogs. And eat the bread."

He isn't listening. He has his face turned toward the sky, and his eyes are crinkled shut as he breathes deep lungfuls of air and touches the smooth skin of his chest in wonder and relief.

He will need a new shirt, Nell thinks to herself. *But not a shroud, at least.*

And since her job is done and she has no reason to linger, she turns away and starts walking. Home. She will go home now and see to the chicken. Then she will scour the cauldron and start brewing something.

"Wait!"

She stops and looks back.

"Do you not seek payment, Mistress Nell, for your healing? I have no purse with me. But I will see to it that you are rewarded, and handsomely, for saving my life this day."

The boy's voice rings out at her, full of authority, good breeding, and a desire to do the right thing.

Nell sighs. She has no regrets anymore about saving this person, but she has her own life to get on with, and it is nothing like his. There is no point prolonging this encounter, nor does she want to, for all it might improve her chances of eating well for a while.

Anyway, she didn't heal him. Not really. The fairybaby's caul did that. And what price do you put on a fairybaby's caul? A king's ransom? A flower? A smile?

The boy owes her nothing, she decides. Although . . .

"There is something," she calls to him. "But not money. I don't want your money. A lad from the village—Sam Towser by name. He went away, to fight for the King, and no word has come from him since. If you hear tell what became of him—whether he be dead or alive—his father, the blacksmith, would find comfort in knowing."

So would Grace Madden, she thinks to herself. *And the minister. And me. In fact if that frolicking rascal be alive still, I will track him down and drag him home myself, to do the right thing by his Merrybegot.*

Surprised, amused, the boy agrees willingly to such a simple request.

"I will make enquiries," he tells her. "I promise."

Shivering a little in the thin sunshine, he pulls the tatters of his shirt across his chest. Although the material remains torn, the bloodstain has vanished. He checks the bracken. Not a splash of red anywhere. Amazing.

His attention has shifted for only a few seconds, but when he looks up, Nell has gone.

He opens his mouth to call her back but thinks better of it. Instead he picks up the bread she left next to the boulder and sets off in the opposite direction.

Left behind, the remains of the fairybaby's caul flutter where they hang. Torn though it is and completely drained of its lifesaving power, there is just enough magic left in its tatters to make it a once-in-a-lifetime's find for any passing piskie. Unraveled, its threads could be used to sew a tiny garment whose wearer would know flashes of inexplicable bliss. Wadded into soft balls, it would make nose plugs so effective that the lucky recipient would sleep through anything, even a triple murder right next to its ditch. Worn as a neckerchief, it would lend such radiance to the face that its owner would attract a constant stream of admirers, all bearing gifts and singing love songs, in a most unpiskie-like fashion.

But the piskies won't venture this far from the village. Even those who catch a whiff of what's out here won't risk it. So the caul just hangs, like a wraith's entrails, droops, and finally falls. And eventually, it melts away as if it had never been—as if it had never saved a life or, in doing so, changed the course of history.

October 31st. All Hallows' Eve. The one night of the year when the veil between the worlds is so thin that communing with ancestors can be as easy as having a chat with a neighbor over a garden gate. To those with the Knowledge, it has always been so. Others, with no understanding of these matters, hang wild garlic on their doors to deter ghosts and warn those most vulnerable to strange visitations—children, cider-drinkers, unwed maids, and the splutter-minded—to stay away from the churchyard.

The minister has made it clear that Satan and his minions treat All Hallows' Eve like one big feast and will be abroad with a particular vengeance this year, cavorting in who knows what shape or form. And paying calls to witches.

The Watchers are trimming their lanterns. They have taken

it upon themselves to mount a vigil after dark, in case Satan and his minions have a mind to drop in on the cunning woman's granddaughter.

Silas Denby intends to get roaring drunk.

It has been a wet, sorrowful day. And as dusk falls, the shapes of things—trees, scarecrows, hedges—darken and drip and seem ready to walk.

Nell has been busy. She has cleaned the cottage from top to bottom, prepared a syrup of angelica stalks to cure coughs and colds over the winter, and spent quality time with the dun chicken. She knows full well what night this is and intends to mark it properly with a ritual.

The jar of ointment she will need sits ready and waiting beside the cauldron. The top of it is sealed with a pig's bladder and marked with a black cross. The black cross means the contents are baneful and must be used sparingly. Belladonna, hemp, and other secret ingredients, shredded, powdered, and steeped in hog's lard, buried for a year and a day, and charged by the Powers of the north.

Flying ointment.

Nell is going to fly.

Matthew Hopkins, Witch-finder General, is polishing his boots. The minister's housekeeper would have done it, but he is a meticulous man and likes the job done properly. It doesn't matter that in a few hours' time both the boots and the hem of his expensive cloak will be splattered with mud. It is part of his personal ritual to look as imposing as possible before setting out to trap a witch.

He could, of course, ride out to the cunning woman's cottage on horseback. But it is important that he walk the whole way, carrying a lantern as big as a pumpkin and accompanied by the minister. It is important that he get noticed passing through the village and that as many people as possible decide to join along. Witnesses, all . . .

The witch-finder has no idea what the cunning woman's granddaughter will be doing when he reaches her, but even if she is merely sleeping, he has enough evidence now to condemn whatever she is up to as diabolical. She could be eating a bowl of stew, and he will say there is human flesh on her spoon. She could be mending a dress, and he will denounce her for wishing to look her best for Satan.

On the washstand, beside the witch-finder's honey-water hair tonic, silver ear pick, and a small pot of tooth powder, lies the dun chicken's feather. When the witch-finder is ready, he will slip it into a cloth pouch, along with the roll of parchment upon which he has written the testimonies of the minister's daughters and enough other information to make the case watertight.

The minister had been keen to include his elder daughter in the night's affairs, for the mere sight of the cunning woman's granddaughter on All Hallows' Eve would send her into a frenzy for certain. But the witch-finder did not think her presence was necessary. There might be womenfolk looking on who would take one glance at Grace Madden's belly and make awkward connections. Best she stays out of sight—tonight and for what he calculates to be another three months, at least.

The younger daughter, though . . .

Easing on his boots, the witch-finder thinks of Patience Madden. A strange, fanciful child, not altogether correct in the head. Pious, though, and obedient to her father. It will do no harm, he decides, to have her in tow. At least her belly is flat.

Colors. Flashes of amber and topaz against the cottage walls. And voices. Women's voices calling, "Hellooooo . . . *here* you are!" The sound is as jumbled yet as sweet as a chorus of blackbirds, cuckoos, and wood pigeons on a spring morning.

Lying prone in the firelight, tingling from head to toe, Nell feels the sweat breaking on her, counts the escalating beats of her heart, and tells herself not to panic.

No evil . . . no evil. Safe as anything, surely? For I have sprinkled salt . . . called on all the Powers for protection . . . and placed the silver knife just so, with the blade pointing south.

Uncertain how much of the ointment to use, she was sparing with it at first, rubbing just the teeniest blob onto her wrists and the base of her throat, where the pulses are, before lying down next to the hearth. Better, she knew, to be out in the elements to experience fully the exhilaration of this flying ritual. But because she is alone and scared of being seen, she has made do with leaving the cottage door open, so the wind and the rain can blow in. The fire is raging so fiercely that nothing will put it out. The dun chicken, for fear of being roasted, has retreated under the bench.

Tradition also required Nell to be naked: sky-clad as nature made her. But being by herself with the door open made her wary of going that far. As a compromise, she has slipped her granny's dress over her bare skin, fastening the loose folds across her breast with the jeweled frog.

For a long time—too long, it seemed to her—she just lay there, waiting to feel something, while the chicken grumbled hotly across the room.

"Bogger this," she muttered eventually, reaching out for the jar of ointment.

Too much.

She has larded too much of the stuff onto herself. Impatiently, foolishly, convinced that she knew what she was doing—that a smidgen more wouldn't hurt—she has let such a powerful, baneful dose of herbs into her system that she is flying, all right: looping the loop like a crazy thing, while her body lies drugged and rigid on the ground.

And the colors and the women's voices are just the start of it all—like sailing out of a choppy harbor, feeling just a little queasy, but not unduly worried until you're out there on the open seas, fighting a storm.

No wonder the ones with the Knowledge—the women taken as witches—spoke of wild dancing and demons and leaping flames when required to confess what happened when they flew. For this is a trip of the most terrifying kind, so weird yet so utterly believable that to suffer it is to know yourself at the mercy of whatever devils your mind cares to spit in your face.

And so Nell, flying higher and wilder than she ever intended this night, sees fairies swarming and dead babies by the score . . .

Looks down from a great height upon the cauldron to find it full of wasps and earthworms, discussing a surefire cure for the pox . . .

Follows the ghost of her mother up the chimney and away over the moors, until the lovely, misty figure turns into a hare, thumps its hind feet, and disappears . . .

Weaves among the trunks of apple trees, touching wet bark and the rough shape of a heart . . .

Hears the dun chicken squawk a warning . . . sees it kicked by a boot, a highly polished boot with a silver spur on the heel . . . watches it flap and scuttle, dazed and bleeding, out of the doorway and into the night while other boots take aim at its stupid head and rough voices call it an "imp" and a "devil."

Real. This last bit seems horribly real. But it cannot be. *It cannot be.*

Can it?

"She's wearing the clasp!" a girl's voice cries out. "The witch is wearing my mother's clasp—the one she stole to work her spells with! The one she is using to harm my sister! She is using it now! Stop her! Stop her!"

And because she cannot speak, because she is still flying, Nell offers no resistance when the minister hauls her body up and sits it on a stool. Nor does she struggle when he and the man with the silver spurs tie her body with rope, to stop it keeling over.

Swooping and soaring she is . . . a little bumpily now . . . but still enough to have no clear idea at all about what is really happening.

Only when a clammy hand reaches out to tear the jeweled frog away does she come to her senses enough to respond—instinctively and automatically.

"Devil's spawn!" cries the minister, jumping away. "She bit me!"

And his face is truly a parsnip. A pale root with a hat on. And because, in Nell's drug-glazed eyes, he is just a vegetable, with tendrils for fingers and toes, it seems perfectly reasonable to have taken a chunk out of him. Reasonable and funny—very, very funny.

"Into the pot!" Nell cries, her voice rasping and peculiar as it returns to her throat. "Into the pot you go, and I will have you for my supper."

And as she sits and rocks with laughter—between the worlds still and beyond the bounds of time—the Watchers press forward in gleeful fascination. And even those villagers who did not want to believe, who had come to see fair play and would have sent the witch-finder packing had he overstepped the mark— even they can only gawp, openmouthed, before melting away, hurrying home as quickly as possible lest one look or word from the cunning woman's gibbering granddaughter should endanger their own precious souls.

Home they go, to bolt their doors, check on their children, and drink cider to calm their nerves. For Satan is abroad this All Hallows' Eve, and the minister was right all along. There is a witch among them. Young Nell is a witch. And the sooner she admits to it, the better.

The Confession of Patience Madden
THE YEAR OF OUR LORD 1692

*It took three nights and two days, so 'twas rumored, for the
cunning woman's granddaughter to be trapped. I was there, on
All Hallows' Eve, when my father and the witch-finder went to
her. Half the village was there, actually. It was a spectacle.*

*The poor girl was fair terrified. Her chicken flew at the
witch-finder, and he kicked it away. I expected it to change shape
or to curse, since it was supposed to be an imp in disguise. But it
just ran away, squawking in pain and alarm. Only a bird after
all. Only a fat old hen, its side slit by the witch-finder's spur.*

*I stayed by the open door throughout the proceedings and
said nothing. I just listened and watched. Was this girl really so
powerful that she could make someone's belly swell like dough?
She didn't look it.*

*My sister had remained at home. I thought that strange. I
had expected her to jump at the chance of seeing the witch and
her familiar get their comeuppance. She always did like to*

gloat. I thought she would have wanted to be there, among us, in case the witch repented and took the bloating sickness from her there and then.

I know now, of course, exactly why she stayed away—why she dared not show her belly in public.

What a goose I was. What an innocent fool.

The cunning woman's granddaughter got tied to a stool.

Then the witch-finder read out the charges against her:

1. That on May Morning, the year of our Lord 1645, she did use vile witchcraft to beguile Sam Towser, the son of John Towser (blacksmith), so that he became aimless and distracted about his work and did leave the village unexpectedly, with no word come from him since.

2. That in July 1645 she did conspire with her grandmother, Eleanor Thwaite (deceased), to bring a wasting sickness upon Silas Denby (farmhand).

3. That sometime between April and August 1645 she did enter the home of Elias Madden (minister) and steal from there an emerald and ruby clasp, which she did use for the purposes of vile witchcraft.

4. That on August 9, 1645, she did call upon the minister's daughters, Grace and Patience Madden, and finding them abed and ailing, did use vile witchcraft to inflict further sickness upon Grace Madden.

5. That she did consort with an imp, being in the shape of a dun chicken, and did use its feathers for the purposes of vile witchcraft.

The cunning woman's granddaughter did not admit or deny these things. She seemed dazed. So the witch-finder announced that he would stay for as long as it took for her to respond to the charges. And he chose a woman from the village to remain with him as a witness. The rest of us, he sent home.

What transpired that night and over the two days and two more nights that followed, I cannot fully account for. But I can well imagine what the cunning woman's granddaughter suffered, and as the Lord is my witness, I am sorry for it.

She was watched. I know that much. Kept tied to the stool, denied sleep, victuals, and water, and watched for signs that the Devil had her. Stubborn, though. She was mighty stubborn, that girl, and would not break or speak or give an inch, for all she must have been weak with hunger and thirst and half crazed from lack of sleep.

'Tis said her familiar dragged itself through the open doorway at dawn on the third day and that she screamed at it to stay away. To fly, to run, to hide. And that the witch-finder went after it, speaking the Lord's words as he prepared to stamp on its neck.

And 'twas then the girl broke down, all stubborness gone.

Our housekeeper could scarce keep the excitement from her voice as she brought news of all this to my sister and me. It was early morning, four days after All Hallows' Eve, and we must have been the last to know. I saw a mist hanging cold and gray beyond the window of our bedchamber. I watched the housekeeper licking her lips as if the information spilling from them was sticky and sweet.

"Has she confessed?" Grace demanded. "Has the witch confessed to planting the Devil's spawn inside me?"

"She must have done," the housekeeper replied. "She must have confessed to everything. For the witch-finder is well satisfied and eating a hearty breakfast."

"Good," said Grace.

I cleared my throat.

"What's the Devil's spawn?" I asked.

A look flashed between Grace and the housekeeper.

Then: "All in good time," my sister answered, almost kindly. "I cannot talk of it while the witch lives. But I will explain it to you in due course."

I let the matter lie, content that I had not been rebuffed or pinched for my curiosity.

"What happened to the chicken?" I asked instead.

The housekeeper said she didn't know. "But 'tis said the witch bears the familiar's marks, all right," she told us. "Raised red spots where that fat chicken did suck her blood."

They could have been flea bites, those marks. They could have been any kind of rash. But I needed to hear, and to believe, that they were truly the Devil's brands. For to think otherwise as I lay safe in my bed, was to know myself part of a scheme to trap an innocent girl.

After the housekeeper had gone to ply the witch-finder with more porridge and ale, I got up and began dressing. Grace stayed in bed. She had permission because of the bloating.

We said nothing further to each other about any of it. I, for one, did not want to dwell a moment longer upon the things that had happened to the cunning woman's granddaughter. I

*particularly did not want to think about the next thing—the
very last thing—that was going to happen to her now that she
had been trapped.*

*I just wanted my sister back to the way she was. I wanted
everything to be all right.*

*You believe me, don't you, brothers? You are trusting in
what I say? For I am a God-fearing woman and have never
born false witness in my life.*

NOVEMBER
1645

The piskies are angry. Mutinous. Fit to bite the ankle regions of anyone foolish enough to walk too close to their nesting places. How can they sleep? How can anything possibly sleep with so much tension in the air?

And now the banging.

Bang! Bang! Bang! Every thud shakes the plugs in their nostrils and brings information so tantalizing that even the offspring, who would usually hibernate through anything, cannot ignore it.

Bang! Bang! Bang!

It isn't even all that close, this din. It's coming from the crossroads, a good walk from the village. And if it was simply a carpenter making a cradle or a farmer mending a barn door, it would barely register.

But this is no cradle or door being hammered together. It is a gallows pole. And that, for most piskies, is impossible to ignore.

Away up the hill the minister's housekeeper is making whit-pot, a pudding of bread, cream, eggs, currants, and spices. It is comfort food. It will make everyone feel warmer. She, too, hears the banging drifting on the wind and stops what she is doing to cross herself.

In the parlor the minister's daughters are putting the final stitches in their samplers.

"What's that noise?" asks the younger one, looking up.

"Nothing," Grace Madden replies. "Just the wind howling in the trees."

But her thimble has fallen from her finger to roll upon the floor, and she can feel her Merrybegot kicking and kicking inside her, as if it knows its mother for a deceiver and a murderess.

"Liar," says the younger girl before snipping carefully through a wisp of red thread.

Grace Madden stares across at her sister, and for no reason she can recognize, feels suddenly afraid.

"Don't call me a liar," she says, speaking fast and clenching her cold fists to ease the strange and sudden fear. "For *you* are the biggest liar in this house. You have been dreaming up falsehoods all your life—and speaking them, too, when it suits your purpose. You know you have. You cannot deny it."

Patience Madden shrugs to show she doesn't care a fig what her sister or anyone else says about the tales she can weave in her head or speak aloud if she has to.

Then: "What do you think?" she asks, holding up her finished sampler.

Grace Madden considers the work. It has all the right stitches in it—buttonhole, braid, chain, overlapping herringbone, satin, tent, cross and half cross, long-stemmed cross and Italian cross—

but is hardly a thing of beauty. The unicorn is misshapen, and the border of lilies and moths is ill-spaced and puckered.

The text in the center, painstakingly worked in funereal black, reads:

DEATH LIKE AN OVERFLOWING STREAM

SWEEPS US AWAY—OUR LIFE'S A DREAM

Grace Madden shivers and reaches for her thimble. The baby in her belly has gone very still. The hanging will be the day after tomorrow, a Monday. She will be kept away and so will Patience, and for that, at least, she is grateful.

"I cannot tell for the life of me what your unicorn is," she says sullenly to her sister. "It could be anything. It could be a dog playing a trumpet or a white cow with a hat on."

"I don't care," the younger girl replies gaily. "I don't care what it looks like. It's done and that's that."

Bang! Bang! Bang!

"Now I'll tell you a story," Patience Madden says to her sister. "About the witch Jezebel, who was thrown from a tower so that her blood splattered and sprinkled the wall. And lo and behold, they went to bury her, because she was a king's daughter, but found no more of her than the skull, the feet, and the palms of the hands. . . ."

Across the hall the minister is shut away in his study, going over the words he will recite at the foot of the gallows pole. The emerald and ruby frog sits on his desk, glinting at him. The girl gave it up eventually, when she had no spirit remaining to fight for it and no strength left to bite.

Bang!

The minister pours himself a splash of claret. His fingers tremble. "Wine is a mocker, strong drink is raging: and whosoever is deceived thereby is not wise."

The Lord will forgive me this small transgression, he decides. *For He knows the yoke I bear is a heavy one.*

The minister will be glad when all this is over—when the whole matter is closed. He has been meeting for many weeks now with Puritan leaders across the border, men of vision, like himself, with plans to sail for the New World. Come spring, he and his daughters are to sail with them. They will start a new life, where no one knows them among God-fearing folk in a land wide open to new beginnings.

It is all arranged.

Meanwhile he must see to it that no breath of scandal touches his family. For nothing must sully the reputations of those embarking on this voyage in the Lord's name. Nothing.

The cunning woman's granddaughter will be silenced on Monday, and the witch-finder has been paid. The housekeeper, too, will hold her tongue and be rewarded handsomely for doing so.

All that remains is for nature to take its course. The result will also be dealt with, and then they will leave, he and Grace and Patience. And all anyone here will ever know and believe is that a witch cast her evil eye on the minister's daughters, causing a mysterious illness that eventually passed.

Bang! Bang! Bang!

The jeweled frog looks poised to leap away. It is a beautiful thing, a gorgeous thing, but the minister cannot look at it for long. Before sailing for the New World, he will find the time to visit his wife's grave, for all it is two days' ride away and the roads in winter might prove impassable. He made it his business a long time ago to discover his wife's final resting place, and he goes there, when he can. Torn between weeping and cursing, he usually just stands with his hat in his hands, despising himself for continuing to love a woman who died in sin and shame, giving birth to another man's child.

He never thinks of the brat. He doesn't know if it was a boy or a girl, let alone whether it lived or what became of it if it did.

"Witch . . . ," he murmurs, blinking at the jeweled frog. She was a witch, all right—a practitioner of the ancient arts. He married the one person he could never hope to strike the fear of God in, and she haunts him still. It is the cross he bears. His secret shame.

Bang! Bang!

He shuts the frog away in a drawer and pours another drink.

The cart comes for Nell just after dawn. She has been kept locked away for more than a fortnight, and when they open the door, the light pains her eyes.

She doesn't recognize the ones who yank her up and hurry her out into the miserable morning. She doesn't feel the cold, either, even though she wears only a shift.

The people huddled in groups around the gaol shuffle forward, gawping. Their faces are ugly with anticipation, yet they dare not come too close, and some of the children cover their eyes with mittened or frostbitten fingers—too scared to even peep.

"Witch!" someone hisses from a safe distance.

Dully, mechanically, Nell registers the tying of her ankles so that the hem of her shift will not billow out. They always do that to women or girls, so they will not be shamed by men looking up their skirts while they hang. As if she cares. As if modesty is a concern this day. As if they are doing her a favor.

They leave her hands free, to enable her to pray. Another favor.

The cart is small and drawn by a horse so old, it shambles. It isn't far to the crossroads, but the lanes are deep in muck and mire, so what with the horse and the mud and the ruts in the lanes, the going is slow. Nell has to stand on her tethered feet, gripping the sides of the cart as it slews and jerks along.

There are more people gathered along the way. Someone throws an apple—a rotten one. Nell feels it hit her shoulder, but doesn't even flinch.

As they lurch over a slope she sees, up ahead, the biggest crowd of all. And the pole—the gallows pole—rising up from the crossroads like some abominable, leafless tree.

That's for me, she tells herself, but somehow her mind will not accept the truth of it. And she is not afraid as the old, broken horse stumbles on, for what is happening to her this day seems so unreal that it might as well be happening to some other poor man-handled girl. It is nature's way, she knows, this shutting down of the senses in response to unbearable pain . . . a kindness from within, when all without is beyond both kindness and reason.

The crowd—a sea of smug, excited faces—is parting now, and they are nearly there. Nell can see the minister standing right next to the pole and the witch-finder beside him. She cannot bring herself to look among the crowd, although she knows full well the Watchers will be there, their eyes boring into her, their big feet firmly planted in the mud so that no one can budge them from the spot they have chosen—the spot with the best view.

Some of the others jostling for space were surely birthed by her granny or are holding infants she herself helped bring into the world. It is the worst sorrow, that they they have come here now to see her, to watch what is about to happen.

As the cart trundles the last few yards the people closest to it reach out to prod and pinch. Some think it lucky to touch a condemned witch. Others are simply cruel.

Someone has hold of her hand and is trying to put something there, between her fingers.

What is it? A crucifix? A bone? A lock of someone's hair?

She looks down, for this touch is not nasty, just insistent.

It is Mistress Bramlow, pressed up against the slats of the cart by other jostling bodies and struggling to keep her footing in the mud. Her face is gray with sorrow, but there is strength and purpose in her voice as she whispers: "Take it. Take it now."

Instantly Nell understands. And as her fingers close upon the snippet of belladonna—enough to send her into a mindless stupor, should she swallow it in the next few moments—she has to struggle not to let this one small act of kindness undo her in a way that cruelty has so far failed to do.

For she will not cry. Not for any of them. Not now. It would be taken as a sign of repentance, and she repents of nothing—except, perhaps, of having been so lavish with the flying ointment that she sealed her own fate.

As daft as the chicken, she thinks dizzily as the cart jerks to a halt. *I have been as daft as the poor old chicken.*

The crowd is roaring now, and the pole, with its dangling rope, is so close that she could reach out and touch the splintered wood.

The chips or cuttings of a gibbet or gallows on which one or more persons have been executed or exposed, if worn next to the skin or round the neck in a bag, will cure the ague or prevent it.

The piece of belladonna, clenched in her fist, seems to throb there, like a trapped spider.

Take it. Take it now.

But she won't. Stubborn to the last, she will stand up straight, showing neither weakness nor remorse. Yes, she will. *Yes, she will.* . . . A witch? Well, yes, she confessed to that in the end, since having the Knowledge, like her granny and her mother before her, truly made her one. But guilty of hobnobbing with Satan and causing harm? Never.

A sliver of wood, taken from the gallows pole, will cure the aching of a tooth, particularly if tamped down on the ache with the inner rind of an elder tree, made into a paste with three drops of sage water and a little pepper.

Busy. Her mind is busy, sifting through recipes, potions, and spells, taking her away from this moment, this place.

And the rope is round her neck, as thick as an arm, and the minister is right in front of her, telling her to make peace with the Lord. To beg His forgiveness while there is still time.

And as the hangman adjusts the noose, she keeps her head up and looks the minister straight in the eye. Appalled he stares back at her, his speech faltering, the pages of his Bible fluttering in the wind.

For it is as if . . . as if . . .

He looks blindly away, across the moor, then back again. But there is no mistaking it, no mistaking the light in those eyes, the defiant curling of the lips, the tilt of the pointed chin above the chafing rope. He has seen that same look before, on the face of his wife . . . the mother of his children . . . the woman he loved. It is uncanny. It is—impossible.

He knows he must finish what he has to say before giving the signal for the cart to be pulled away, leaving the witch to dangle and choke.

But he cannot speak. He cannot move. And the Lord's words are sticking in his throat, like fish bones.

"Re . . . pent!" he cries, but it comes out squeaking.

And as the crowd shifts restlessly, there is a drumming in his ears that can only be the sound of his own thudding heart. Can it not?

Confused, he turns around.

Everyone turns around.

For those are hoofbeats they can all hear, approaching from the west. And then . . . here they come, over the crest of the hill, a party of the King's men—and favored ones, too, by the look of their horses and the billowing of their fine cloaks in the bitter wind.

The Watchers crane their thick necks. This is good fodder for their gossip—fine gentlemen come to see the hanging. Word must have got round that a witch is to swing this day, and these four, five, six young bucks are just in time to enjoy it.

"Get out of my way!"

The rider at the front is approaching at such a gallop that those in his path are at serious risk of getting their own necks broken or their bodies trampled by flying hooves.

With little shrieks and muffled curses, women and men grab their children and scatter, creating a space that the white mare and its rider seem to stream along before rearing to a spectacular halt right in front of the gallows.

The other riders rein in their horses on the very edge of the stumbling crowd, keeping their eyes on the one who led them here as he leaps from his saddle and points straight at Nell.

"Remove the noose," he commands.

The hangman opens his mouth, then closes it again. He isn't quite sure. He *thinks* he recognizes this person, this boy, but he can't be absolutely—

"Hurry up, man! I haven't got all day."

Nell feels as if she is falling. This person's words are swirling in her head, and she doesn't know what to make of them. Is it a prank? It is bound to be a prank—and a mighty cruel one, at that.

Past caring, though . . . Beyond feeling anything . . . Nature's way . . .

She cannot move much for the constriction of the rope around her neck, but by tilting her jaw very carefully, she can just about see the speaker standing below her, next to the cart. He is wearing a heavy buff coat over armor and a hat with a plumed feather. She doesn't recognize him, nor does she care, until his voice rings out again:

"Are you deaf, man? Or simply stupid? Remove the noose, I say."

And then she remembers.

What manner of creature are you? . . . Do you not seek payment, Mistress Nell?

It is him. The boy she found wounded up on the moor.

She closes her eyes, blocking him out. Blocking them all out. Foolish boy. Stupid bogger. Means well, but will be hanged alongside her, for certain, for his audacity this day.

"No. Wait!"

It is the witch-finder speaking. Or hissing, rather, through gritted teeth.

"Aha!" cries the boy. "Matthew Hopkins, is it not? I should have known you'd be in at the kill, sir. How much did they pay you for this one? Your rate is twenty shillings a witch, I hear. Or is that just for one-legged old crones?"

The hangman dithers, his fingers slack against the noose and loathsome on Nell's throat. The crowd has fallen silent, and the witch-finder's face is boiling red as he splutters: "I work for the good of us all, Sire, and in accordance with the law of the land. His Majesty, I dare to suggest, would find no fault here."

The boy raises one eyebrow.

"His Majesty, as you are doubtless aware, has other matters on his mind at present. He is leaving this one to me. Let her go."

"But the verdict is sound, Sire, and the punishment fitting. The witch must hang."

Nell sways and swallows. *His Majesty? . . . Sire?* What are they blathering on about?

Then the minister chimes in:

"'Thou shalt not suffer a witch to live!' Thus saith the Lord! Exodus, chapter 22, verse 18!"

His voice is as loud as ever, but there's a wobble to it.

"Amen!" echoes the witch-finder. "'Tis fitting, wouldn't you agree, Sire, for the Lord to have the final say?"

"Ordinarily, yes," snaps back the boy. "But the Lord also speaks through His Majesty from time to time, don't forget—or, if it's easier, through me. And I'm not asking you, my friend, I am *telling* you. Let. Her. Go."

Nell is sure she can feel the noose tightening while the men and the boy from the moor haggle over whether she swings or walks. *Be done with it either way,* she thinks wildly. *Just be done. For all this . . . this tussling . . . it shames me somehow.*

She closes her eyes. Waits for the crowd to roar its own "Amen" in support of the minister. Waits for the hangman to step away and for the signal to be given. But the crowd is holding its collective tongue and keeping a respectful distance. Everyone is gaping at the boy in a kind of gormless amazement. And a few of the women are wondering whether to kneel.

"Be it really him?" someone whispers to one of the Watchers.

Yes, the Watcher nods. Yes, it be him, all right. The young Prince Charles, sent to the west country a few months back to rally troops for the Royalist cause. The King's heir, come to whisk the cunning woman's granddaughter from the very brink of damnation. If he can. If they let him.

The Watcher blinks and smirks. Any piskies nesting nearby will be wide awake by now—wide awake, goggle-eyed, and sneezing fit to bust.

"What say you, good people?"

The boy-prince has swung round to face the crowd. They are his future subjects, God willing, but Royalist supporters, all? He cannot say for sure. He can only hope that most of them are and that a dazzle of words will win over the rest.

"Is it not the divine right of kings—God's representatives here on earth—to be merciful at any time of their choosing?" he appeals, throwing both arms wide as if he owns everything—the people, the land, the cold gray air—and would embrace the lot, given half a chance.

A murmur of assent ripples slowly through the crowd.

"Has it not always been so?"

More ripples of agreement and a flurry of nodding heads.

He relaxes then. Whatever their usual sympathies, they are all of one mind at the moment—touched by the presence of a prince, as if by magic.

Madness. Nell is shivering now in the cart. Shivering so hard that she must clench her teeth to stop them rattling. *This boy is talking madness and blasphemy and will be knocked down and killed for it in a minute.*

"Well?" the Prince persists, smiling into the crowd. "Do we pardon this girl in the King's name or not?"

And with still more noddings and mumblings and a few bobs and curtsies, the crowd lets it be known that if the heir to the throne, God bless and protect him, sees fit to show mercy to the cunning woman's granddaughter, then who are they to stop him?

"Just don't put her to dwell among us no more," shouts Silas Denby, rubbing his big gut a little doubtfully. "Or I, for one, won't be accountable. We want her three counties away, at least."

His wife digs a bony elbow into the fat between his ribs.

"I mean, should it please Your Gracious Majesty," he adds. "Sire."

The Prince isn't listening. His men are signaling that it is time to go. He has stayed long enough, and it is dangerous. There are nests of rebel soldiers hereabouts, and this is hardly an ideal time or place to be expounding on the divine right of kings.

The Prince nods and casts a final smile upon the crowd. "I thank you all," he shouts, "for your benevolence this day." Then he leaps easily back onto his horse and turns his smile upon the hangman.

"Go on, then," he says. "Let her go. It's what everybody wants."

Slowly the hangman loosens the noose, then lifts it away from Nell's face and over the top of her head.

"Now untie her feet."

The hangman does as he's told.

The minister and the witch-finder step forward as one man.

"Save your breath," the Prince tells them.

Nell grips the sides of the cart. She cannot speak, nor does she think she will be able to move.

But: "Quick!" the Prince is saying, reaching down to grab her hands. "Put your left foot in the stirrup and jump."

So she takes his hands and scrambles and jumps as best she can while he hauls her up in front of him. And as the white mare wheels round, and she clutches its mane to keep from falling, she gets a fleeting glimpse of Mistress Bramlow's face, beaming and beaming, before the Prince digs his spurs into his animal's flanks and they are off.

"That was close, wasn't it?" he yells in her ear as they gallop away. "There's a coach waiting over the hill. Are you all right?"

She doesn't answer. Cannot. All she can think is, *I could have been dead. They were going to hang me. Me. I could have been dead. I could have been . . .*

And her teeth begin to chatter again and her knees to knock. And they are still chattering and knocking a good half an hour later as she sits huddled in a coach, being taken to a place of safety.

She has never been in a coach before.

"We're heading for Falmouth," says the Prince. "It's on the coast."

She has never been to the coast before, either.

I should be swinging, she thinks. *Had I not taken the caul with me that morning. Had I not saved this person's life. Had I not told him my name. Had he not learned of the hanging. Had he not been honorable. Had he arrived just a few minutes later. . . .*

I would have been turned off.

Finding her voice again feels strange—as if almost being hanged might have changed it somehow; as if it might babble, or curse, or howl for having so nearly been silenced forever.

"So you're the King's son, then?" is the first thing she says, the words gravelly in her throat.

"I am," he replies. "But don't stand on ceremony. I get tired of people fawning around me like lapdogs."

She is quiet again for a while. He has given her his coat to wear. It wraps her twice round and is slowly warming her through.

Then: "You shouldn't have pardoned me," she tells him.

"What?"

"You shouldn't have pardoned me in front of the minister and them others. I never did the things they said, so I didn't need forgiveness—not yours, the King's, the Lord's, nor anyone else's."

He looks at her in astonishment—her mutinous face, her raggedy hair—then bursts out laughing.

"I've just saved you from the gallows!" he chortles. "And . . . and . . ."

"I *know.*" Watching him—this boy, this *prince*—rocking with laughter, Nell feels her own mouth start to twitch.

"You did say not to fawn," she adds, a big grin breaking on her face. "And I did save *your* life first."

"Yes, but . . ."

"'Tis true."

"But . . ."

"Well then . . ."

They are both laughing now, laughing so hard that it hurts. And it seems to Nell as if the carriage is laughing too as it bumps and jolts along.

All of a sudden she wishes her granny was with them. Her granny would have been cackling louder than either of them, out of sheer relief for the continuing of Nell's life. And wouldn't she so love to have seen the coast?!

Sea sand, Nell thinks to herself as her giggles subside. *Coral, white and red; foam of the sea; stone pumice; sea salt and crabs claws; a feather from the back of a gull bird . . . We could have done with some of those things, Granny, couldn't we?*

And the answer comes slipping into her head as she leans back against her seat, suddenly exhausted.

So gather them yourself. And use them.

Do your job, girl.

And be happy.

The Witch-finder General leaves the village at first light the following day—with half his usual fee. It is fair to say that he is not a happy man. The minister's housekeeper watches him go, his heavy cloak flaring like his temper as he clatters out of the courtyard on his fine horse, without so much as a "fare thee well" or a "thank you" for his hearty breakfast.

A rude person, the housekeeper decides, turning away from the kitchen window. Ill-bred for all his smart talk and the tremendous shine on his boots.

A gust of rain smacks the window glass. The housekeeper

sniffs. He will have a filthy ride of it, that witch-finder, all the way back to Essex. And serves him right. Arrogant bogger.

The kitchen door creaks open, and in sidles the minister's younger daughter.

"What is you want at this gray hour?" snaps the housekeeper. "Creeping round in your shift like an ill-bred wench. For shame!"

Patience Madden ignores all of this.

"What will happen to the witch's body?" she says, her voice high-pitched and feverish. "Will she be divided into twelve pieces, like the Levite's concubine, and sent to all the coasts of England? Or will she be eaten by dogs, like Jezebel?"

The housekeeper takes three steps toward the door, her face grim and angry.

"Shoo!" she hisses, pushing the girl from the room. "Go back to your bedchamber this instant, missy. You and your poisonous fancies!"

Closing the door, she marches back across the kitchen and sticks her hands in a bowl of groats, left to steep all night in a quart of hog's blood.

They will need a good meal this day, the minister and his daughters. Something heavy and meaty for their jumpy bellies to work on. Something to distract them from their nerves, which are going to be as tight as lute strings now that the witch is pardoned and as free as a bird.

Lucky brat, she muses. *Lucky, lucky little chit.* To have been saved from the gallows like that, in the perfect nick of time. What were the odds? What power, presence, or spell made that come about?

The minister's housekeeper adds cream, chopped thyme,

parsley, succory, endive, sorrel, mace, pepper, and a shower of suet to the bowl and begins pummeling the mixture as if it were somebody's face.

She has never set much store by magic. Piskies, yes, she believes in them, having seen one so recently with her own two eyes. But magic? The stuff of dreamers, weaklings, and gullible oafs, she's always thought. Yet what else but magic—and the most extraordinary spell, at that—would bring a prince of the realm galloping to the rescue of a common girl?

"Poppycock," she mutters to herself as she pounds and squishes away at the ingredients for blood pudding. "Fiddle-faddle, bafflegab . . . pie in the sky."

And when she's done taking her anger and spite out on the food, she slaps it into a pot and boils it ferociously.

Later it will give the minister heartburn and make Grace Madden puke. Patience, being wiser than anyone has noticed, will take one sniff and refuse to eat it.

For who's to say what the difference is between a love potion concocted with kindness on a waxing moon and a blood pudding mixed in anger on a filthy winter's morning? Who's to say what has an effect? What is magical, what isn't, and why?

Who truly understands?

No one has set foot in the cunning woman's cottage since the mob came to trap Nell for a witch. For one thing it would take a brave soul to cross the threshold of a place where Satan was often made welcome. For another every villager knows there is nothing in there worth stealing, except a good solid cauldron—and as Mistress Denby keeps pointing out, who would fancy making stew in a witch's pot that has probably held everything from rats' tails to babies' bones in its time?

So although the cottage door remains ajar behind a thicket of dead stems and twigs, nothing has been disturbed. The cinders in the hearth are cold and gray, and the cunning woman's broom has snails inching up its handle. Upstairs the turnip-shaped hole in the thatch has widened some more, and the blanket on the pallet is so wet, you could wring it out.

Mistress Bramlow enters quietly and stands beside the empty cauldron, remembering.

She has no fear of this place.

"Chook," she calls softly. "Chook, chook chook."

In her heart of hearts, she does not expect anything to happen. Still, it is worth a try.

"Chook? Chook, chook, chookie?"

Nothing.

With a sigh, she turns to go.

Then she hears it. A single cluck so faint that it sounds like a piskie's hiccup.

Quickly she moves to the ladder and starts to climb.

It is so cold up in the roof space that her breath comes out in clouds.

"Chook, chook?"

Perhaps she is imagining things. Perhaps that sound was no more than the skittering of a mouse in the eaves or the twinge of a floorboard.

But, no . . . there it is again.

And over on the pallet, right in the middle: a slow movement as if some small thing has decided to get out of bed.

Mistress Bramlow holds her breath and stays where she is, standing at the top of the ladder, her cold hands gripping the topmost rung. It might be a piskie, after all. She has never seen a piskie and isn't sure how she will fare if one pops up right here and now. It won't be pleased, she knows, to have been woken from its winter sleep. It will be in no mood to answer a question. It might even bite.

Another rustling, a little louder this time, and there the thing is.

Mistress Bramlow sighs with relief as a stupid brown head with a wobbly red comb lifts and slowly turns.

"Come along then, chookie," she murmurs, climbing all the way into the roof space and walking slowly toward the pallet, with both hands outstretched. "Come along now."

The dun chicken is too weak to struggle as she lifts it up and checks it over. The wound ripped by the witch-finder's spur is still there, but it is miraculously clean and beginning to heal. And the rest of its body, although somewhat shrunken, is nowhere near as wasted as one would expect, given that no one can have fed, watered, or cuddled this creature for almost a month.

The weakness, Mistress Bramlow realizes, has more to do with misery than injury or starvation. The dun chicken has simply lost the will to live.

"Come on now," she croons, tucking it gently beneath one arm. "You'll be all right now, chookie. You'll be all right with us."

It must have found a stash of corn, she decides, going carefully back down the ladder. Or an old loaf. It must have drunk water from the washing bowl in the roof space—although how it got up there in the first place, with its leg all cut open, is a mystery.

Leaving the cottage, she has a go at closing the door, but

the great wodge of dead honeysuckle is in the way, and unless she puts the chicken down and spends time cutting twigs back, the door is never going to shut.

"Oh, leave it," she mutters to herself, turning away.

Nyit, nyit. Wise choice.

Left alone again in the cunning woman's cottage, half a dozen piskies adjust their nose plugs and drift back to sleep. Five of them are up in the roof space, burrowed deep inside the mattress like lumps in a pan of porridge. Only one of them woke up when the sad-mother-one appeared to take the chicken away. And it was too snug in the soft darkness to even think about biting or flashing its arse.

It is glad that the chicken has gone. Smelly old thing. They had all felt sorry for it at first and had been perfectly willing to carry it up the ladder, to share their wonderful nesting place. They had even fetched water for it when it clucked in a parched-sounding way and fed it corn when it got too gurgly in the stomach region. One of the female piskies had even gone so far as to rub a salve of crushed juniper berries on its injured leg region, so the wound wouldn't fester.

That was a particularly nice thing for a piskie to have done, but as it said at the time, who wants to wake up in the spring to find a dead chicken moldering in the nest?

Anyway the chicken has gone now, which means they can all snooze soundly throughout the winter.

Nyit. Smelly old bird.

In the downstairs room one piskie sleeps alone. The others don't want it, because it snores too much and shouts out when it dreams. It is a male piskie, this one, and has a lot of sleep to

214

catch up on after missing the start of hibernation to run the Errand.

Two others helped, but not much. And neither of them would have bothered if the oldest female in the tribe hadn't insisted. You didn't argue with this particular female. *Oooooo no.* Too mad, and too nasty, with sons in every ditch and a claim on all the best pickings.

One piskie to gather information. Another to write it down. A third to run the Errand—but only as far as the border. That's what the mad old female had decreed, before taking to its nest in the minister's garden.

The information had been easily gleaned.

Bang! Bang! Bang!

There'd been no ignoring it. Not for any of them.

Bang! Bang! Bang!

The piskie scribe had done a patchy job, using mud to make the words on bark peeled from a silver birch.

All of two minutes it had taken. Hardly an arduous chore.

Running the Errand, though . . . even without crossing the border. *Ooooo what a challenge!* What a footsore and miserable task to land on any male piskie looking forward to its winter sleep.

It had done it, though. *Ooooo yes.* Plod, plod across the moor with the message tied to its back region and a dozen will-o'-the-wisps lighting the way.

The fairymanchild and his horse had been waiting, as arranged, on neutral ground at the very edge of the border. A rare thing, cooperation between piskies and fairies. As rare as a blizzard in August.

Only for a Merrybegot would they declare a temporary truce—and then only with little love lost in the doing of it.

Give it here and begone, you smelly creature, the fairymanchild had hissed.

Oooo! Pretty is as pretty does. Drunken idiot! Shimmering fool! the piskie had spat back before unshouldering the burden of its message and handing it over.

The fairymanchild had looked upon the piece of bark with obvious distaste.

The fairies would have done a more beautiful job, using proper parchment and ink pressed from scarlet berries. But at least the words had been legible:

Healer girl to hang
Monday at first light
Crossroads

Bah!

The fairymanchild had tucked the message into a fine velvet pouch and wheeled his horse around. No time to waste. No time for a nap or a quick cup of blackberry wine. The hours would have to be stilled, if not sent backward, if he was to get to Falmouth and alert the Prince before it was too late.

So off he had galloped in a shower of glitter, without bothering to say good-bye—which was just as well, since had he seen the piskie's parting gesture, he might have stayed to fight and it could have led to war.

As it was he did his duty and completed the Errand according to plan. He woke the Prince by tickling his toes, then vanished, leaving the message where it would be seen and understood. And he slowed time just long enough for the Prince and his men to get to where they had to go, to rescue the fairy midwife.

And then he went home, put on his slippers, and drank himself into a stupor, deep in the ribs of the hill.

The piskie is exhausted. It doesn't mind that the others have banned it from the cunning woman's pallet, for it is a loner by nature and prefers a hard sleeping surface, anyway, to somewhere as soft and claggy as the inside of a mattress.

After a bit of scratching around, it has found somewhere that suits it perfectly—a wooden box, so well hidden that nothing and no one is going to disturb it. The lid was a bit stiff, and there was stuff inside that needed lifting out: a bit of old rope, a knife, a goblet, and a box of salt.

It has put all these things to one side, where it will see them when it wakes up.

The rope will be useful, come the warmer weather, for making a ladder or lots of belts for holding trousers up. And the goblet has sparkly bits round the rim, which the female piskies will want to wear in their hair. Even the salt might come in handy, for throwing in people's eyes.

These objects, the piskie knows, must have been important to somebody once, to have been hidden away so carefully.

Still . . .

Finders keepers, it chunters, curling up in the empty box.

Nyit nyit. Zzzzzzzzz.

The Confession of Patience Madden

THE YEAR OF OUR LORD 1692

We were never told, Grace and I, the exact circumstances of
the witch's escape. Our housekeeper knew the full story but
kept her counsel. Father knew it too, and it put him in
the foulest of tempers for many a moon. I believe he
brooded on it for the rest of his life. I believe he never
quite got over it.

My sister became greatly agitated when it became clear to us
that there had been no hanging and that the cunning woman's
granddaughter was alive and well and off who knew where with
the one who had saved her from the noose.

"'Twas surely the Devil that took her!" she shrieked. "Satan
on his black charger, striking sparks from the earth!"

"Enough of your conjurings, missy," our housekeeper
scolded. "'Twas a horse as white as milk and a gentleman as real
as anyone. And there's nothing can be done about it, so best you
make what you can of a bad business."

It was morning time. We were supposed to be dressing. We were supposed to be as we were.

I looked hard at my sister's stomach, as big as a cannonball still, beneath her shift.

"What will happen to your belly now?" I asked. "Will it stay like that forever?"

Perhaps she'll die, *I thought.* Perhaps she'll keep getting bigger and bigger until she bursts like a seedpod.

I hoped it wouldn't happen anywhere near me. I hoped it wouldn't happen at all.

I hoped the cunning woman's granddaughter would forget about hexing my sister and that the bloating would cease.

"Be still!" Grace roared before turning clumsily to our housekeeper and grabbing her big red hands.

"What if the witch talks?" she hissed. "What if she blabs, and word gets round? What if it means we can't go to the New World after all? Father will surely kill me!"

What? What? What?

"Go where?" I cried. "What new world are you talking about? Tell me!"

I was fit to weep. They could have been planning a secret voyage to the moon, for all I knew about it.

Our housekeeper looked at me, her lip curling as if I was something that needed sweeping up or putting away.

"Leave us," she said to Grace. "I'll tell her what she needs to know."

Dragging her feet, my sister threw a shawl around herself and left the room.

And our housekeeper sat down on the edge of the bed and

told me: Come spring, my father, Grace, and I would be sailing across the world to live among our fellow Puritans in a new land. But first, before we went, we had to wait for my sister to be relieved of the Devil's spawn.

"Now what else would you be asking?" she said. "Be quick, for I've a pudding on the boil."

I had a dozen questions about the voyage to the new world. But they could wait.

"What is the Devil's spawn?" I asked. "And how did it get there?"

The explanation took many minutes. I sensed my sister hovering beyond the door, but her presence was of no consequence to me. I listened, openmouthed, as our housekeeper explained frolicking to me in no uncertain terms.

"Well, that's the measure of it," she snapped at last. "Only it didn't happen like that with Miss Grace, as well you know, for you were right here when the witch threw her nasty charm, and it landed slap bang on your poor sister's tummy."

I said nothing, only stared at her, hard.

"'Twas like the Holy Spirit descending on the Virgin Mary," she continued, warming to her tale, "except there was nothing good or holy about it, for it begat the Devil's spawn."

She patted my hand, mistaking my expression.

"There is nothing to fear," she said briskly. "Just trust in the Lord, be kind to your sister, and breathe not a word of this to anyone. Your father knows what to do and will take care of matters when the time comes."

The bed creaked as she stood up.

"Are you coming with us to the New World?" I said. "You and your little girl?"

She didn't answer, only gave me a look before leaving the room. It was a look that said she could imagine no other future for herself other than with us—or with Father, anyway.

I wonder what became of her?

Anyway I did not bother saying anything further, and she clattered away down the stairs, to check on her pudding. Grace sidled back into the room. Her face was flushed and her glance almost humble.

"Are you all right?" she said. "Do you understand everything a little better now?"

"I have no wish to discuss it," I replied, turning my back on her so that she would not see my face.

My poor mind, I have to tell you, was in turmoil.

Did they really take me for such a fool—my sister, my father, and our housekeeper? Did they truly think I had cobwebs for brains?

Oh, it was all as clear as daybreak suddenly.

For had I not borne witness to my sister leaving our bedchamber night after night? And had I not seen the wanton disarray of her as she parted from her suitor at the gate? And heard her foolish sighings with my own two ears?

If I had only known, back then, what it all meant . . . what it could lead to. If I had only understood . . .

It made my blood boil, to think of the part I had played in blaming the cunning woman's granddaughter for my sister's condition. For the thing in Grace's belly was not put there by a charm. I knew that now. It was put there by the one she had frolicked with so shamelessly in the woods below our home.

But who was he? Who could he have been?

The answer came to me during evening prayers as if the Lord Himself had whispered the name in my ear.

I did not want to believe it. At first I refused to believe it, even though it made perfect sense. I convinced myself it could not have been; that my sister, Grace—the learned one, the pretty one—would never have fallen for the likes of him, however craftily he had gone about beguiling her.

But when Grace's time came, and I saw what she birthed, I feared—no, I knew—I had been right after all.

And when I found the wooden heart, branded through with the letters "S" and "G," I could no longer doubt it.

DECEMBER
1645

The coach comes for the dun chicken two weeks before Yule.

"Oh my," murmurs Mistress Bramlow as it clatters to a halt outside her cottage. "Oh my, oh my."

Her daughters press against her.

"Can I come too? Please let me!"

"I'm the oldest. Let me go!"

"I'll hold the chicken for you. I'll be good."

"Me! Me! I'll hold the chicken."

"I want to!"

Outside the lanes are iced with frost; the moor is stiff with frozen bracken. It is too cold to snow, which bodes well for the longest journey of Mistress Bramlow's life.

"I'll be home for Yule," she tells her husband. "God and the weather willing."

Jack Bramlow touches her cheek. "We'll be waiting," he says.

The coachman is waiting at the door. He is holding a purple velvet cushion like a squishy tea tray between his hands. It is a very fine cushion with golden tassels trailing from each corner.

"Is that for the chicken?" the Bramlows' eldest girl asks.

The coachman grins and nods.

"It'll make a proper mess of it," the girl tells him. "And it'll peck off them dangly bits like they was fancy worms."

The coachman shrugs and grins some more.

"Right, then." Jack Bramlow clears his throat. "You've a long journey ahead, wife. Best make a start."

Mistress Bramlow feels like crying. But her daughters are laughing as they pet the chicken—perched on the cushion now and eyeing the golden tassels. So she laughs with them as they all troop out into the cold, and she is still smiling as she steps up into the coach.

A small crowd has gathered to watch her leave.

"All this for a bogging hen," someone mutters. "All this for a stupid bird that don't even lay!"

The Watchers tut and draw dark woollen shawls tighter round their shoulders.

But they make way, respectfully enough, as the coachman strides past and reaches up to deposit the dun chicken, on its velvet cushion, in Mistress Bramlow's arms.

The village children are enthralled. Even the ones too small to run after the coach as it pulls away will always remember how fine it looked and how excited everyone was to think that it had been sent all the way from Falmouth, by royal command.

Many years later, when the story has faded to legend and people are starting to say it never really happened, one very old man will be badgered by his great-grandchildren to "tell the chicken story" and will grin to remember the way that daft bird inclined its head and fluffed its wings, for all the world like the queen of all living things, bidding lowlier beings farewell.

"Did Charles II really give it corn in a golden bowl and let it poop in the palace?" one great-grandson will want to know.

"Ah, now that I cannot tell you," the old man will say. "But I wouldn't be at all surprised."

By the time they reach the outskirts of Falmouth, Mistress Bramlow is exhausted from being jolted over miles and miles of rough ground—and is pretty fed up with the chicken.

She has dined sumptuously along the way and rested at quality inns. No highwayman, ghost, or rebel soldier has stopped the coach, nor has it lost a wheel or been stalled by blizzards. As journeys go in this wild region, in the cold season *and* with a war raging, the whole trip has been surprisingly uneventful.

The dun chicken, however, has been a restless, flapping, poop-scattering pain in the arse. Used to ranging wherever it wants, the coach just seems to it like a cage on the move, and the velvet cushion is no substitute for a dust bath or a good wallow in old cinders. Daft though it is, it vaguely misses home. And it isn't going to settle until it feels safe.

It is late evening and too dark to see when the coach swerves onto a slippery quay and comes to a final halt.

The coachman jumps down and comes round to open the door.

"I must tend to the horses," he tells Mistress Bramlow, keeping his voice low. "Best you wait here, Mistress. Only, don't step too close to the water's edge. And hang on tight to that bird."

Mistress Bramlow would have been glad of a lantern and a bit more information before being left in pitch blackness with the dun chicken tucked grumpily under one arm and the unfamiliar sound of seawater sloshing scarily close to her ankles.

There is a small inn not many steps away. But it seems

deserted, with no sounds of revelry and just one candle burning low in an upstairs window. Above and behind the building, the thick, twisting shapes of winter trees blend with the night and stretch away along the edge of a creek as far as who knows where.

The air smells of seaweed and crabs' claws, and Mistress Bramlow dare not move.

Then she hears it: a faint but regular splashing sound as if a seal or some other swimming-creature is heading for the quay. The dun chicken hears it too and starts to cluck.

"Hush," Mistress Bramlow tells it, straining her eyes in the dark as the splashing grows closer and louder.

It is a boat. A boat with one figure rowing and another trailing his left hand idly through the inky water and humming a jaunty tune. There are no barrels or boxes on board, so they cannot be smugglers.

The one humming wears a good thick coat and a plumed hat. As the boat reaches the quay he lights and raises a lantern, spies Mistress Bramlow, and beams.

"Got the chicken?" he says, leaping from the boat. "Aha. I see you have. Excellent. Follow me."

Mistress Bramlow manages a clumsy curtsy before falling into step behind the swinging glow of the lantern. *Don't you poop down my skirt,* she begs the chicken silently as they head toward the inn. *Not in front of royalty.*

Nell is sorting seaweed when she hears footsteps creaking on the stairs. She has already noted the arrival of a coach and is vaguely wondering who else has come to stay at this out-of-the-way place, hidden like a secret among the thick woods beside the water.

This little room, overlooking the quay, has been her refuge

for several weeks now. It is warm, clean, and safe, with meals and a good fire provided and a feather mattress on the bed.

The Prince has been visiting almost daily, rowing over from his base at Pendennis Castle to make sure she is all right and has everything she needs. He has told her that his father, the King, keeps nagging him to sail for France, or Denmark, or some other foreign shore, and to stay there until the rebels are defeated and it is safe for him to return.

"I'll take you with me," he has told her. "So don't worry."

Nell isn't worried. For what is there to worry about? The Prince has been kindness itself. Like a brother. Like a friend. She was on her guard to start with, not knowing what would happen, what he might expect of her, now that they have saved each other's lives.

It crossed her mind, in a niggling way, that he might try to frolic with her, having set her up so nicely in a cozy room with a feather bed in it. He is a prince, after all, and used to getting what he wants. She worried about that for a while, until he noticed how tense and distant she had become and asked why.

"I keep expecting you to try to frolic with me," she told him, blushing to the roots of her raggedy hair and staring fiercely into the fire. "And I don't want you to. In fact if you so much as touch me at all, in that kind of way, I'll fix it so you never frolic again. Not with anyone. I can do that, you know. With the Knowledge. On a waning moon. My granny taught me."

He had laughed his merry laugh at that and had given her a playful shove on the arm. And she had felt a great sense of relief, realizing that he did not think of her as a frolicker after all and was no more likely to frolic with her than to take ale with the piskies.

Since then she has been more like herself. Only not completely so, for the Prince has told her it isn't safe to venture out. When they are both far away in another place, he says, she will be able to roam where she pleases. For now, though, she must stay here, eating and dreaming and waiting to go.

There is sense to what he says, but it irks her to be kept here all the time. Like a prisoner. Or a pet.

A knock at her door startles her, for she isn't expecting the Prince tonight. Perhaps, she thinks, it is the innkeeper's wife, come to check on the fire or bring more soup.

"Come in," she says.

"Surprise!" the Prince calls out. "Close your eyes!"

Nell smiles, but faintly.

"Are they closed? No peeping. You must promise not to cheat."

"All right. I promise."

What now? she wonders. *What has he found for me this time? More seaweed? Another bag of shells? Or a clutch of feathers from a gull bird?* He brings such things all the time, knowing that they interest her and have something to do with the Knowledge. She hasn't the heart to tell him that a true healer gathers her own bits and pieces, giving due consideration to the phases of the moon and taking care to honor the Powers of earth, air, fire, and water, depending what she picks, catches, or cuts.

Even the richest takings from sea and shore are no good for healing if collected by someone without the Knowledge. And anyway she has no means of preparing them—no cauldron, no knife, and no stock of magical juices, waters, oils, or powders for mixing.

Instead, to pass the time and keep the Prince happy, she has been arranging the seaweed, shells, and feathers into pleasing shapes on the floor. A face shape; a tree shape; and today, the shape of a bird outlined in weed, filled in with feathers and with shells for a beak and an eye.

Some more white shells would be useful and some of the particularly stringy weed. Then she could do a whole person shape, perhaps. Or a cantering horse with a flowing tail and mane.

Her eyes are tight shut, as required, when the door opens and footsteps enter the room. She senses rather than sees that there is more than one person in front of her, and fear flashes through her brain and lodges deep in the pit of her stomach.

Who is it? Who can the Prince have brought to visit her, when her presence here at the inn is supposed to be secret? And why has he told her not to peep?

Wildly, irrationally, it dawns on her that the other person might be the witch-finder. Or a hangman. Perhaps telling the Prince little bits about the Knowledge has been a terrible mistake. Her granny always said it was best kept secret from outsiders, particularly during troubled times. Perhaps the Prince has decided she is a dangerous girl after all and wants nothing more to do with her.

Perhaps—

"Hold out your hands," the Prince tells her.

He doesn't sound grim or sorry. He sounds gleeful. But then, he has royal blood in his veins, doesn't he? And maybe boys of royal blood always sound gleeful when they are about to chop someone's head off or hang them from the nearest tree.

Slowly, too terrified now to peep or even protest, Nell holds out her hands and waits to feel the cut of leather or rope binding her wrists.

Feathers . . . warmth . . . the familiar weight of . . .

No. It cannot be. 'Tis a gull bird, that's all. He has brought me

*a living gull bird, thinking, perhaps, to call it my familiar and have
some sport before—*

But a gull bird wouldn't cluck like the creature in her arms.
It would cry like a brokenhearted sailor. Nor would one be snug-
gling against her chest or bobbing its daft head against her chin
in spasms of sheer delight.

Certain, almost certain . . . Nell opens her eyes.

It is!

It really, really is!

And there stands Mistress Bramlow, of all people. And the
Prince, behind her, beaming to see Nell so lost for words, so
clearly astounded by the brilliance of his latest surprise.

"It didn't die after Hopkins kicked it," he tells her. "It's got
a bit of a limp now, but that's all."

Nell nods, unable to speak.

"I thought about keeping quiet and just getting you another
one," he continues happily. "A younger one that would lay eggs.
But I knew it wouldn't be the same."

Nell looks at him. She will never fear or mistrust him again.
Never. He looks so pleased for her right now that anyone would
think she had given *him* a present.

And Mistress Bramlow, too, is smiling like a saint, despite
having a stream of chicken dung all down the front of her skirt.

All of a sudden there is a lump in Nell's throat as big as a
stone, and she knows she is going to cry. Before she can, though,
the dun chicken—alert now and extremely hungry—leaps, flapping, from her arms and makes a dash for what appears to be the
nearest source of nourishment.

"That really is a *very* foolish animal," the Prince remarks as
its skittering feet send seaweed and feathers flying and its stupid

beak goes *peck, peck, peck* at the tiny shell Nell placed on the floor as the eye on the head of her bird shape.

"It is," Nell agrees, laughing with him through her tears. "And a hungry one. So don't take your hat off, whatever you do, or it will have the brim for sure and take the feather for good measure."

So corn is sent for. And something a little finer, for human consumption. And Mistress Bramlow forgets about the rigors of her journey and the dung on her skirt as she watches Nell, petting the dun chicken in the glow from the fire, and listens to the heir to the English and Scottish thrones chatting away as happily and easily as any village lad known to them since his cradle days.

Later, after the Prince has taken his leave, Mistress Bramlow puts an arm round Nell, just as her granny might have done, and gives her a hug.

"I'll be all right now," Nell tells her.

"I know. I know you will."

For a while they watch the flames, twisting in the grate.

Then: "There be no word on Sam Towser," Nell says. "He could be as dead as a door knocker or alive still. No one knows."

"That's strange," Mistress Bramlow muses. "For enquiries made by the Prince himself should surely have led somewhere. There can't be many Sam Towsers fighting for the King hereabouts."

Nell shrugs. "I expect he changed his name," she says.

Mistress Bramlow looks puzzled. "Why would he do that?"

So Nell tells her about Grace Madden being with child and about it being a Merrybegot and deserving of its life, even though its father couldn't care two pins, and its mother had tried to kill it.

"Well, I never." Mistress Bramlow shakes her head. "I should have guessed. For no one has seen that girl for months.

231

We all thought she was sickly still or too ashamed of her foolish playacting to show her face in church. 'Tis said the whole family be leaving soon, anyway, to sail for the New World. Perhaps they'll take the baby with them and pass it off as an orphan—or as the housekeeper's child, maybe."

"Really?"

Nell hopes Grace Madden's Merrybegot will be all right in the New World. She hopes it will find friends there and that the Powers will look after it all its life.

"I'm a Merrybegot too," she says. "Did you know?"

"Yes." Mistress Bramlow smiles at the wise little face beneath its uneven crop of hair.

"And the Powers have looked after me, haven't they?"

"They certainly have. And His Majesty the Prince will be a kind and loyal protector. You will want for nothing, Nell, I'm sure."

Nell agrees, but her expression grows stubborn as she scratches the dun chicken's neck and stares into the fire as if divining something there.

"He thinks I should grow my hair," she says. "But I don't want to. It would only snarl up."

Mistress Bramlow pats her hand. "Then keep it short," she says. "'Tis your hair, after all."

In the fire something pops and crackles, like a burst of laughter. The dun chicken stretches and squirms on Nell's knees. It is full of corn and seems happy enough, but for some reason it will not settle.

"I shall fend for myself, you know," Nell is saying. "Wherever it is we sail to. I shall make a study of all that lives and grows in the place and be a midwife and a healer there. I will do that, whatever happens."

"I believe you will," Mistress Bramlow tells her softly. "And you will do it well. Your granny—"

She never finishes. For the dun chicken has raised itself up on Nell's lap and is clucking fit to burst.

"Whatever is it?" Nell scolds. "What's the matter?"

Perhaps, she thinks, the witch-finder's spur did more damage than they know. Perhaps the poor old chicken is in pain and they haven't realized.

What to do?

Her granny taught her only the one spell for such a worrying situation. This is it:

A SPELL TO PERK UP
AN AILING CREATURE

Take four red thistle blossoms and place one at each of
the four quarters. Place a flat stone in the center,
and upon it lay the creature, held in place by thine
own hands if necessary. Loudly summon the Powers of
the earth (unless this be a flying creature, in which
case let it be the Powers of the air). Anoint the animal
with three drops of carnation oil while calling,
"Across the ground you'll walk or run,
when this healing work is done" (unless this be a
flying creature, in which case let thy call be:
"Through the air you'll soar anew,
when this healing work is through").
So mote it be.

But Nell has no red thistle blossoms to hand, only seaweed. And she isn't sure whether a chicken that flaps a lot but can

233

barely manage to lift itself off the ground counts as a creature of the earth or of the air.

Too late to wonder. With a final, raucous cluck, her beloved creature-of-no-particular-element launches itself at the ground, landing heavily on its side and dangerously close to the fire.

"Oh!" Nell jumps to her feet and bends to grab it. But it limps and flaps away from her, across the room to where the spoiled bird shape still covers the floor, looking like nothing much anymore, except, perhaps, a map of somewhere very strange.

And as Nell and Mistress Bramlow watch in dismay, the chicken starts to spin and waggle its daft body among the shells and weed and feathers as if it doesn't quite know what to do with itself.

"Perhaps its innards be all upset by the journey," Mistress Bramlow suggests. "Perhaps it's about to poop."

"I don't know," Nell says in distress. "I don't know what the matter is, and I don't know what to do."

The dun chicken flops down among the picture-mess and goes very still.

"Oh no!" says Nell, appalled.

But it isn't dead or even dying. Only concentrating very, very hard, its eyes blinking and blinking and blinking as if it has suddenly seen something unbelievable.

"Aha," says Mistress Bramlow. "I think I know what be happening."

Precisely as she says it, the dun chicken gives a triumphant squawk, shuffles its hindquarters in an important way, then rises up on its ridiculous feet and struts and limps back toward the warmth of the fire.

"Well, I never," says Nell. "Well, I never did."

"That chicken never did, you mean," chuckles Mistress Bramlow. "But it has now."

And both of them stare in astonishment and delight at the big brown egg lying among the scatterings of Nell's bird shape like some kind of landmark or a perfect gift.

All the Bramlow children are standing in the lane, jumping up and down to keep warm while they wait for the coach that is bringing their mother home—in time for Yule as promised.

The youngest one has dropped a mitten near the ditch and cannot find it. She is puzzled by this, since it is a bright red mitten and should be easy to spot among the mess of frozen brambles and fallen leaves.

"Hurrah!" the others cry. They have heard the approaching clatter of hooves and wheels and are jostling to be the first one hugged when their mother arrives.

Squatting down, still searching for her mitten, the youngest girl hears a rustling and sees a small something, with a mucky face and bits of moss on its head, about to burrow deeper into the icy mulch of the ditch. It is holding her mitten.

"That's mine," she tells it. "Give it back."

The thing wrinkles its nose at her.

"Come away from that ditch!" one of the bigger girls shouts, distracting her. "You'll wake the piskies, and they'll drag you in."

The coach is in sight now, and Mistress Bramlow is leaning out, waving madly and blowing kisses.

The youngest daughter looks back at the thing—the piskie.

"You won't drag me in, will you?" she asks it. But this piskie seems in no fit state to drag anything anywhere. It appears to be having some kind of sneezing fit.

"Bless you hugely," says the youngest Bramlow. "I have to go now." And she skips away, not minding about the mitten now that her mother has stepped out of the coach, her arms spread as wide as wings for hugs.

In the ditch the piskie continues to sneeze, racked and rattled by the bits of information stirred up in the air by Mistress Bramlow's return.

Atchoo! Ooooo the death of monarchs . . . Chop, chop, there goes the head of Charles I.

And what of the Prince-one, who sent that coach here, causing such a commotion? Oh, a lucky one—a charmed one . . . A ladies man, he'll be. Oooo yes.

And the girlie, the Merrybegot . . . Atchoo! She'll be fine, she'll be fine . . . A respected midwife and a healer, that's what she'll be. Yes, yes . . . snug as a cat in a whitewashed cottage . . . in Jersey, that's the place. Nice place . . . Rich pickings . . . She won't need no Prince-one helping her out, although she'll let him think she does so he won't get all huffy in the pride region.

And a chicken always with her . . . even when she's old and stooped . . . a daft bird, with a limp. Can't be the same chicken down all the years, can it? Must be. Must be. Smelly old bird . . . Nyit, nyit.

A-A-A-tchoo! . . . More stuff about that Prince-one. Charles II, he'll get to be. And, yes . . . here's the laugh. Here's the wheeze . . . See him old, in his royal bed, surrounded by bishops and ticking clocks . . . about to snuff it . . . almost gone. And what's this? What's this he's saying? And with everyone leaning over his face region, to catch his last words?

"Let not poor Nelly starve."

And who does he mean? Who's he talking about with his last gasp? That chit of an orange seller, Nell Gwyn?

Ha-ha! Wrong!

Atchoo!

The Confession of Patience Madden

THE YEAR OF OUR LORD 1692

I cannot dwell for too long on what happened next. I must tell of it quickly, for the memory, even now, has the power to make me afeared and all of a tremble.

Yule passed without incident, a day of prayer and of waiting, like so many others before it.

I had been given my own chamber: a pokey space, little bigger than a closet, at the opposite end of the house to the room Grace and I had shared. Our housekeeper said it was because I was a grown girl myself now and better suited to solitude.

I knew this to be more of her nonsense, but I kept my counsel. In truth I was glad to be parted from my sister, for she was as big as a whale by then, and I had grown scared of falling asleep next to the thing in her belly that kicked often as if with hooves.

The sky on the day of the birthing was blue-black, like a bruise, and I swear I saw sparks striking from the heavens before they opened, like a wound, and sent a great fall of snow to cover the ground and to seal us all in our homes.

There were other omens, too. A robin found frozen on the step while a crow cawed nastily from the branches of an elm. The howling of a dog somewhere down in the village.

Father kept to his study. I thought he might come out when Grace started to scream, but he didn't. I tried to follow our housekeeper up the stairs, but she spun round and snapped, "Keep to the parlor. And don't come out until you're told."

It was chilly in the parlor, for the logs in the grate were smoking and would not catch aflame. Another bad omen. I had completed my sampler and had no plans for another, so I busied myself for a while sorting the box of threads. It didn't take long, and after that I simply sat.

I don't know how many hours I waited there, listening to my sister's screams. I remember that the sky beyond the window grew blacker still as dusk fell and that snow piled up against the sill, like something trying to get in.

And then the terrible shrieking stopped, leaving a silence that rang at first with echoes and then grew strangely heavy. Unbearable, too. I couldn't bear it. I could not endure sitting there anymore, not knowing.

Outside my father's study I paused and listened.

Nothing.

But my ears were fine-tuned, by then, to the quality of silence, and I knew he was behind that door and in no hurry to come out, even though no one had ordered him to stay put until told otherwise.

I had one foot on the stair and one hand on the banister when the door to our chamber—Grace's chamber—flew open and the housekeeper ran out—really ran, as if the hounds of Hell were hot on her heels, as indeed they had every reason to be.

Down the stairs she clattered, the large bowl she used for mixing held out in front of her. From her face I could tell that the bowl contained something unspeakable—something she could hardly wait to throw away.

When she saw me, she stopped dead halfway down the stairs.

"Get back in the parlor," she hissed. "Now!"

But I stood my ground. Petrified.

For long moments we faced each other.

And then, behind the study door, my father rang a bell. It was what he always did when he wanted another bottle of claret brought or more logs for the fire. Usually he would give one or two short rings, and then wait for the housekeeper to arrive. Only if she was tardy or hadn't heard, would he ring the bell again, more insistently. This time, though, he rang that bell without stopping. Loudly. Madly.

Perhaps he had heard our housekeeper on the stairs but could not understand why her footsteps had not passed his door. Or perhaps the sudden silence—the not knowing—was too much for him as well.

The tinny clanging of the bell made little impression on me, but our housekeeper jumped as if stung, tightened her grip on the rim of the bowl, and resumed her descent of the stairs as if my presence in the hallway was no longer of any consequence.

And I . . . I . . . I moved back just enough to let her pass— to let her run through to the kitchen, where her thick shawl hung on a peg beside the door, and then run out of the door and into the night, still clutching the bowl—out to some place *where the contents of that bowl could be left to freeze. To die.*

I tell you now, our housekeeper did a mighty service that night not only to Grace, my sister, but to all humanity.

For I saw what was in that bowl as she ran past me. I saw, and the memory of it, brothers, haunts me still.

I cannot . . . I cannot . . .

JANUARY
1646

Twelfth Night: Stars, hard and bright as nail heads, studding the sky. Snow, great soft waves of it, clogging the lanes and beginning to freeze.

Shortly after midnight, villagers gather at the edge of the orchard. The snow here rises past their boots and crunches underfoot like the flesh of windfall apples. The villagers are glad that the big white flakes stopped whirling an hour ago, otherwise, they might never have got here, and there would have been no ritual.

One of the Watchers holds a fistful of amulets, stones shaped like bones and cores, swinging from loops of thread. Another carries a basin filled with squares of toast soaked in cider. Everyone else has brought pot and pans and sticks or spoons to bang them with.

The trees loom in a straggly huddle, their topmost branches interlinked like the arms of arthritic friends. The oldest tree of all has piskies nesting under its roots—robust male piskies who don't mind being woken every January by an infernal clatter, since it always ends with the leaving of boozy bread that lines their stomach regions and gives them cheery dreams for the rest of their winter sleep.

This year these piskies are already awake before the first pot is banged. For something else roused them earlier. Something quite unexpected and so tingly on the nostrils that it was impossible to ignore.

And now, right on time, here come the Apple Howlers.

The noise begins, as it always does, with an earsplitting blast of gunfire. Three men—it is always three—pepper the sky above the treetops with musket shot. And then:

"Hats full! Caps full! Bushels, bushels, sacks full!"

Then the villagers invade the orchard, shouting and whooping and banging their pots and pans loud enough to shatter icicles. In single file they come, wading and crunching through snow to the oldest tree of all.

If there are bad spirits wintering here, no one is sure anymore who or what they are. All anyone knows is that this ritual—to banish evil, to humor the piskies, and to protect the next apple harvest—is as much a part of village life as the birthing of pot lids, the shoeing of horses, and the slow turn of seasons.

The oldest tree's boughs dip heavily, weighed down at their tips by diamonds of ice. The Watcher with the amulets is the first to approach it. She has the first stone in one of her big chapped hands and is reaching to fasten it to a convenient twig, when one of her feet—

"Eek! Get back, neighbors! Step away! 'Tis a piskie brat, as sure as I live and breathe!"

The amulet falls from her fingers, lands with a soft plop in the snow, and disappears.

A piskie brat?

The villagers crunch and scuffle backward, their mouths cold Os of surprise. Silas Denby holds his pot in front of his stomach, like an inadequate shield, and raises his spoon. He has known enough strange goings-on these past months to last him a lifetime. Any sign of trouble from piskies, and he will fight as brave and dirty as any soldier, for all he is armed not quite to the teeth with kitchen wares and so sozzled on cider that the trees here look like they're dancing a jig.

"Squash the boggers!" he bellows, jabbing his spoon in the vague and general direction of the stars. "Stamp 'em out!"

But before he can either attack or fall over, the spoon is whisked from his grasp, and a woman—Mistress Bramlow, it looks like—is down on her knees beneath the oldest tree, spooning away snow and crying: "No! This is no piskie child, neighbors. This is . . . this is . . . Oh, the mite. The poor little mite!"

Silas Denby can barely focus on the oldest tree's trunk, never mind the thing half buried beneath it. *What?* he wonders. *What is it, then? A badger? A fairy? An apple with legs?* He belches uneasily as other villagers push him aside, craning their necks and raising their lanterns to see.

Mistress Bramlow is bent low over whatever it is she has scrabbled up and is chafing and rubbing away at it with bare freezing hands.

What is it? Will it bite her? Is she mad?

The villagers wait, poised to run if necessary. The silence has a tingle to it, and the stars seem to throb minutely, above and between the branches of the trees.

Then the thing on the ground opens its mouth and begins to cry.

No one can mistake that sound. It goes straight to their hearts.

"A boy," Mistress Bramlow marvels, a sob catching in her throat. "A perfect baby boy." And she holds him up to the light of stars and lanterns, so that everyone can see how human he is. How human and how alive.

The Watchers cluck softly. A newborn. Just a few hours old, at most, and very small.

Tsssk.

Their sharp eyes scan the ground for some sign that a birthing took place here this night, with only the trees to bear witness.

No mess. No blood on the ground. And no footprints remaining either, to show that someone carried this newborn here and laid him naked in the drifting snow as if upon a lamb's fleece.

Poor scrap. Poor little mite.

"Will you take him in, Mistress?" The Watcher in charge of the piskies' toast doesn't often speak. Her voice comes out rasping and as rough as a man's.

Mistress Bramlow is swaddling the baby in her shawl and breathing on his nose to keep new ice from forming there.

"Of course," she replies. "Of course I will."

The baby is quiet now, looking up at her with eyes so dark, they seem black. He has a cleft in his chin so deep, it might have been pressed there by his guardian angel, and his hair, now that it is no longer filmed with frozen snow, looks like being fair. He will be beautiful one day. The promise of it is all about him.

Other women are stepping forward, offering advice, their own shawls, and helping hands as Mistress Bramlow gets shakily to her feet, clutching the newborn tight.

"Thank you," Mistress Bramlow murmurs. "Yes, let's take him home." In her mind she is thinking back . . . counting moons . . . working out whether this child is who she thinks he is.

Her mind is whirring, working fast.

Tomorrow she will visit the big house and tell the minister that a foundling has been discovered and that she is of a mind to raise him as her own. She will see what kind of a response she gets to that and take her course from there.

The baby wriggles in her arms. The soft weight of him as they trudge down the hill is like and yet not like the way little Amos felt when she held him. For a moment it hurts to think of her own lost son. Her boy, dead before anyone could truly know him or the person he might have become.

This boy, this foundling, will never take the place of baby Amos. But he will be like another son, for all that, and she and Jack and the girls will grow to love him for himself.

And up in the tree, its face coarse and gray between sparkles of ice, a piskie blinks once, twice, and wishes this special pot lid well. A good person, he'll grow to be. Happy in the heart and mind regions and devoted to the land. Seven sons of his own, he'll have one day, and not one of them a ranter. How about that, then? *Oooo yes.*

"'Tis cold enough to freeze Hell over," one of the other women mutters as they crunch into the village. "That be one lucky newborn, to survive so. The piskies must've tended to him, I reckon. I'd give him a good rub with rowan oil, if I were you, Mistress, in case he be tainted."

Mistress Bramlow smiles in the dark and hugs the baby closer.

Never mind the piskies, she thinks. *The Powers look after their own.* And this infant, she is almost certain, isn't tainted. Only special. A child sacred to nature.

A Merrybegot.

It is still bitterly cold the following morning, but the threat of more snow has passed, and the sky, as Mistress Bramlow pushes open the gate to the minister's house, is the exact shade of blue that used to light up the stained-glass window in the church. The blue of forget-me-nots and the Virgin's robes. The aching blue of heaven.

She has come here alone, leaving her husband and the girls to mind the baby. Having taken to goat's milk and survived the night, he is sleeping soundly. Mistress Bramlow believes he will live. She is sure he will live. But there are two matters over which she must set her mind at rest—matters things only the minister can resolve.

The path leading up to the house is as tangled over as ever with the arching stems of brambles. Walking beneath the arbors, Mistress Bramlow is surrounded by spikiness—thorns, blackened thistles, and dripping icicles—with little scraps of blue above and between, making the sky look torn up.

At the front step she hesitates. Really, she should go round the back, to the entrance used by servants and tradesmen.

But, no.

She bangs with the door knocker, listens to the sound of it bouncing away into the house, and waits.

After a while, just when she is beginning to wonder whether the minister and his household have already fled the place, the housekeeper opens the door.

Mistress Bramlow can tell straightaway that this person knows something. For there is a shiftiness about her and a look in her eyes that speaks of a sorry deed, recently done and only partly repented.

"I must talk to the minister," Mistress Bramlow tells her.

The housekeeper flushes red as a radish but says not a word, only points across the hallway at a closed door, behind which the minister is brooding and drinking and wishing that he could snap his fingers and find himself transported, magically and immediately, to the New World. Alone.

He makes no reply to the knock at his study door, but Mistress Bramlow goes in anyway and stands there, hard-eyed.

Again she can tell, just by looking at the minister, that something has happened in this house.

"A foundling was discovered last night," she tells him. "Half frozen in the snow."

He returns her gaze without moving a muscle or betraying any feeling at all.

"Dead or alive?" he asks, his voice so carefully neutral that Mistress Bramlow knows beyond a shadow of a doubt that the existence of the newborn—whoever it was who birthed him—comes as no surprise.

"Alive," she snaps. "By some miracle."

She waits for him to say more, but he is too busy digesting

her words. Watching him is like watching a man trying to swallow a big lump of something sour.

Mistress Bramlow would like to give her tongue full rein. She would like to tell this twisty-faced, mealymouthed hypocrite that a man—*any* man, but particularly one who speaks for the Lord—would be deserving of nothing but contempt—nay, a stoning—should he have left a healthy newborn to die or knowingly allowed such a terrible thing to happen.

She is tempted to hit him, actually, but whatever she does, she mustn't spoil her chances of keeping the baby. She must hold her temper in check and say only what is necessary to keep the infant safe in her care.

"I have taken the child in, "she says. "I wish to raise it as my own."

At that the minister flinches.

She presses on. "I take it that no one would wish to stop me? There is no mother that you know of, who might want the child returned?"

With a hand that is visibly shaking, the minister lifts a bottle from the table beside him and pours himself a drink.

"The mother," Mistress Bramlow repeats. "Do you know of any unfortunate woman or maid hereabouts who might want this baby back, knowing it to be alive still?"

The minister tips the drink down his throat and sets the glass on the table with a movement that is both bitter and resigned.

"No," he replies through gritted teeth. "I know of no such person."

"So I may keep the child?"

"I suppose so. If you must."

Mistress Bramlow breathes a little easier. That's the first matter cleared. Now for the second.

"So you will baptize it immediately—today?"

The minister splutters and looks at the floor.

"I don't think—I don't believe—I can."

"Why not?"

"Because . . . I cannot spare the time. And anyway, he is a foundling, is he not? A bastard child, steeped already in sin and shame."

Mistress Bramlow steps closer. She is furious, absolutely furious, but her voice remains steady as she tells him, "I do not recall saying whether this be a boy-child or a girl-child."

That's it. She has him. She has him well and truly cornered. Trapped, in fact.

"This child—this boy—is a Merrybegot," she continues calmly. "The Powers will look after him, whatever happens. But you will baptize him anyway, for good measure, and you will do it today. And then we will speak no more, and I will forever keep my counsel on the matter of his birthing. Do we have an agreement?"

The minister will not look at her, but he nods.

"And your daughter Grace," Mistress Bramlow adds, just to make things absolutely clear between them. "She is well? Or as well as can be expected?"

Utterly defeated and finally shamed, the minister nods again.

"Then I will take my leave and await your visit this afternoon for the baptism of my . . . my son."

At the door she pauses.

"I will call him Nathan," she says softly. "Which means 'a gift.'"

Nathan.

A gift.

The minister will dream about this grandson of his, intermittently, for the rest of his life. The dream will trouble him, but not as much as the one in which he sees again the look of his wife on the face of the cunning woman's granddaughter. That dream will haunt him forever, but he will blame it on the climate or too much cheese at supper. Awake he will refuse to dwell on it or recognize the likeness as anything more than a trick of the light. Awake he will push that likeness far away, to a place in his head where it cannot be seen.

Mistress Bramlow crosses the hallway, opens the front door, and steps outside. Coming from the dark of the house, she is dazzled by the white of the snow and the blue of the sky. Feeling dizzy, too, after such a difficult encounter, she cannot for the moment think about walking home.

I will sit down for a minute, she thinks. *Just for a minute, to calm my nerves and gather my thoughts.* She does not want to be seen hanging around the front of the house, so she walks shakily round to the side, where she finds a bench set beneath the kitchen window. Its seat is covered with snow, but she brushes a clear space and sits.

It takes a while for her legs to stop trembling. *That was no easy task,* she thinks, closing her eyes. *But I did it.*

Above her head, someone has scattered crumbs on the kitchen windowsill and left the window slightly ajar. So when the shouting starts, Mistress Bramlow cannot fail to hear it.

"My instructions could not have been clearer, woman! 'Take it where it will not be found,' I said, 'and bury it.' And yet it lives!"

"I took it as far as I was able to walk, sir. Far enough away for no fingers to point at this house, should its remains be discovered one day. But the ground was too hard for me to dig. Too frozen—"

"Well, a pretty pass we've come to now, with it down in the village and tongues wagging nineteen to the dozen, I'll wager."

"Then 'tis a miracle, sir, for 'twas cold enough outdoors last night to kill a grown man in the skin of a bear."

Mistress Bramlow has heard enough. She stands abruptly, not caring if she's seen or heard, and turns away from the kitchen window to walk back along the side of the house and away from this place as quickly as possible.

And then she realizes she is being watched.

Startled, but not unduly worried, she picks her way across the snow to where a girl is standing as still as a bush.

Patience Madden. The minister's younger daughter.

"Good day," Mistress Bramlow says to her. "Aren't you cold?" For the girl has no shawl over her dress, and her bare hands are almost purple.

The girl does not reply, only continues to stare, as if she hasn't properly understood.

Ah, yes, thinks Mistress Bramlow. *The simple one. And what can this be at her feet, embedded in the snow?*

A bird. A dead robin, placed in a scooped out hollow but not yet covered over. And she has fashioned a small cross out of twigs and rimmed the edge of the grave with tiny stones, holly berries, and pins.

"Oh," says Mistress Bramlow. "Poor thing. But it's kind of you to bury him."

The girl looks at her strangely.

"I'm not burying him," she says. "He's too pretty. I'm going to leave him like this, where I can still see him."

Her voice is slurred as if she is not used to speaking.

"Oh," Mistress Bramlow says. "I see. Well . . ."

She looks again at the dead robin, then back at the plain blank face in front of her. *Poor child,* she muses. *Stuck here in this bleak place with such a one as a father and no mother to see that she at least wraps up warm before going outdoors. And how much does she know, I wonder, of her sister's plight?*

"I've been to see the minister," she tells her gently. "Because a baby was found last night, up in the orchard. He's a handsome little baby and lucky to be alive. Your father has promised to baptize him."

The girl says nothing, only glances quickly across at the house—up to a window, a bedroom window—and then back again.

She knows, Mistress Bramlow realizes. *She knows everything.*

"Are you all right?" she quizzes her softly. "I have five daughters of my own, you know. You can talk to me, my dear, should there be something the matter—some troublesome thing on your mind."

She reaches out to touch the girl's arm in a motherly way, but Patience Madden rears back, like a young cat that has never been stroked.

Mistress Bramlow is genuinely upset. "Please . . . it doesn't matter," she soothes, holding out her hand still, but to reassure this time instead of touch. "I didn't mean to frighten you. It's just . . ." She feels completely at a loss now and not sure what else to say.

"Your sister, Grace," she murmurs eventually. "Is *she* all right?"

The girl nods mutely.

"Then . . . you will be leaving for the New World soon? The two of you, with your father?"

She nods again.

"Well, that's good. I'm sure you and your sister must be very dear to each other. So if . . . if she needed help or was sick in some way, you would say so, I'm sure. Would you not?"

And then, for the first time, the girl's expression changes. And Mistress Bramlow realizes that there is little point in talking to her anymore. For she has never seen hatred written so clearly on anybody's features. Her own girls have their differences occasionally. All sisters do. But this . . .

That child be not right in the head, she thinks, stepping quickly from the garden and letting the iron gate clang so hard behind her that great drops of melting snow rain down on her head and shoulders.

Months—even years—later she will sometimes remember the way Patience Madden stood in the snow, with a frozen robin at her feet and flashes of loathing in her eyes. And she will wonder what became of her and her sister, far away in the New World.

Most of the time, though, she will be too busy enjoying her own family—her five daughters and little Nathan, her dark-eyed, golden-haired Merrybegot—to spare them any thought at all.

The Confession of Patience Madden

And so we sailed from Plymouth in the spring of 1646, Father, Grace, and I, and arrived here in the New World to begin our lives afresh.

And my sister married, as you know, and had five children, three of whom are living still. And I did my duty, as was expected of me, keeping house for Father until the Lord called him home in the winter of 1669.

In time the events of 1645 grew faint in my mind, the way certain colors do on the patches of a quilt—so slowly that you don't always notice unless someone else points out that what is now a faded pink was once the deep red of tomato fruits or a summer poppy.

The scent of a poppy can send you to sleep. Did you know that, brothers? I long to sleep. My mind spins so, for the lack of it. But I must finish my story, so that you will understand.

There were poppies in the corn the night I met the Devil. There were foxgloves in the hedgerows, curving like pink scythes above my head. And I . . . I had no idea, no idea at all, why the Devil should take it for granted that I was waiting for him there beside the orchard. Or that I would willingly jump up on his horrible horse and go with him straight to Hell.

But I worked it out. Oh, yes. I put two and two together long ago. Only I kept my counsel for my dear father's sake and to give my much-loved sister, Grace, a chance to repent of her terrible sin and live a decent life here in the land of new beginnings.

And I believed she had repented and made her peace with the Lord. I truly did.

Until now.

When the girls of this neighborhood—Betty Parris and Abigail Williams—took to their beds with strange fits and visions, I prayed day and night for an end to their affliction. When it grew worse, I dared to hope they were merely playacting, as I once did, out of ignorance and fear—and because my sister made me.

But when Annie Putnam saw yellow birds dipping and diving in the meetinghouse and fell to the ground in agony at being pinched by fingers no one else could see, I knew she could not be pretending.

I knew that Satan was here among us. And I knew why.

Ah. I see there are more of you now, come to hear the ending of my tale. It has been a long one, I know, and I have been glad of your patience in listening so intently. Glad, too, that you have written it down, for every word is true and, as such, should be recorded.

Forgive me . . . yes . . . I will continue.

The girls who pointed their fingers at me at the

meetinghouse . . . two moons ago now . . . the ones who call me a witch. Don't you see, brothers, how mistaken they are? I have been locked away in this place a long time now— too long—and believe me, it is not I who should be here.

The cunning woman was innocent, and so was her granddaughter. They were not witches, brothers, and neither am I. Don't you see how Satan moves? How he covers his tracks and looks after his own?

That night I met the Devil—do you know why he thought I would go willingly? Because he had already met with my sister. He had frolicked with my sister, in the woods below our home. That night and all the others before.

Don't you see?

We were the minister's daughters, Grace and I. And that made us special. Mary by Gods. *I was not mistaken.*

Don't you see it all clearly now?

The heart I found beneath our mattress. The wooden heart branded through with the letters "S" and "G." It was his mark burned there, next to "G" for "Grace." That awful, twisting "S." Satan's brand.

He took Grace first because she was the prettiest. And willing. He thought I would be easy prey too. But he never took me. I didn't let him.

And all that followed—the fits and the spitting of pins, the lies about the frogs, the trapping of the cunning woman's granddaughter—it was all deceit, all trickery played out by my sister, with me as her dupe so that no one would guess that the thing growing in her belly was . . . was . . . truly the Devil's spawn.

I saw it—yes, I did—before the housekeeper took it away. I saw it in the basin, and the sight of it . . . I can barely . . .

It was as black as your hats, brothers, I swear it was. And with yellow-green eyes wide open . . . wide open and flickering like twin fires, newly lit. And instead of feet and hands, it had hooves—cloven hooves, like those of a goat.

Forgive me, I can speak of it no more.

The wooden heart?

Yes, I have it still, and you may take it for your evidence. You will find it in a box, buried to the depth of my arm, six paces from the door to my father's house. A baneful thing. A nasty thing. But I have never dared destroy it or try to throw it away, for fear of Satan's wrath. Buried deep, it has done no harm. But be careful, brothers, how you raise it. And do not touch the "S."

The jeweled frog?

I know not what became of that.

Perchance my sister has it. If so, be sure to take it from her, for I fear she has been using it with baneful intent.

Well now, I can see by your faces, brothers, that my words are no longer falling on deaf ears. I am glad of that. For it is not I who should be here. Not I who am a witch.

It is my sister, Grace.

She lives on the outskirts of Salem, in the house grown all around by corn.

Go get her.

Author's Note

I always knew this novel would end in Salem—and why. I'd been reading about witch trials in seventeenth-century New England and discovered that a significant number of accusers were young girls who were either the daughters or the servants of ministers.

All of these girls went in for the kind of writhing, shrieking, and hysterical behavior associated then with demonic possession.

Why? Did they truly believe themselves possessed, or were they just getting a thrill out of behaving very badly indeed?

Something the writer Carol Karlsen said of them stuck in my mind: "As the community looked on, their bodies expressed what they could not: that the enormous pressures put upon them to accept a religiously based male-centered social order was more than they could bear." (*The Devil in the Shape of a Woman: Witchcraft in Colonial New England* [London, 1987].)

It was then that the minister's daughters began to take shape, in my imagination. Grace and Patience Madden. Two very different girls, but both expected, by their Puritannical father, to suppress natural feelings of jealousy, insecurity, and desire.

The height of the witch craze in England occurred in the 1640s. The English Civil War, between Parliament and the monarchy, was at its height then, dividing the loyalties of the people and throwing everyday life into turmoil. Matthew Hopkins, an unsuccessful lawyer, was quick to take advantage of this situation. He convinced the population of Essex that Satan was out to get them. Known before long as the "Witch-finder General," Hopkins made a great deal of money from getting vulnerable individuals to confess to witchcraft—and seeing them hanged.

I took the liberty of "borrowing" Matthew Hopkins and sending him a long way from home.

The young Charles II really was sent to the west country of England in 1645 as a figurehead for the Royalist cause. He hid out at Pendennis Castle in Cornwall before sailing into exile in the spring of 1646. His involvement with the cunning woman's granddaughter is pure make-believe—although it startled me to discover, while plotting the gallows scene, that King Charles I wrote repeatedly to his son between August and November of 1645, urging him to flee the country and "not to delay one hour."

I never did find out why young Charles—fifteen at the time and no lover of hardship—ignored his father's instructions and dithered around the west of England during the filthiest of winters, in constant danger of falling into the rebels' hands. It didn't matter, for I already had an answer. Of course I did. He had to save my Nell!

Charles I was executed in 1649. Young Charles, however, did not ascend the throne until the monarchy was restored in 1660. Remembered historically as "the Merry Monarch," Charles II allegedly devoted as much time to sensual pleasure as diplomatic activity before converting to Catholicism and dying in his own bed in 1685. Nell Gwyn, who is mentioned fleetingly in this book, was one of his many mistresses.

My own Nell and her grandmother typify the countless numbers of single, outspoken, unconventional women and girls, who have been accused of witchcraft in numerous times and places around the world. Their knowledge of herbal remedies and leanings toward pagan ritual were bound to go against them since both could be twisted into "proof" of Satanic practices.

I borrowed heavily from the *Culpeper's* (1616–1654) *Complete Herbal* to conjure the remedies brewed in the cunning woman's cottage and plundered the folklore and superstitions of Devon and Cornwall to create the piskies in the ditches and the fairies in the hill. The spells are based on traditional Wiccan magic with a fanciful twist or two.

The word "Merrybegot" has slipped out of use. But it was spoken long ago—in the west country, anyway—and meant exactly what it means in this story.

Julie Hearn
April 2005
www.julie-hearn.com

For Further Reading

Many of these books are written for readers on the college or graduate-school level, but they offer great insight to those interested in reading further about the setting and lingering myths of this period.

Aronson, Marc. *Witch-Hunt: Mysteries of the Salem Witch Trials.* (New York, NY: Atheneum Books for Young Readers, 2003).

Bunn, Ivan, and Gilbert Geis. *A Trial of Witches: A Seventeenth-Century Witchcraft Prosecution.* (London, England: Routledge, 1997).

Culpeper, Nicholas. *Culpeper's Complete Herbal.* (Whitefish, MT: Kessinger Publishing, 2003).

Gibson, Marion. *Reading Witchcraft: Stories of Early English Witches.* (London, England: Routledge, 1999).

Norton, Mary Beth. *In the Devil's Snare: The Salem Witchcraft Crisis of 1692.* (New York: Knopf, 2002).

Royle, Trevor. *The British Civil War: The War of the Three Kingdoms, 1638–1660.* (New York, NY: Palgrave Macmillan, 2004).

Scot, Reginald. *The Discoverie of Witchcraft.* (Mineola, NY: Dover Publications, 1989, 1930).